BATTLE OF

The Tathas was bigger than any Rikard had ever seen and each of its tendrils was tipped in red. It was this which was broadcasting the devastating psychic weapon.

Rikard's panic was overwhelming. He knew all too well the kind of madness those alien thoughts could engender, the horror of being touched by one of those degenerate things, being dissolved and eaten while still alive. He fought to control his fear, fumbled for his gun. But even as he pulled the gun, his vision blurred from the effects of the Tathas' psychic attack.

He tried to reach under his shirt for the dragongem, the one thing which, once long ago, had helped him against this evil, but he couldn't get his hand to work. There was a gun in it. He let the gun go, tried to raise his head, saw raiders coming out of the balcony, down ramps, across the floor from first level entrances. The Tathas loomed large, its carrier zombies striding, clumsy but purposeful, toward him.

He concentrated all his energy in retaining awareness...

*

CRITICAL RAVES FOR
ALLEN L. WOLD'S PREVIOUS NOVELS:

*

Also by Allen L. Wold

Jewels of the Dragon

Published by
POPULAR LIBRARY

CROWN
OF THE
SERPENT

ALLEN L. WOLD

POPULAR LIBRARY

An Imprint of Warner Books, Inc.

A Warner Communications Company

For Diane, and for Ooglio Babba,
Queen of the Spaceways.

And a special thanks to Brian Thomsen.

POPULAR LIBRARY EDITION

Popular Library®, the fanciful P design, and Questar® are
registered trademarks of Warner Books, Inc.

Cover illustration by Tom Kidd

Popular Library books are published by
Warner Books, Inc.
666 Fifth Avenue
New York, N.Y. 10103

A Warner Communications Company

Printed in the United States of America

First Printing: July, 1989

10 9 8 7 6 5 4 3 2 1

PROLOGUE

The Federation encompasses hundreds of inhabited worlds among thousands of star systems. It is, on the whole, a utopia, at the peak of its golden age. Each world is independent, with its own idea of the good life, free to make its own laws as it sees fit, to define for itself its ideal culture. Thus, not every Federal world is itself a utopia. Some have achieved a stable society that Plato would envy. Others are in a dynamic state of growth and decay, flux, change. Still others, such as Nowarth, have made a wrong turn somewhere.

Most people who live in a utopia are happy with their situation—that's part of what makes it a utopia. Crime and trouble are quite rare. But another aspect of utopia is that it's boring.

Some people are just not content with the easy life. For these, the Gestae, the ancient Chinese curse is not a curse at all— they *seek* interesting times. They live by their wits, moving from world to world, looking for something exciting to see or to do or to be. They do what they do not for wealth, or for power, but for fun. For a Gesta, the greatest thrill comes not from breaking a law but from slipping through the cracks. Which doesn't mean they don't frequently find themselves in trouble.

Nowarth was not a world any Gesta would have chosen to visit, at least not without a rather specific reason. Its towering city-buildings were partially empty or wholly abandoned. Its single, planet-wide government was one of the most conservative and restrictive in the Federation. But the man who was calling himself Jack Begin, and his companion, now known as Ann Tropius, had a reason. It was here that Jack's "client" insisted that they do business.

Jack and Ann had come to Nowarth well ahead of their appointed meeting time. It was a simple matter for them to pick up the local dialect, learn how to wear local clothing, adapt to the average daytime schedules. Good camouflage was, of course, part of the repertoire of any Gesta.

Good camouflage would not, however, help them if they were caught exploring the empty, monolithic city-buildings late at night.

PART
ONE

1

The two Gestae rode up silent lifts toward the top of the abandoned city which, like its neighbors not many kilometers away, was an irregular tower that seemed shorter than it was by virtue of its girth. In fact, when it had been alive, its upper floors had been pressurized to compensate for its height, though now there were too many windows missing, and occasional places where the outer wall had been broken out and, with the cessation of the air-conditioning, pressure had been lost. The tower was only about a kilometer and a half tall, however, so the reduced pressure was little more than an inconvenience.

The tower had not been abandoned that long ago, and for the most part was intact, the only damage being that caused by vandals rather than due to the weathering of the elements. Indeed, though most of the city was dark, many of its systems were still powered, a function of the automatic backup generators and batteries rather than feed from the planetary grid.

There was enough power, at least, so that the gravity lifts were working. There were few lights on in the tower, but the lifts that Jack and Ann chose, and their lobbies, were near the outer edge of the tower, and dimly illumined by the skylight coming through the great window walls. None of the lifts went more than a couple of hundred floors, however, so they had to change frequently. But at last they neared the top, yet still below the penthouse levels, and stepped off the last lift into a small but luxurious lobby.

Jack, as he called himself, was twenty-eight in Earth years, still a youth by the standards of the day when two centuries was the average life expectancy. He was very tall and slender and rather dark, but not very handsome. He moved with a lazy grace that made him seem almost sleepy, though now he was alert to every sound and shadow. Beside him, the woman who called herself Ann seemed even shorter than she was—her head barely came up to his shoulder. She was a couple of years younger than he, attractive in a hard, smooth way, and where Jack seemed lazy, she was like a compressed spring.

There was no one else in the lobby, though they were not the first to have been here, and the corridor on their right showed reflected light from beyond a corner. There was rubbish on the floor—fragments of ragged clothes, papers, broken cardboard boxes, other things less identifiable—and the dust on the now-gray carpet was thick enough to show footprints. The window wall of the lobby was intact, and somebody had smeared something unpleasant across it just at eye height. Beyond the window they could see several other towers, some black and silhouetted against the night sky, others lit or partly lit.

Jack had been carrying a heavy case the whole way, and now he put it down to adjust the belt with its holster and heavy six-shot .75 caliber pistol so that he could draw quickly—his long coat tended to get in the way. "I would have thought," he said, almost in a whisper, "that our friend would have chosen a place where nobody came at all."

"On the contrary," Ann said. In spite of her youth, she had many more years' experience than he. "If you're the only one here, then you can't escape notice. But if you're just one among many, then you won't seem special to anybody who might be watching." Her holstered laser pistol was strapped to her right thigh, just below the edge of her short jacket.

They did not go up the lighted corridor, but instead turned to the left, following the instructions Djentsin had given them when they'd agreed to meet in this place. Their feet crunched occasionally in the near darkness, where they trod on the remains of the baseboard security lights, each of which had been methodically knocked out. Jack felt the scar on the palm of his right hand itching. He flexed his fingers, but did not scratch, did not grab the butt of his gun.

The corridor paralleled the outside of the building. The doors on the inside of the corridor they could just barely make out as they passed. Those on the outside were sometimes solid, others windowed. What light there was in the corridor came from those, from the offices beyond on the outer side of the building, themselves only dimly lit through their window walls. This had once been a very exclusive part of this city, though its decline had begun long before it was abandoned. Most of the rooms that they could see into were empty, the furniture either broken by vandals or removed by scavengers.

They had not gone very far before the broad corridor ended in an L to the left. The corridor around the corner was short, without any doors that they could see, and absolutely dark, though at the far end was a pale gray luminance. Jack could not make out anything about what was at the end until they got there and found themselves in a large, interior plaza.

The dim luminance came down from security lights on the narrow balcony along all four sides on the floor above them. There were three other corridors entering the plaza; benches arranged in sociable clusters; containers that held now-dead trees and plants and, around the outside wall, the remains of a few small service shops, their contents stolen or smashed. A central lift, unenclosed, stood in the center of the plaza. A broad and ornamental stair spiraled squarely around it to an intermediate landing below the balcony, then to another landing that surrounded the lift at the balcony level and with narrow walkways leading to it, then rising uninterrupted to a deeper mezzanine one floor above that.

They paused to listen, but there was no sound other than their breathing. Jack thought he could even hear his pulse. He turned to look at the dark corridor behind him, but heard nothing anywhere.

This was just the way Djentsin had told them it would be, but that didn't make Jack feel any easier. He and Ann had met Djentsin on Balshpor a quarter of a standard year previously, when trying to find a buyer for certain cultural artifacts they had "liberated" after having taken care of certain other obligations of a more public nature. They had been using different names then, as had Djentsin, not the ones they had been known by during their more public business. But though Djentsin had made them an offer they found hard to refuse, he was not a Gesta. He'd tried to pretend to be one, and Jack didn't trust him. This place was too good for an ambush.

"So what do you think?" Jack asked at last. It was hard to speak above a whisper. The security lights on the balcony, reflecting as they did off the carpeted floor and then back from the mezzanine above, cast too many shadows for his comfort. In spite of that, the plaza was all but black.

"Too good to believe," Ann answered. "But if he had wanted

to just pick us off, there were plenty of opportunities at all the lift changes we had to make."

"But none of the lobbies offered as many opportunities as this."

"You only need one clear shot," Ann said.

In spite of the itching scar on his right palm, Jack did not put his hand on his pistol butt. He took a deep breath and stepped out into the plaza. Nothing happened. He turned to look back at Ann, who was standing where she had been, almost invisible in the darkness.

"Not taking any chances?" he asked.

He could not see her smile, but he knew it was there. She stepped out to stand with him. Together they walked to the lift.

But the lift wasn't working. Either the power had been cut off at this level, or the lift itself had been disconnected. They went to the broad, shallow-stepped stairs that climbed around it, and went up.

At the first landing they paused. There was no movement, no sound. They went on to the balcony level. Still everything was silent and dead. Jack's hand itched abominably. They went up to the mezzanine.

It was, except for the opening to the lower levels, one vast lobby. The security lights were lit up here. Eight alcoves, in the center of each wall and in each corner, opened off the mezzanine, which held only couches in groups, planters of dead things, and low tables with low comfortable chairs. "Right corner from the top of the stairs," Ann said, reciting Djentsin's instructions.

So that was where they went, and found a smaller lobby opening off the alcove, and a stair going up, as they had been told. They went up, to another lobby over the one below but not open to it, with corridors where the alcoves had been on the lower level. Set into the walls between the corridor entrances were at least one restaurant, what looked like it might have been a hair parlor, a bar now totally demolished, and several other suites that they could not identify. This had been for the convenience of the penthouse residents only.

They could go no higher here. Only a hundred of the richest and most important families of this city could have lived in the penthouses to which these corridors gave access.

"Seems like he's making it awfully difficult," Jack said.

The residences were on the outer edge of the tower, surrounding this last lobby area, large enough in itself to have accommodated a dozen families on the world in which Jack had grown up. He and Ann did not pause to look around, but went up the corridor, directly opposite the top of the stairs, its security lights still intact but shining only dimly, and took the left hand of the T at its end. The doors on this corridor opened only off the outer side, double doors, massive and ornate, each with a symbol instead of a number. At the far end of the transverse corridor was a thin edge of light near the floor, as if the door there were just slightly ajar.

And that was where they found the symbol they were looking for, a triskelion in green and yellow and black, the significance of which Jack did not know, over leather-padded double doors that were, indeed, slightly ajar. With a tentative hand, Ann pushed open the right-hand leaf.

Beyond was a foyer as large as the average living room, with closets on either side, and another double door opposite the entrance. This stood open, and was from whence the light was coming. They entered the foyer and now could see past the inner door to a spacious living room, even by this tower's standards. The outer wall, which had once been all window, was smashed and open to the high night air. They were impressed in spite of themselves.

As they went on into the living room they could hear, through the gaping window wall, the dim sounds of night outside—the noise of the living cities not that far away, the susurration of the wind. After the darkness of the outer halls, the skylight seemed bright, and it was that only which they had seen through the hairline crack below the leathern double doors.

To their right was a spacious dining room which, lit by its own intact window wall, seemed large enough for a banquet of twenty or more. To their left, through an arch, was a parlor, less formal than the living room, the place where, obviously, the family that had once lived here had spent most of its time. Unlike the lower floors of the penthouse level, this place had not been vandalized. Its outer doors must have remained locked until just recently.

Another arch opened off the far side of the parlor, and from there a corridor, its security lights in the baseboard still glowing, led back into the private part of the suite. There was a bathroom, an office, a library, a study, and at the end a sitting room with three other doors. They were all shut tight, and if there were lights behind any of them, they could not be seen.

They chose the door in the middle, as they had been instructed. There was light on inside, enough to let them see a luxuriously comfortable but understated sitting room, separated by a broad arch from the bedroom beyond where, sitting in the dim light of a table lamp beside the bed, was a man, looking at them as if waiting for them. It was Djentsin. In his lap was a 6cm scattergun pistol, a "defender." "Come in," he said as he let his hand rest on the butt of his gun. "You're right on time."

Jack tried to make his movements seem casual as he went halfway to the middle of the room and stopped. On his right, Ann walked easily but angled away from him a bit so as to make a more difficult target if Djentsin should decide to shoot. The "defender," at that distance, could hit anything within half a meter of its aiming point.

Djentsin, as they did this, remained seated, looking very calm. "You brought it with you?" he asked.

"We did," Jack said. He put the case down on the floor. "You have the Leaves?"

"Just one this time. It's on the bed." He did not gesture or take his eyes off Jack.

Jack turned to the bed, where he could see the dim glimmer of the elongated diamond shape of a silver Leaf of Ba'Gashi. But even as he took the first step toward it, Djentsin raised his gun and pointed it steadily at Jack's head.

"You're in no hurry," Djentsin said. "You can see the Leaf, but where's the Shanteliar?"

Jack glanced down at the case. "In there."

"Like hell it is, unless you've broken it up. And if you've done that, you're dead."

"It's a special case," Ann said. "It's a lot bigger than it looks."

Djentsin's eyes never flickered, his hand did not waver. "I'll just bet it is," he said.

Jack had to admire his poise. "The only way to find out," he said, "is to look inside." He gave a small smile. "Do you want to open it or shall I?"

"You open it," Djentsin said.

Jack went to kneel behind the case and turned it on its side so he could work the latch. For the first time Djentsin's eyes moved to Ann. "You," he said to her, "stand behind Msr. Begin, with your hands on his shoulders where I can see them."

Jack waited until he could feel Ann's hands on him. There was no tremor, but then the armor under his clothes wouldn't have let him feel anything as delicate as that. The armor wouldn't do him any good, however, if Djentsin shot him in the head.

He thumbed the catches on either side of the case and it split in half. He raised the top half and let it open all the way back to the floor. The inside appeared to be solid. He glanced up at Djentsin. The man was watching his eyes.

In the middle of each of the two newly exposed surfaces was another catch, recessed into the interior cover. Jack reached for them and—

"How convenient," came a male voice from beyond the doorway behind him.

Jack was so startled that he almost knocked Ann off her feet as he half turned to see who was there. She barely regained her balance by clutching his shoulder so hard that it hurt, and they both stared into the doorway, but it was too dark to see the intruder. Jack caught his breath, and heard a small rustle of coat sleeves folding as Djentsin changed his aim.

"Easy," said the unseen man, "easy." His voice was smooth but uncultured, his accent that of a lower-class local. "I got a hair trigger on this thing," he went on, "and it can take out the whole room." Then the shadows moved and the man stepped forward, just into the doorway and the edge of the light. In his right hand was a battered blaster, aimed negligently in their general direction.

"What do you want?" Djentsin asked. Jack glanced back to see Djentsin's "defender" now pointed unwaveringly at the intruder. He let his right hand fall negligently to the butt of his own pistol, but a fold of his coat was covering it.

"I want," the intruder said, "whatever you've got. You're trespassing, this is my scally. Now you just riff out your pockets, and you can go home. Otherwise I'll drop a bolt in front of your chair and the whole room will go out the wall."

"That won't leave you much," Jack said. He tried to ease the flap of his coat from the butt of his gun.

"I'll just pick up whatever's left and be clear of you."

"Maybe that blaster doesn't work anymore," Ann said. "It looks pretty old."

"One sure way to find out," the man said with a smile. "Now you, unbuckle that laser and let it drop."

Ann did so without hesitation, but the man wasn't looking at her. He was smiling at Djentsin. With a snort, Djentsin tossed his gun on the bed, just beyond the Leaf. The man didn't blink, but just turned his gaze to Jack. "You too," he said. It had been a long time since Jack had seen eyes that hard.

Jack held a beat, then pulled his coat aside and, with both hands, getting to his feet as he did so, undid the buckle of his holster. He let the belt fall.

"Now," the man said, "let's see what you've got. Back away."

Jack moved to one side of the case, Ann to the other. The man smiled softly, and they backed further.

The man came up to within a meter of the case and looked down at it but did not crouch. "Fancy bag," he said. "I'll look into it later. Now, empty your pockets, put everything down on the floor. You, fella, get to your feet."

They did as they were told. Then, while the man was looking at Ann, Jack reached under his collar, as if to adjust the chain he wore around his neck, as if to ensure that it was properly concealed. And as he had hoped, the man noticed this small action.

"What you got there?" the man asked even as Jack let his hands fall to his sides. Jack stepped back just a little bit. "Come on," the man insisted. His head was slightly tilted to one side. "Let's see what it is."

Jack, feigning reluctance, reached up with both hands and took the chain from under the collar at the back of his neck, so that when he drew it over his head, the end down the front of his shirt was still concealed. He hesitated, then the man reached out and took the chain and pulled it away from Jack's shirt. Dangling from the long loop was a large gem set in a simple gold clasp.

The man's eyes flickered when he saw it, and a slow smile crept over his face. "Pretty fancy for a guy to be wearing, ain't it." He stepped back a couple of paces, then jerked the chain so that the gem swung up into the palm of his hand, all the while keeping his eyes on Jack. "This just might make it worth the trouble you've caused me," he said. He held his blaster steady, aimed at the floor between Jack and Ann where the bolt would take them both out if he fired.

Then he opened his other hand palm up, glanced down at the gem, held a beat, glanced back up at Jack with a very odd expression on his face, looked down at his hand again, which he brought closer to his face, the better to see the fire-colored gem sparkling on his palm. His eyes widened, he took a deep breath, then he stopped moving, as if he had been hypnotized.

Jack glanced at Ann. She was smiling. Then he stepped up to the man and bent down to look up into his enraptured face.

"What . . .?" Djentsin started to ask.

Jack did not touch the gem, but gently removed the blaster from the man's right hand. He looked over the weapon and turned back to Djentsin. "It's old," he said, holding out the blaster, "but it works." Then he returned to the case and knelt again, put the blaster down beside it, looked up at Djentsin, and said, "I really want to make this deal."

Ann bent down to retrieve her laser as Djentsin came around Jack to look at the immobile man. Jack knelt back. This would take a moment. Djentsin stared into the man's face, then looked at the gem in his hand, and started to touch it.

"Leave it be," Ann said, "or he'll wake up again."

Djentsin pulled his hand back and looked down at Jack. "That's dialithite," he said, waving vaguely at their paralyzed intruder. Jack said nothing. "You don't need the Leaves," Djentsin went on, "that gem is worth more than all of them put together."

"That may be," Jack said. "If I wanted to sell the stone, it would certainly bring enough to let Ann and me live comfortably for the rest of our lives. But then I wouldn't have it anymore, and sometimes the effect it has on people is worth more than money—like right now for example. Shall I open the case, or do you want to call the deal off?"

Djentsin stared at him a long moment, then, "Open the case," he said.

Djentsin didn't seem concerned for his safety anymore, or for any possible treachery. He stood beside the case as Jack thumbed the inner catches. The case seemed to split in two once more, in the other direction this time, and Jack opened the two sides away from each other, so that now the case was twice as wide and twice as long and a quarter as deep as it had originally been. But once again the inside was covered by panels.

"Damn funny case," Djentsin said.

"It is that," Jack said. "Cost a small fortune, but like the dragongem, it comes in handy." He undid four more recessed latches, in the middle corners of the panels, and one by one opened them. The space beneath them was very dark, and something about it made the eyes dance. He reached in, his hands seemingly swallowed by shadow darker than it should be, and grabbed at something invisible within. He got to one foot, pulled up, and drew out a thing like a double scroll, wrapped in figured leather, the staff-ends long and elaborately carved. It was almost two meters tall and half a meter wide.

Djentsin's breath changed, deep and slow.

"What would you rather have," Ann said, "the dragongem or this and the rest of the Reliquiture?"

"It's the Shanteliar," Djentsin said. His voice was almost reverential. "God damn. But . . . what else you got in there?"

"Just this this time," Ann said as Jack handed the object to Djentsin. "It's about all that would fit, actually."

The Shanteliar was heavy. Djentsin took it from Jack carefully and reverently. It was as if the apartment, Jack and Ann, and their strangely hypnotized intruder had all ceased to exist. He carried the leather-covered double scroll over to the bed, and carefully propped it up against it, so that it was almost vertical. Then he stood back and looked at it.

"This," he said, "has been lost since my people left the Valrein Worlds in the middle of the Old Federation." He turned a very serious face to Jack. "The symbolism of the Shanteliar and the other things that were lost with it are still remembered. They are the core of what makes us who we are. If I could bring this back to the Archipopulos on Derolos, I would be the hero of my people." He looked at the Shanteliar for a long time. When he turned back to Jack and Ann, his face was more than grim, it was also exultant. "Do you really have the rest of the Reliquiture?"

"We do," Jack said. "As art objects, they are probably worth more than the Leaves."

"But you don't want the Leaves because of their artistic value," Djentsin said, "or because of the money you might gain from their sale. Do you? Neither do I want this and the rest of the Reliquiture because of their monetary value. I think you understand me. I don't need money. My present occupation provides me with more than I could spend in a lifetime—unless I learn some new vices. But this—" And again he gazed at the twin scrolls of the Shanteliar, with their stave-ends like miniature crowns. "If I can restore the Reliquiture, I will become the hero of my people, and more than that no man could ask." He took a deep breath and turned to face Jack and Ann again.

Ann went around to the other side of the bed and picked up the Leaf. This time Djentsin didn't object. She held it up to him, until he took notice. "Fair trade?"

"I feel like I'm cheating you," Djentsin said. There was an odd, wry smile on his face.

"Not at all," Jack said. "The Shanteliar and the other things are worth only money to me, the Leaves only money to you. Neither one of us will lose on this deal."

"That is for sure," Djentsin said. His smile was broad, but there was fear somewhere underneath his composure. He could hardly breathe. "It so very seldom works out that way. But reassure me, what more do you have?"

"There is a kind of cloak," Ann said, "with a heavy collar but no hood, though it looks as though there should have been one." Djentsin just stared at her. "Then there are two staffs, one like a walking stick but very crooked, with what looks like odd chunks of iron embedded in it, and the other more than two meters tall, also crooked and seemingly wrapped in varin thread or silk." Djentsin's face became absolutely blank.

"There's a large goblet," Jack said. "I think it's made of silver, or maybe platinum since it hasn't tarnished, narrower at the lip than in the body, and a large platter kind of thing with gems around the outer edge, and a small table with what looks like solid ivory legs, inlayed with a geometric pattern I don't recognize."

"That's it," Djentsin said. His breathing was heavy, his smile wolfish. "That's the full Reliquiture. I can hardly believe that it's true."

"And you?" Ann asked. "How many Leaves do you have?"

"Twelve more." His breath was a pant. "That's all there were."

"That's right," Jack said. "Where shall we make the trade?"

It took Djentsin a moment to respond. "Not here," he said at last, "I was just being cautious. Do you know Total Foam?"

"I've been there," Jack said.

"Fine. It will take me at least two quarters to get the rest of the Leaves and get there."

"We might need a bit more time than that," Ann said. "The

rest of the Reliquiture are still—where they've been all this time. Say three quarters of a standard year?"

"All right," Djentsin said. "That will give me time to put the Shanteliar in a safe place, where the senechals can find it if I don't get back. I'll meet you at the Chessi Morphica Hotel, you know where that is?"

"That's where I stayed," Jack said.

"Excellent. In twenty-seven decads then."

2

"Wait a minute," Ann said. Her words brought them all back to the present. Jack glanced at her, then followed her staring eyes to the far side of the bedroom. It should have been dark. Instead, a comcon screen was glowing. Djentsin looked too.

"How long has that been on?" Jack said. He started to walk toward it.

"I don't know," Ann said as she dropped the Leaf into Jack's case. "It was on when I looked up."

"Some of his friends?" Djentsin asked, gesturing to the still immobile intruder.

"We should be so lucky," Jack said, "but it doesn't fit in with his mode of entry." He stopped halfway to the comcon. He didn't want its camera, if it were on, to pick up his face.

"Let's assume it's the cops," Ann said in a low voice. "Which means they knew somebody would be here tonight." She looked at Djentsin, but his face betrayed no guilt, only anxiety.

"Shall we just wait at the hotel?" Jack asked Djentsin.

"I'll be there before you. I'll be visible—for someone like you."

"Then let's get out of here," Ann said, and even as she spoke they could hear the distant echoes of footsteps coming from the shops area at the center of the tower—heavy, mechanical footsteps that could only be made by troopers wearing battle armor.

"Holy shit," Jack whispered. He strode to where his gun belt was lying and hurriedly picked it up and put it on.

Djentsin picked up the Shanteliar and lugged it to a side door. "Have you got a way out?" he asked in a hoarse whisper from the doorway.

"We can make it," Jack said as he closed up his case.

"I'll see you there, then," Djentsin said, and hefted the double scroll out the door. A moment later, over the sound of the approaching troopers, Jack could hear the faint snick of a hatch closing, and almost immediatly the subtle hum of a gravity drive coming on. The window on that side of the bedroom brightened, as if a vehicle were pulling away from another window or a hole in the wall.

"What are we going to do?" Ann whispered. The sounds of the troopers—and the clank of some kind of automated machinery—were getting nearer. The steps did not hesitate or turn aside to check out alternate routes. The cops knew exactly where they were going. "Shall we follow Djentsin?"

"That's probably the first place they'll look," Jack said. He went to their uninvited visitor and gently took the dragongem from his hand. For a moment the man stood as he had, but even as they left the bedroom by the way they had come, he began to awaken from the trance.

They hurried up the hall toward the sound of the approaching troopers and into the living room. They could even hear muttered voices now, and see reflected lights coming up the outer corridor. Quickly, and carefully, they went out the broken main window onto a narrow ledge on the outer side of the city tower. Jack led the way along the ledge, as broad as his foot was long, away from the window to a projecting spine.

From where they clung they could see the room brightening, then lights flashing around inside. The troopers had been closer than Jack had thought. He worked his way around the spine, which wasn't easy with the heavy case he was carrying. Ann followed close behind. Then they heard shouts coming from the apartment they had just left. One voice was unmistakably that of their surprise intruder. There were shots, then a blaster bolt that blew out a whole section of the wall into the night. After that, a hesitation, then more shots, then silence.

Then the lights inside began to move again, and they could hear the heavy steps of the troopers. The projecting spine offered some protection, but if anybody leaned out the window or the new hole in the wall and looked in their direction, they would be easily seen.

They crept along the ledge, away from the apartment, to a recessed section of the wall. The windows all along the inner face were intact, and never meant to open against the reduced atmospheric pressure at this height. But there was decorative work on the inside corners of the recess, not much, but enough to let them slowly climb down several floors toward a broader ledge.

Even as they went they could hear voices coming from up above. Most were muffled and unintelligible, but one came clearly. "There's nobody out here, he must have had a flier." He was answered by someone within, then started to say something more, but the voice was drowned out by the whine of vehicles landing on the roof of the penthouse.

"That wasn't just a casual search," Ann said as she joined Jack on the half-meter ledge.

"It's either us or Djentsin," Jack said. He leaned out over the edge and looked down. The wall was smooth there, but at the far end of the ledge was another column of decorative work. "Maybe we can find another broken window."

They went to the decorative column and started down. The descent here was trickier, and the next ledge was only five floors lower. Below this was a two-hundred floor drop to a roof. Jack held Ann as she leaned out to scan the walls to either side.

"Nothing," she said, "unless we want to go back." She looked up. The dim reflections of rotating red and blue lights revealed the continued presence of the police vehicles.

The sky off in the east was no longer a dead flat black. Beyond the lights of the tower cities nearby were the first signs of approaching dawn. The near silence of the night air was no longer perfect either—distant traffic traveling between lit cities could now be heard, and within another hour or so there would be plenty of air traffic around this abandoned city. Directly across from them, only two kilometers away, was a tower fully lit. Even at that distance, in the upcoming dawn, they could be too easily seen if anybody happened to look out while they were moving.

"I hate to do it," Jack said, "but I don't see any other way."

"It's what we brought them for," Ann reminded him.

Jack carefully crouched down on the projecting ledge and set down the case between him and Ann. There wasn't much room on the ledge, and it took both of them to keep the case in place while Jack undid first one set of latches, then the inner set, and at last the four security panels. As it was, he couldn't open it all the way.

He reached inside, his arm going in up to the shoulder though the case was only twenty centimeters thick. He groped around for a moment, then pulled out a cumbersome thing that looked like part of a floater engine, fitted with straps and harness. Ann took it from him, and rested it on the ledge behind her but had to hold it with one hand to keep it from falling. With the other hand she kept a firm and steadying grip on the case while Jack reached in again and brought out another similar device. With one hand he then closed up the case again, until he could set it safely down on the ledge.

The objects were heavy. Their weight had been partially compensated for by nullifiers built into Jack's case. Now Jack and Ann had to bear the full weight, and it was tricky getting them up onto their backs and securely strapped in place while maintaining their balance on the ledge. The harness buckled in front, where there was a set of jury-rigged controls with trailing wires that ran over the shoulder to the devices on their backs. What looked liked parts of floater engines were in fact the scavenged parts of floater engines, the floater plates themselves, refitted to work along the long axis, and with minimal power provided by batteries.

Jack turned his on. There was a faint hum and he felt his weight drop to about ten percent of normal. "I wasn't sure it would work this high up," he said. Floater coils were designed to neutralize large masses close to the ground. Fliers and aircars used other means to gain altitude. But Jack had never intended to fly with these things. Ann switched hers on too.

They turned to face the wall and, holding the case between them to share its weight and to keep them from getting separated, they stepped backward off the ledge and started falling down the side of the wall. Below the first roof was another drop of twenty floors, which ended on a narrow ledge with overlooking windows. One of these had been broken out, and rather than continue their descent outside in the first light of dawn, they went in.

Beyond the broken window was what had probably been a private apartment, though little enough of what it had once contained remained intact. As soon as they were safely inside they removed their floater packs and put them back in the case. Ann couldn't help but glance at the comcon screen against the wall. It was smashed.

From the apartment they felt their way along dark corridors, not to the lift shaft by which they had come up, which would be watched by the police, but to a different set of lifts far on the other side of the city tower. There were no guards there.

They went down. The security lights within the shaft were not all working, so for the most part they descended in darkness. They had to change lifts several times on the way down, but they met no one. At last they came to the bottom of the express shafts just above the ten floors of the main public levels.

From here they had to use larger lifts that went only a floor or two, or sometimes broad, public stairs, and at last a back stair to get down to the parking levels under the city. They went at a fast walk, sometimes running down ramps, ever deeper into the underground. Near the bottom were many cars and service vehicles that had been abandoned along with the city.

Still legible codes on support posts told them their position, and they quickly found their way to the right place, where their car was just one among many. Jack put the case in the trunk while Ann got into the driver's seat and started the car. Then Jack got in the other side and unbuckled his gun. Ann glanced at him, then did the same. He took her belt and gun and put it with his in the backseat.

She drove slowly, without lights, toward one of the back ramps. They went up level after level, the silence broken only by the faint hum of their own vehicle. At last they came to the top level, with only one more ramp to go to the paved apron that surrounded the city. The exit was a brighter square in the darkness.

"Shut it down," Jack whispered suddenly. Ann switched off the ignition, and the floater settled to the concrete on residual power. In the silence they could both hear the hum of another, more powerful vehicle, just outside near the top of the ramp. A few seconds later the exit darkened as a large car pulled slowly up to block the way out. It shone no lights, but the outline of a patrol car was unmistakable.

Jack hoped that the cops would think this vehicle was just a derelict—except that there were no other derelicts here. Then doors opened on either side and two cops got out. Both were heavily armed. They came around to the front of the patrol car and stood there a moment, whispering to each other. Then they drew their sidearms and started down the last ramp into the parking deck.

The scar on the palm of Jack's right hand itched intolerably, but he resisted the urge to scratch it. He glanced at Ann, saw her catch his eye. Their guns were in the backseat, no sense trying to go for them—besides, they were caught. As the cops halved the distance to them, Jack heaved a very audible sigh, muttered "damn."

He saw Ann glance at him, then nod as she agreed with his plan, as flimsy as it was. "I told you we should have gone to my place," she whispered. Jack bet that, even though the whisper was soft, the cops had heard it.

But if they had they didn't care. They came on, one toward each side of the car and well separated, guns raised but not directly aimed.

"Not a good place for a makeout," the cop, a woman, on Ann's side said.

"Just get out nice and easy," the other cop said, "and keep your hands in view all the time."

Jack couldn't think of anything to say, so he kept silent as he carefully opened the door and, with his hands up in front of him, slid out of the seat.

"We were just looking for some privacy," Ann said from the other side of the floater.

"Wrong place to find it," the cop on her side said. "Now turn around, hands on the roof, two steps back."

They took the standard position for the search. The cops were quick, thorough, and not unnecessarily intimate. Jack watched Ann's immobile face across the roof of the car.

"All right," Jack's cop said when the search was done, "you can stand up now, but keep your hands up."

They did as they were told, and the patrol car at the top of the ramp came to life. Now with its lights on, it backed around till it was heading toward them. Its headlights were on bright. The cops were carrying 10 mm machine pistols, a bit heavy for standard patrol work.

"Put your hands out," Jack's cop told him. He took a security flex out of its case on his belt. The driver of the patrol car was talking on the mike.

"But officer," Jack protested as the cop put the node between his hands and the metal cables coiled around his wrists. "What have we done?"

"Trespassing, for starters. Now get in the car." He stood back to give Jack room to walk to the patrol car.

"Just in the parking level," Ann said. She too was handcuffed. "We didn't even get out of the car."

"Good enough," the cop with her said. She was holding the keys to the floater. "Now get moving."

Two other patrol cars pulled into the space on either side of the first, their headlights illumining the whole scene. Jack and Ann walked to the arresting car. Its backdoors opened automatically, and they got in. Jack's cop got in front with the driver, while the one with Ann's keys went back to the floater and started it up.

The two other patrol cars backed away, the one they were in backed out and turned around. Jack caught a glimpse of their floater following before the cop in the front told him to face forward.

The patrol cars were wheeled vehicles, and in spite of the heavy suspension the ride over long unused highways was rough. There was a security panel between the front and backseats, but there was also a speaker grill, and it was open, presumably so the cops could hear anything Jack and Ann might say to each other. They didn't say anything.

But they could hear the cops too. There wasn't much talk, and what there was, in the brief phrases people use when they don't have to explain things to each other, seemed to be about the search at the top of the abandoned city. From what he could make out, Jack figured it wasn't them the search had been after, but Djentsin, though the name by which he knew the man wasn't used.

Apparently three cops had been killed by the outlaw who had intruded on Jack and Ann, when the cops had come on him, still dazed but in possession of his blaster. The outlaw, in turn, had been shredded by riot-gun fire.

What the cops in the front seat were most concerned about was having been posted on the ground and missing the real action. Still, it was lucky that they hadn't been one of the three fatalities. How they had known Jack and Ann were in the parking levels was never mentioned.

After a while the passenger cop turned around to look back at Jack and Ann. "You just kind of picked the wrong place," he

said. "There are a lot of squatters in there who are going to go
to jail tonight—if they don't get killed resisting arrest. If you're
clean, all we'll charge you with is trespassing and vagrancy—
we'll let the violation of curfew go. If you're not clean, tough
shit." He turned away.

All Jack could think was that they must have wanted Djentsin
very badly.

At last they came to a city-tower, one of those nearest the one
where they'd been arrested, and were driven directly into the
building to the police station on one of the lower levels.

They were searched again, separately, and very thoroughly.
The police found Jack's dragongem and were more than a little
impressed, but they knew what it was and handled it gingerly.
Jack wasn't afraid that they might "lose" it—their own regulations were too strict.

The search included a complete X ray, and the cops could
make nothing of the implant in Jack's hand, arm, and skull,
which was fine with him, but it made them suspicious. Their
retinas were also recorded to be compared with the IDs they
carried—again Jack wasn't too concerned; he'd forged the IDs
carefully to include retinal identification. And then they were
taken, together, to routine interrogation.

The questioning, which was just a preliminary, lasted four
hours or so, and was for the most part rather low-key. The
arresting officers, who had to be present, were a bit more
cheerful than they had been, since the presence of a .75 pistol in
Jack's car qualified them for special credit, and bonuses for
hazardous service. No one on Nowarth could own firearms
without special permits, and lasers were strictly for military and
police use, but .75s were illegal in and of themselves. All other
charges, even the cops' inability to open Jack's case all the way,
hardly mattered compared with that.

Jack and Ann stuck to their story, saying as little as possible.
Everything they had done since their arrival, up to the time
they'd gone to the abandoned city-tower, they admitted to, but
let their real anxiety lend authenticity to their act of confusion,
fear, reluctance. Apparently the cops bought it.

At last the interrogation was finished, and Jack and Ann were
led to the temporary detention block and locked up in adjoining
cells, where they could see and talk to each other. They did not
avail themselves of the opportunity, there was no sense giving

the cops anything more to work on. Instead they decided to catch up on some sleep.

They were wakened by the arrival of the public prosecutor with the lawyer who had been assigned to handle their case—whose presence had not been necessary during the preliminaries. They were taken from the cells and led into an interview room.

The lawyer was a woman, Msr. Cheevy, somewhere in her second century. "I'm here to protect you as much as I can," she told them. She set an attaché case on the table opposite which Jack and Ann were sitting, and opened it. "I've checked the records of your arrest," she went on as she started the recorder inside, "and everything seems to have been done according to the law." She then told them what they could and couldn't say and do during the interview with the prosecutor.

He, a man of around sixty or so named Dregoff and rather young for his position, started out by putting their ID cards on the table. "If I didn't know for a fact," he said, "that you are not who these say you are, I'd swear they were authentic. In fact, they're so good that I don't think I could make a charge stick. Traveling under false names, yes, but not forgery."

The young man who'd been calling himself Jack Begin leaned back in his chair and looked at his companion. Her face was blank, her expression rigidly controlled. He forced a small smile, then turned back to Dregoff. "Who are we then?" he asked.

"Rikard Braeth," Dregoff said, "and Darcy Glemtide. You might have gotten away with it except for the fact that you were rather thoroughly identified and recorded when you were involved with that business on Seltique. I guess I heard something about it back then, though I don't pay much attention to things like that. I've read all the reports now, of course. Quite a piece of work it was."

"So what happens now," Darcy Glemtide asked.

"Not quite what we'd planned," Dregoff said. "You're famous, you know, in your own way—at least in certain circles. We still intend to press all charges, including illegal entry and possession of false credentials. But I expect some pressure from the Federal government to ease up on you because of what you did for the Taarshome and the Belshpaer. And I can sympathize with that. But the laws you broke you broke here under our jurisdiction—"

"That hasn't been proven yet," the lawyer said.

"Pardon me, Msr. Cheevy. The laws you are suspected of breaking are Nowarth laws, not Federal laws, and as such the prosecution is under our jurisdiction, not Federal jurisdiction. You will stand trial. And I have every confidence that we will prove our case." He got to his feet and glanced at the lawyer. "They're all yours, Msr. Cheevy." Then he left. The door closed with a rather final sound.

Cheevy put some papers down on the table and sorted them, more to enforce a pause than anything else. "I'm going to be straight with you," she said with a sigh. "I'll do everything I can to get the charges dismissed, but I don't think you have much of a chance.

"The trespassing charge is pretty solid, but it might be reduced to a misdemeanor. The guns were in your car, and hence technically in your possession, but we might be able to keep Msr. Dregoff from proving that you had knowledge of them. As for the false credentials . . ."

She sighed again as she looked at one of the papers, a list. "And that case they found in your trunk, they'll get it open eventually, even if they have to destroy it in the process—you'll be compensated for its cost, of course, unless it, too, proves to be a confiscatable item like the guns.

"If everything goes perfectly, and the courts are lenient and take your work on Seltique into account, you might get off with transportation and a fine—the dialithite crystal they found on you"—she tapped the list—"should cover most of that. But if they have their way, you're looking at exemplary punishment —they won't want people to think, just because you *are* famous, that you can get away with anything. That would mean up to twenty years of cognizant stasis and possibly partial re-programming."

"We have resources," Rikard said. "We can afford to pay for anything you can legitimately use." But he looked at her in a way that said he'd be willing to pay, too, for work that was less than legitimate.

"That might help," Cheevy said, "but I wouldn't count on it. Msr. Glemtide is known to be a Gesta, and you are assumed to be one by association. That in and of itself makes you persona non grata here."

"But we haven't done anything," Darcy said, "other than park for a while in the bottom of that tower."

"If you even got out of the car," Cheevy said, "they'd get

you for attempted vandalism as well. And what about those ID cards?"

"A legitimate name change," Rikard said. "We couldn't find any privacy after we introduced the Taarshome to the Senate chambers and reinstated the Belshpaer. Wherever we went the news services always found us. We don't like being famous, Msr. Cheevy."

"You'll have to provide me with information so I can get the records of the change," Cheevy said. "If they exist. Of all the worlds in the Federation to come visit, why did you choose this one?"

"It seemed like a good idea at the time," Darcy said.

"Well, it wasn't. I'll do the best I can. You should know, that according to the laws of Nowarth, you can be questioned while under the influence of certain electronic devices and chemical substances. You won't feel any pain. And you won't be damaged. If you are, the inquisitor loses her job and your compensation would be enough to hurt the city budget. But you *will* be examined."

"You don't sound very encouraging," Rikard said.

"I wish I could be. Unlike Msr. Dregoff, I did follow the events on Seltique. I have to admit that I admire you for what you did, what you were able to do. I'll do my best for you."

She stood up, and guards came in to escort Rikard and Darcy back to their cells.

They didn't have much of a respite before the inquisitors came.

3

It was a dark tunnel, slimed with fungus, and the only light was that coming from Rikard's father as he burned, leaping in the flames of the enemy's weapon. Though Rikard knew, in some remote corner of his mind, that this was just a ploy of his tormentors, he still felt his heart lurch, as it had when this had been real, felt his bowels wrench, still felt the tremendous sense of loss.

The man beside him said, "Those floater packs were very clever. Where did you get them?"

Rikard turned toward his interlocutor, redly lit in the light of his father's fire. "You leave my father out of this!"

"Those packs can't help you this time," the man said. "What were you doing in the city?"

Rikard tried to shut the answer out of his mind. How much had he told them? Were they guessing?

"I'm ashamed of you," his father said. "You knew the laws and yet you deliberately broke them."

His father, now, was as Rikard had last seen him—old, ragged, slightly crazy with years of isolation. The police had no way of knowing about that. And the police had no way of knowing that his father would have been proud, not ashamed, of Rikard's deeds, if regretful at his getting caught. That was the truth. His father smiled, proudly, secretly, sharing the secret knowledge with him. "Between gray stones," his father said.

Another thing the police could not have known about. Rikard remembered the stones, and the electrical stimulation that was supercharging his imagination let him see a dragongem in each hand. In the Tathas darkness, it linked his mind with the sky of reality, instead of the caves of insanity. He felt color return, saw superimposed on his mental image the true vision of his hands, strapped to the arms of a heavy chair built in with electronics. The field surrounded his body, radiating from the device enclosing his head.

"I can't stand this anymore," Darcy said, though she wasn't there. "I've worked so hard to block those memories out. Please, Rikard, let's cut our losses."

She did not look at all well. She was strong, he knew, stronger than he, but perhaps with darker secrets. Would she break? Had she already? Was that how they knew about—don't think about it.

A man sat at a console a couple of meters in front of Rikard's chair, his back to him. He adjusted controls, readouts changed, telltales flickered, dials registered new values. A woman, standing beside the man, looked at Rikard with unconcerned attention. "Where did you first meet Djentsin?" she asked.

Who the hell was Djentsin? Rikard opened a huge scroll wound around silver staves, capped with elaborate ornaments.

On the scroll were words written in a strange language, in strange characters, that nonetheless seemed to make sense. A man looked over his shoulder. "Where is the Reliquiture?" he asked.

Rikard turned away with an effort, tried to push the too-close image from his mind, and saw a door open in a wall of shadow. The woman who entered his suite, at the Carolinga Hotel, was a stranger on Godwin IV. That was important; no such woman had ever visited him there. It should be a man, and it should be on . . . he clamped down on the memories, even as her face began to assume a familiar form, and wrapped himself in darkness.

His body rotated in space. He felt Darcy lying next to him. He had never been very successful with girls, and it astonished him that he and Darcy should be lovers. He reached his arm across her, felt himself becoming aroused.

"What the hell is going on here?" a woman said. "You people get your kicks from this?"

"Do you get your kicks from watching?" Rikard asked back. Then the left half of his field of view became bright. There were two technicians, standing sullenly at their machines. Rikard, strapped naked in his chair, felt acute embarrassment. If they were doing this to him, what were they doing to Darcy?

Somewhere a man said, "You have no authority here. This is planetary business, and I'll ask you not to interfere."

"I make my own authority," Rikard said.

A man on Rikard's right spoke. "I'm afraid she does have the authority." The rest of the room brightened, revealing the stranger woman, other technicians, his interrogators. "I've just gotten a call from the Secretary. We have to let Braeth go."

Rikard looked at the man, the woman beside him, his father between them. His father's expression was sorrowful, not angry, not disappointed. Then his clothes began to smoke, his skin blackened, small flames danced on his head, his shoulders, across his chest. "God damn you!" Rikard screamed.

The woman glanced at her male companion, oblivious to the charring corpse of Rikard's father between them. "How long will he be like this?"

"It will wear off in a few hours," the man said. He was older, and carried himself with an air of resigned authority. The woman carried authority too, but anything but resigned. She looked at Rikard with distaste.

Rikard, without being drunk, felt as though his brain were swimming in alcohol. This was reality, he knew that now. The false perceptions of his father, Darcy, other places and times, faded but lingered as a dark background to his consciousness.

Rikard tried to focus on the woman's face, but her features seemed to be rippling, as if seen through disturbed water. She said, "I want this man, and his companion, to be ready to leave within half an hour."

The man hesitated a beat, then nodded. Around the room, the technicians started switching off their equipment. Rikard watched as the lights went dead, the dials swung to zero, the readouts went blank. Everybody's face was rippling. Sometimes he couldn't tell if a person was a man or a woman. An enveloping blackness pulsed in and out around him.

"We'll straighten him up as quickly as we can," the man said, "but it will take at least two days to do the paperwork."

"So do it after we're gone," the woman said. She was dark complected, tall and muscular, and something about her posture hinted that she had been born on a world less hospitable than Nowarth. "Now where's Glemtide?"

"We cannot release this man," the man said with angry intensity, "until the proper forms have been filled out, the required—"

"Now, Korijian!" the woman said. "You deal with your business however you choose, but Braeth and Glemtide go with me now. Where is she?"

"In the next lab," Korijian said, barely controlling himself. "But I must insist—"

"I informed you," the woman said, "over a standard day ago that I had a warrant for these people. Upon that notification, the matter was legally out of your hands. Federal law required that you make these people ready for me. Why haven't you complied?"

"We were hoping we could get just a little more information on an important crime. There has been—"

"I know something about this world, and I doubt that any crime committed here is important to the Federation. I expect full cooperation from you from here on. Now let's get out of here."

Two technicians came up to Rikard and began releasing the straps, the probes, the contacts. His skin felt fuzzy, half numb, half supersensitive. They stepped back when they were done and Rikard tried to stand, but he couldn't lift himself out of the chair.

"See?" Korijian said. "He needs more time."

"He'd have had it if you'd stopped your interrogation when I first communicated with you. Are you going to help him walk, or shall I call in my own crew?"

Korijian just stared at her, but the two technicians helped Rikard out of the chair. The woman turned toward the door, Korijian went with her, and the technicians, with Rikard wobbly between them, followed. As the woman stepped out into the hallway she looked back at Rikard.

"Don't you think it would be a good idea," she said with malicious sarcasm, "to give him back his clothes first?"

She stood in the open doorway, with Korijian fidgeting beside her, waiting as the technicians, with some help from one or two others, started to put Rikard's clothes on. Then she and Korijian left.

When Rikard was dressed, the same two technicians helped him walk, first up one hall, then down another, until at last they came to a door that let them into the back rooms of an office complex, and from there into the office proper, spacious and well decorated. Korijian was seated at the desk, a broad expanse of polished dark wood, uncluttered except for the insets of several specialized communications and control devices. The woman was sitting in one of the side chairs. Rikard's escorts took him to another chair, immediately in front of the desk, sat him down, and then left.

Korijian and the woman were both angry, she sitting in stony silence, he staring off into space. Rikard expected them to react to his presence, but they did not. He had a long, uncomfortable moment to wonder how much he had told the police under their interrogation. It didn't help any that the room seemed to be shifting off balance, that he felt puffed and pringly all over. Then he began, belatedly, to wonder who this woman was, that she could order a city police commissioner around the way she did. He was almost going to ask her when a movement beside him distracted him.

It was Darcy. How long had she been there? He didn't remember another chair being there when he came in. She looked awful, as bad as he felt. He reached out to touch her, and she noticed him for the first time. He tried to smile at her, didn't know if he succeeded or not. She leaned over the arm of her chair and put her arms around his neck. He tried to hug her back, though the distance between the chairs made it awkward. How much had she told? He said, "Are you all right?"

"No." Her voice was weak, and broke even on a single sylla- ble. "I'm not. You don't look too good either."

"If these people have been damaged," the woman said, "the colonel will not be happy."

"Your colonel," Korijian said thinly, "has no say on how we conduct our interrogations."

"That is true, but he may have something to say about your continuing those interrogations after you have been officially notified of the subjects being required by the Federation."

Korijian just sat there, tight-lipped.

The woman turned tiredly to Rikard and Darcy. Her gaze was disapproving, almost disgusted. "You're pretty lucky, you know," she said. "If I'd come one day later, your brains would be jelly."

"Who are you?" Rikard asked at last. His voice sounded strangely metallic in his ears.

"My name is Orin Sukiro, I'm a special agent with the Fed- eral Police. The colonel has been looking for you. Do you feel well enough to travel?"

"We can go any time," Darcy said. "Who cares what we feel like?"

"I don't," Sukiro said. She got to her feet.

"I'll need to register your authorization," the administrator told her.

"I've registered three times already, I think that's enough."

"You'll do it again," Korijian almost yelled, "as often as necessary, or these people don't go anywhere but back into in- terrogation."

Sukiro glared at him a moment, then slowly, stiffly, she took a thick card out of an inner pocket of her jacket. Korijian reached for it, but she held it away from him, and plugged it herself into a slot on the desk. Korijian stifled a comment, then reached for the card again, but Sukiro kept her hand on the protruding edge.

"Not," she said, "that I'm afraid you might take it from me."

Korijian glared at her and sat back in his chair. There was a tone from the desk, and the card popped up. Sukiro took it and put it back in her pocket.

"But if I lost it," she went on, "you might claim I'd never had it." Her smile was nasty. Korijian just glowered.

"Now," Sukiro said, "let's go. And I want all their personal belongings, as specified in the warrant and registered—again —just now."

"They're being brought," Korijian said with poor grace.

Even as he spoke the outer door to his office opened, and an officer entered, guiding a floater tray, on which were the gravity packs, Rikard's 4D case, and other things they had left at their hotel. Rikard got unsteadily to his feet. He wanted to make sure everything was really on the tray. But the officer guarding it held out his hand to stop him.

"I'm sorry," he said, "you're not allowed to handle this until you're out of Nowarth's jurisdiction."

"What if something's missing?"

"File a form 407-C39F. It will take about thirty standard days to process."

"You're kidding," Rikard said. He tried to take an inventory of the tray without touching it. "Where's my gun?"

"It's been confiscated," Korijian said. "You won't be getting that back."

"Now wait a minute, Darcy's gun is there—"

"Msr. Korijian," Sukiro interrupted, "the warrant is very clear. Please check any of the four copies you now have. I am to take custody of Rikard Braeth, Darcy Glemtide, and *any and all* of their possessions, specifically including that gun!"

"That gun, Agent Sukiro, is contraband. It is illegal for any person on this planet to own a gun of that type, for any reason, under any circumstances, and that includes officers of the law, security patrol, and planetary guard. Our laws are very clear also, and that weapon is to be destroyed."

"And I happen to know," Sukiro said softly, "that *my* gun falls into the same category." She pulled back the tail of her jacket, revealing a holster containing a heavy police blaster. "Do you intend to confiscate that too?"

"You are a Federal agent, and there's nothing I can do about that."

"Fine, and there's nothing you can do about that man's weapon, either, since as of my notification to you of my warrant, that gun became officially Federal Government property. It must be returned to me, if not to him, or you will face Federal charges."

"I'm sorry," Korijian said, "it can't be done."

Sukiro stared at him. Korijian stared back. After a moment, a small smile of triumph crossed his face.

Without taking her eyes from Korijian, Sukiro reached over his desk and started punching buttons. Korijian was too surprised to protest at first, and by the time he recovered, the call had gone through.

"Department of the Interior," the voice from the comcon said, "may I help you?"

Sukiro moved around the desk so she could see the screen and be seen by the person at the other end. "I'm Federal Agent Orin Sukiro," she said, as she slipped a card into the comcon slot. "May I speak with Secretary Jakoby, please?"

"What do you think you're doing?" Korijian protested. But he was helpless to interfere. Sukiro paid him no attention.

"Jakoby here," a new voice came from the comcon. "What can I do for you, Msr. Sukiro?"

Succinctly, but in detail, Sukiro explained her problem in getting Rikard's gun released. When she finished, Jakoby asked to speak to Korijian.

"Let her have the gun," he said. He sounded tired, and a bit reluctant. "I've had the warrant checked, and it's explicit, and in order."

"Yes, sir," Korijian said. Sukiro reached out and broke the connection.

"But not here," Korijian said to her. "I'll deliver the gun to your ship."

"That's fine. Now let's for God's sake go."

Korijian's resistance at last seemed to be broken. He arranged for an escort, who took Rikard and Darcy, along with Sukiro, to internal transport through the city-tower to a government garage on the outside of the building, at ground level, where they got into a floater.

Rikard and Darcy shared the backseat with one of their escorts, while Sukiro rode in front with the other. Rikard's mind was becoming ever more clear now, and he wanted to talk to Darcy, to ask her how she was, to find out what she had experienced. But the presence of other people stifled him, and he had to content himself with just holding her, as she held him, as they went past one city-tower, then another.

The shuttleport was not a tower, but rather a ring of lower structures, surrounding the landing aprons. The shuttles themselves were invisible behind the service buildings, but one craft stuck up, the unmistakable spindle shape of a starship.

It was small, as starships go, but a starship nonetheless. Starships do not land on planets, their structure can't withstand the strain of gravity or atmospheric disturbance. The flicker drives can't move a ship with more than a thousand kilometer accuracy, and even if they could, using a flicker drive near a mass like a planet, or even a large space station, would cause immense damage to the planet or station, due to the momentary spatial distortions of the drive. Yet there it stood, so it had to be one of the special Federal Patrol craft, unique in being fully equipped for surface landings.

By the time they got close enough to read whatever markings it might have had, it was obscured by the even nearer buildings which, though not towers, were nonetheless mostly forty to fifty stories tall. The driver swung the floater around to one side, then pulled into a government garage, where they all got out.

One of their escorts guided the floater tray with Rikard and Darcy's belongings, while the other led them through a section of emigration usually reserved for diplomats. Only once did Sukiro have to say anything to the officious personnel.

The regular shuttle ramps wouldn't connect them to the starship, so they took a small open car out onto the apron and drove to where the Patrol craft stood, on its self-contained landing scaffold like a spider's legs. The tip of its flicker-drive spike hung just meters above the concrete. As they neared, a G-vator platform lowered on a guide wire from the transport ring right under the main saucer. It touched ground just as the car stopped and Sukiro got out.

Rikard was able to walk unaided now, and Darcy, too, seemed pretty steady. One of the escorts unloaded the floater tray and guided it toward the vator platform. Sukiro turned to the other.

"I'll take Msr. Braeth's gun now," she said.

"I don't know anything about that," the woman answered, and for the first time Rikard wondered why Sukiro was making such a fuss about the weapon. The Federal Police couldn't know anything about its special features, it must just be Sukiro's way.

"All right then," Sukiro was saying, "then find out."

"I'm supposed to stay with you."

Sukiro didn't say anything, didn't change expression, just stared at the officer until she colored, got back in the car, and drove back toward the service ring. The other officer, having finished with the tray, watched uncomprehendingly as she drove off.

"She'll be back in just a minute," Sukiro told him. "At least, she'd better be."

The minute went by, and Rikard decided to sit down on the vator platform. He was still feeling weak and confused, but the sun was shining, there was a pleasant breeze across the apron, and if he just sat, he could turn his mind off for a moment. He was hardly aware of Darcy sitting down beside him.

Several other minutes went by. Rikard thought about lying back and maybe taking a nap. But Sukiro was getting impatient. She got on the platform and touched the controls. Rikard watched the remaining officer, left on the apron, shrink as the platform rose to the ship's transport ring.

He could almost feel Sukiro's tension as she led him and Darcy through the narrow companionways to the inside lift shaft, and up to the tiny bridge. Two Federal officers, in uniform, were sitting at the command stations. There was barely enough room for Sukiro and her charges to stand. The agent put a hand on the second officer's shoulder.

"There's a floater tray below," she said. "Stow it, will you?"

The man nodded and left, and Sukiro took his place, where she turned on the comcon and called the police commissioner. "I want that gun, Korijian," she said without preamble when he came on. "And I want it now."

"I'm pushing through the protocol just as fast as I can," Korijian replied. Rikard could see, over Sukiro's shoulder, the man's face on the comcon screen, looking stubborn and frazzled.

"That should have been taken care of long ago," Sukiro said. "I've had enough. You have failed to conform to standard Federal agreements and procedures, you've resisted Federal authority, and I think it's about time I lodged a formal complaint."

"There's no need—" Korijian started to say, but Sukiro cut him off, redialed, the ship's log symbol came on the screen. She then proceeded, in concise detail, to do just what she had threatened. Even as she was signing off by stamping the report with her ID card, the second stuck his head in.

"We got the gun," he said. "I put it in safe three."

"Good enough," Sukiro said. She got up and let the second resume his place. "Let's go."

She took Rikard and Darcy, not down, but out into the tiny living area that surrounded the bridge, under the ship's dome. "We don't have any extra cabins," she explained. "You'll have to make do on the couches here."

Telltales by the bridge hatch were blinking, so Rikard and Darcy got themselves comfortable. Liftoff from a planet on a shuttle was usually very easy, but a ship like this was not designed for atmospheric movement, and if there was any turbulence, its gravity system would not be quick enough to keep them from being knocked off their feet. Sukiro took a chair near them, and even as she sat the ship went up—very fast if Rikard could judge by the rapid change in hue of the sky overhead. Even in a patrol craft, the dome was fully provided with external screens. Internal lights came on as they ascended past the atmosphere, the screens darkened where the sun was, and after a few moments Nowarth came into view as the ship rotated into orbit.

They did not stop at the planetary station, which Rikard could see as a quarter disk off near the limb of the planet, but drove on inertials away from Nowarth toward the jump-slot at the star's north pole, a bit farther out than Nowarth itself. It seemed that Sukiro was going to spend that part of the trip with them.

"What are we charged with?" Rikard asked her. It was something he should have asked long before.

Sukiro looked at him a moment, then at Darcy. "There are no charges," she said.

"But that warrant—" Darcy started to say.

"Enjoy your trip," Sukiro said, and looked away.

"Now wait a minute," Rikard said. Though he was still a bit fuzzy, his mind was now clear enough that he could feel anger again, and the palm of his right hand began to itch. "Just what is this business all about?"

"What it's about," Sukiro said with exaggerated condescension, "is that the Federal Police want you, and you're going."

"In other words," Darcy said, "you're kidnapping us." Sukiro just smiled. "Let me see that warrant." Sukiro, still smiling, just turned away.

"I can lodge formal complaints too," Darcy went on, "and I know that this ship is monitored, and the tapes will be read when we get to wherever we are going. I have a right, as a Federal citizen, to know where you are taking me and why."

Sukiro stopped smiling, though it seemed more because of fatigue than anger. She took out the warrant card and handed it to Darcy, who just stared at it a moment. Sukiro smirked—without a reader, the card was useless.

But Darcy just went to the console next to the bridge hatch, touched a button that opened a panel, stuck the card in the slot, and read what it displayed on the screen. "It's the damndest thing," she said, turning to Rikard. "No charges at all, it just says that Nowarth is to turn us over to Sukiro, with all possessions. It mentions your seventy-five specifically. And it's authorized by the Federal Secretary of Internal Affairs."

"I guess Korijian's in trouble," Rikard said. He got up to read the warrant for himself, then looked back at Sukiro, who was smirking again. "Another interesting point," he went on. "This warrant is addressed to the Nowarth police and government, not to us. They have to give us to you, but nowhere does it say we have to go with you." Sukiro did not stop smirking. Rikard went to stand in front of her chair. "Unless you have another warrant," he said, "that specifically authorizes you to take us into custody, then I'll insist that you set us down on the nearest world. Other than Nowarth."

That didn't seem to faze Sukiro at all. Indeed, her smile got broader. "There's nothing I'd like to do better."

"I don't understand," Rikard said.

"Neither do I," Darcy said, coming to stand beside him, "and I don't like it. How about it, Sukiro, will you let us go?"

"If you insist," Sukiro said. "And then I can tell Colonel Polski that you refused to come."

"Leonid Polski?" Rikard asked.

But before Sukiro could answer, the jump alarm sounded. Rikard and Darcy hurriedly got back to their places on the couch and set the safety on.

"We can't be at the jump-slot yet," Darcy said as the mild stasis field clamped down on them.

"We're not," Sukiro said. "But we're far enough from No-warth to jump."

The dome overhead, showing stars, shimmered as the flicker drive came on and the first jump was made. The stars shifted their positions, held steady for half a second, then moved again, and again, as the flicker came up to full power. Now the stars, visible only in the microseconds between each jump, flowed past them, or seemed to, as the ship drove at what was effectively super-light speed.

"This will take a while," Sukiro said as she got out of her chair. At full power, there was no need for security fields. "We've got a long way to go, you might as well make yourselves comfortable."

"Did Polski send you?" Rikard asked as he turned off the safety on the couch.

"He did."

"What's it all about?" Darcy asked.

"You'll have to ask him."

"Come on," Darcy said, "I've known Leonid for a long time—"

She stopped at Sukiro's smirk, as if the agent had known that she and Polski had once been lovers.

"It's not like Polski," Rikard said in the embarrassed silence, "to throw his weight around like this. Why did he send for us?"

"He sent for you, Msr. Braeth. Not for Msr. Glemtide." Her words were intended to hurt.

"My name is on that warrant too," Darcy said.

"That's as may be, but it's Braeth he wants."

They waited for her to say more, but she just turned with a feigned nonchalance and started toward the bridge hatch.

"Why?" Rikard asked.

Sukiro, her hand not quite touching the latch plate, looked at him distastefully and sighed. "He's got this idea that you can help him with an investigation. I'm sorry, you'll have to ask him about that."

"But why me?"

Sukiro touched the latch, the hatch slid open. She stepped in, then turned to look back at them one more time. "That's what I keep asking myself," she said.

"So why," Darcy said, "did Leonid *say* he wanted Rikard, dammit?"

Sukiro was enjoying herself. "Because of his work with the Taarshome and the Belshpaer. And because the colonel seems to think Msr. Braeth can take care of himself, evidence of which seems lacking to me." Then her face got grim again, and she almost snarled, saying, "And because Braeth is not a cop."

That, it seemed, was what really rankled. Sukiro touched the inner plate and the hatch slid closed.

PART
<u>TWO</u>

PART
TWO

1

Patrol craft are fast. A trip that would have taken a commercial liner ten days took Sukiro's courier only half that time. Which was, however, four and a half days too long as far as the people on board were concerned, cramped as they were into quarters that were meant for three but that had to accommodate five. The two crew were amiable enough but carefully kept a professional distance, and refused to say anything about their business. When not on the bridge they stayed in their tiny cabin as much as they could.

Sukiro's patent dislike for both Rikard and Darcy, even more than the crowding, was what made the trip so unpleasant, and unfortunately the three had to share the habitation deck, as did the crew for meals and exercise.

And that meant that Rikard and Darcy didn't have much opportunity to talk, except about trivialities. The ship was monitored, and anything they might say about the Reliquiture or the Leaves of Ba'Gashi could be legally used against them. And if the subject of their anticipated meeting with Leonid Polski came up, Sukiro was either cruelly taunting or angrily defensive. Rikard got the impression that she regarded the colonel as something of a hero—which in fact he was, of course.

The only incident of note occurred about two hours after the craft left the Nowarth system jump-slot. A signal came in from Polski's gunship—there are no private communication lines on a Patrol craft, so everybody heard the message and the first officer's response—telling Sukiro to go to someplace called Natimarie instead of Dorflyn, saying that Polski would meet them there. Sukiro acknowledged but did not offer the others an explanation.

Their arrival at the Natimarie system was anything but typical. Instead of slowing the drive during the last lightyear or so of travel they came in at full flicker, then went on inertials immediately after the last jump. From jump-slot to the main station took them just under ten standard hours, instead of the twenty-five or so usually required. Traffic control aboard the station wasn't too happy about this, but the Patrol craft came to a relative halt with plenty of clearance. They docked immediately, ahead of other ships that had arrived in a more sedate manner.

Sukiro did not stand upon ceremony but off-boarded Rikard and Darcy at once and towed their luggage floater herself. The boarding tube led them to a lobby filled with the average collection of passengers, most of them Human. They were met by a Federal officer in uniform, wearing a sergeant's stripes, who greeted Sukiro by name and took them through immigration without their having to pass inspection or present credentials.

Natimarie Station was no different from any of the others Rikard had been on during the last fifteen years or so, a bit smaller than some, perhaps, but organized in the same way. They were quickly led through the public areas to a private lounge that had apparently been appropriated for the use of Polski's crew because the only people at the bar and seated on the grouped couches wore the tan and black Federal police uniforms.

They went through the lounge to an inner room. There were only five other people here, seated, each after their own fashion, around a low table. Polski, flanked by a captain and a major, had his back to the door. The other two seated on the floor across the table from him were not Human, but centauroid Senola, the native sentients of Natimarie.

Polski turned as they entered. He looked tired, as if he had not slept much lately, and there was now a touch of gray in his hair. But his smile, when he saw who it was, was broad and genuine. Rikard grinned back.

"How you doing, kid?" Polski said as he got to his feet. He was as tall as Rikard, and handsome in the way Rikard had always wished he could be. He strode up and shook Rikard's hand as if he were truly glad to see him.

"Confused," Rikard said, "but otherwise okay."

"We've got a lot to talk about," Polski said, then turned to Darcy. It might have been Rikard's imagination, but he thought he detected a bit of reserve in Polski's smile for her, in his offered hand. "How are you, Darcy?" Polski asked. "It's been a long time."

"Two years," Darcy said. And though she smiled and shook his hand with vigor, there was something other than the joy of greeting going on in her mind.

After all, Darcy and Polski had been a lot more than just friends before Rikard had come along. She'd chosen to go with Rikard, but she was still fond of her old lover and sometime nemesis. They had been on opposite sides of the law several times, and only the fact that Polski had never caught her at her somewhat less than legal procurement of lost art objects had kept them from becoming enemies. There was still something between them. Rikard could see this in her face, though maybe Darcy wasn't aware of it herself.

"Delivered as ordered, Colonel," Sukiro said. Her tone was a touch too peremptory, too formal.

"Exactly as ordered," Polski said to her. "You got the gun, too?"

"Right here," Sukiro said with a negligent wave at the luggage floater. "I had to pull some strings. They wanted to destroy it."

Polski grinned at her as if he knew what strings she had pulled, and how she had pulled them. "I'll read your report as soon as I can," he told her. "Right now I want to fill you in on what's been going on."

He told the sergeant to put the luggage aboard his gunship, then introduced the newcomers to the other four people, who had been standing politely by their table. Captain Brenner was as tall as Rikard or Polski, but almost fragilely slender and very pale, as if born on a small world orbiting a dim star. Major Chiang was a handsome woman who exuded an aura of competency bettered only by that of Polski himself. The two Senola were named Anaviir, a police captain who was Polski's chief liaison on Natimarie, and Meshatham, a member of the Federal diplomatic corps who was serving as cultural interpreter.

The Senola had slender but deep-chested, horizontal lower bodies, and narrow upper torsos—the lungs being in the lower body. Their four legs were long and slender, though they stood no taller than an average Human. Their faces were narrow and long, with small batlike ears and very large purple, almost red eyes. Their arms were long enough to reach the ground when they stood, and their feet were doubly cloven hooves. Their skins were ivory colored, shading to ocher, hairless except for full manes of dark, rich brown hair.

Their clothes, though accommodating their centauroid form, were not otherwise exotically cut. Anaviir wore a uniform of deep blue with white trim, and Meshatham's civilian jacket, shirt, and trousers were of a subtly patterned fabric in greens and browns, with just a touch of maroon for color. When they spoke, their voices were mellow and resonant, and their mouths showed lots of carnivorous teeth. They had no tails, and no distinguishing sexual characteristics, as far as Rikard could tell.

"All right," Polski said when greetings were finished, "we'd better get going."

"How bad is it?" Sukiro asked him as they left the inner lounge.

"About as bad as it could be, even though we got here before they finished the job. How they knew we were coming I don't know, but they were gone when we landed. They left an awful lot of survivors this time. I don't think they got through the whole area before they left."

There was no further discussion until they got to the privacy of a specially chartered station shuttle. Most of the seats were for Humans, but a quarter of the spaces had been reworked to accommodate the Senola, who had no space technology of their own, and who depended on Federation services for interplanetary trade and transport.

Rikard threw himself into a chair, slunched down, crossed his long legs, and looked Polski square in the eye. "So what the hell is going on?" he said.

"That's what we're trying to find out. About a standard year ago somebody raided a small town on Gentian. Ninety percent of the population, just under ten thousand people, wound up missing, the rest dead, except for five or six survivors who were totally mindless. Since then about forty other worlds have been similarly hit—always small towns, isolated from the rest of their society. That's almost the only pattern there is."

Rikard could only sit and stare at the grim faces around him. At least, he assumed that the Senola faces were grim, too.

It was Darcy who broke the silence. "How many people are we talking about?" she asked.

"Half a million so far," Polski said. "Not as many as died at Banatree, but that was a single incident. What makes this so bad is that we never know who's going to be hit next—and they're being hit, Darcy, every ten to fifteen standard days."

"And they just kidnap ten thousand people at a time," Rikard said.

"It's worse than that," Polski told him. "We don't know the numbers for sure, but we have reason to believe that they're killing about half the people before they take them away. I have no idea what they want with the bodies. They take out their brains, and the major nervous systems. We discovered that only recently."

"You don't mean that literally," Rikard interjected.

"I do. We haven't found any of the nervous material, but we have found a few bodies with empty skulls and spinal columns."

"But what the hell do they do with it?" Darcy asked.

"We have no idea. We've been collecting data like crazy, but none of it makes much sense, either about that or about how they move around and choose targets. A raid can occur almost anywhere, first this side of the Federation, then the other, then right next door, then somewhere else. There seems to be no preference as to the species of the victims, almost every race in the Federation has been 'collected' at one time or another. There is some indication that the raiders are comprised of more than one species, but which species we have no idea. We don't know anything about the weapons they use, how they subdue the population, what kind of ship or ships they have, or any idea where they might be coming from. Or what their motives might be."

"Is *this* why you sprang us?" Rikard asked incredulously. "Good God, Leonid, what the hell do you think *I* can do?"

"These raiders are working out of some kind of base," Major Chiang said. She glanced at Polski, who leaned back to let her talk. "They're not just marching across the Federation from one side to the other," she went on. "We don't know where their base is yet, but we've got our analysts working on it, and as soon as we have an idea, we'd like you to go in and penetrate it."

"Now wait just a minute," Rikard started to say.

"Take it easy, kid," Polski said. "Wait until you hear the whole story. I know you have other business, and I'm not going to force you into anything. But at least give me the chance to try to persuade you."

". . . All right, tell me about it."

"It all depends on our getting some kind of clue as to where their base might be. All we can be sure of at the moment is that it is within the Federation somewhere, and that it has to be able to keep them in supplies, energy, and enough material to launch all these raids, and have some kind of depot where they can keep their victims, assuming they don't just toss them out a lock somewhere in deep space."

"You'd need at least a good-sized city for that," Darcy said, "and that means an inhabited planet. But how could these raiders work out of *any* Federation world without people knowing about them?"

"They've been able to get on and off forty worlds without being detected," Major Chiang said. "At least so far. We'll find out more when we get downstairs. And if they can do that, they're using ships like Patrol craft, or special couriers—"

"Which means they had a lot of money and power to begin with," Captain Brenner put in.

"—and that means," Chiang went on, "that if they're careful, as obviously they have been so far, their base planet may have no idea that they're even there, let alone what they're up to."

"And that's where you come in, kid," Polski said. "As soon as our analysts come up with some possibilities, I want you to go in, as my special agent, to see if you can locate the raiders more precisely, identify them if you can, possibly penetrate them, and get word to us, so we can move on them in force."

And that, Rikard realized, was part, at least, of what was bothering Sukiro. "Why don't you use her?" he asked, jerking a thumb in her direction.

"It wouldn't work," Polski said. Sukiro turned a stony face away. "Police think and act too much like police, even under cover. We're all wired, and that can be detected, and if it is you've got a dead cop. And if we did send someone like Sukiro in under cover, we'd have to work for maybe a year to provide a good background. You can't have somebody just pop up out of nowhere, they'd be blocked out or killed as soon as they said 'Hello.'"

"But I'm different," Rikard said quietly.

"Exactly."

"But I'm known."

"You are. But not just because of all that publicity on Seltique. You may not be aware of it, kid, but you've got a reputation for doing certain kinds of things that no good cop would tolerate—well, professionally, at least. You're a Gesta, and as such you could have any number of motives for being anywhere you wanted to be, any time, without any background other than what you take with you. You can just walk in without explanations and nobody will question that—except the local police, of course."

"Don't give me more credit than I deserve," Rikard said. "Darcy's the clever one, you should ask her, not me."

"Not on your life," Darcy said.

"You could do it," Polski told her. "But the kid's got one advantage that makes him the ideal choice."

"His gun."

"Exactly."

"I've been wondering about that," Sukiro said. "Seventy-fives aren't all that common, but I could have gotten him another one out of the Black Room. What's so special about this one?"

Rikard looked down at the scar on the palm of his right hand. "I'm wired for it," he said, then looked up at Sukiro. "When I hold it, with my glove on, it gives me a built-in self-correcting heads-up range-finder, and speeds up my perceptions by about a factor of ten."

"Holy shit."

"You might say," Polski said.

"I've seen him snap off all six shots in less than a second," Darcy said, "and every one a bull's-eye."

"If it weren't for that," Polski said to Darcy, "you'd have been my first choice. You've had a lot more experience than Rik, and I know you're good enough to do the job, but with that gun of his. . . . Now look, kid," he said to Rikard, "what I'm asking you is a favor. You don't have to do it. But I think you *can* do it, and it could make the difference between stopping these raiders now, or letting dozens of thousands of people be carried off for God knows what purpose."

"You're putting me in kind of a bind," Rikard said. Everybody was watching him. "I do have some unfinished business, and time could be very important."

"I think I have some idea of what you're talking about," Polski said. "Sukiro isn't the only agent I sent out looking for you. But she's the best, so I sent her where I thought you would most likely be. I knew that a man named Djentsin was on Nowarth, and that he had at least one of the Leaves of Ba'Gashi—" There were restrained murmers of surprise from the others.

"—and I knew that you two had been looking for them ever since you left Seltique."

"I thought we were being pretty discreet," Darcy said.

"You were, but I *know* you, Darcy, and I think I know you pretty well too, Rik. It was just a matter of making some shrewd guesses based on where you went and who you talked to."

"You were spying on us?" Darcy asked.

"For purely personal reasons," Polski said dryly.

Darcy flushed.

Of course. Polski was still in love with Darcy. He hadn't tried to keep her from falling for Rikard, or tried to put Rikard out of the picture, as he so easily could have.

"Maybe we're lucky," Rikard said. "They had us cold on Nowarth, I hate to think what would have happened to us if you hadn't pulled us out."

"I do too," Polski said. "And if it weren't for this business, I couldn't have done it. But if you agree to do what I ask, you may not think yourself so lucky after all."

"It's not exactly the kind of business I've had much experience with," Rikard said dryly.

"What about me?" Darcy asked. "Or do you want Rikard to do this by himself?"

"What I want," Polski said, "has nothing to do with it. You two have been a team for a couple of years now. If Rik went alone, he might have to explain himself to people who would find his being there without you very suspicious. But you'll have to make up your own mind about it, just as Rik will. We'll be landing in a couple of minutes, let's see what we find here first." Then Polski sat back and was silent for the rest of the trip.

2

Natimarie was a large world, but rather lacking in heavy elements, such as metals, so most of its technology, which was quite high, was based on wood, porcelains and glasses, and plastics and other organic materials. The population was well under two billion. The town near which the shuttle landed was small by Federation standards, though here it was about average size, just under ten thousand people, surrounded by open grain fields.

Two Patrol craft stood on their landing spiders, hardly disturbing the fully grown but still green crop just a couple of hundred meters from the edge of town. Four other shuttles had, of necessity, caused more damage—not that the inhabitants of that town would care anymore. Two dark tan Federal armored flyers were parked at either end of the impromptu landing field, and surrounding them all were a dozen or so local fliers, and as many wheeled ground vehicles.

But it was the town that held Rikard's attention as he and Darcy came off the shuttle. It rose abruptly from the now-flattened fields that surrounded it and was separated from them only by a circumferential road. Rikard had seen some strange architecture on the worlds he had visited, but nothing quite like this.

At first all he saw were platform floors, suspended in air, connected only by two or three flights of open stairways and occasional columns. Furniture, peculiar to the needs of the Senola, were arranged in groups on each floor, like living rooms, bedrooms, kitchens, studies. He could see through the nearer dwellings into those beyond, and through them into others beyond them; see the trees and bushes on the far sides of the houses, between them, lining the streets, which trees and bushes at some angles obscured his view after only a home or two, at others permitted him to see for blocks and blocks. In those directions the air seemed to grow thick with distance, which was because the houses, shops, public buildings did in fact have walls, but walls made of almost perfectly transparent glass.

"Is the whole town like this?" Darcy asked.

"And every town and city on Natimarie," Major Chiang said. "It takes a while to get used to. Senola don't have much need for privacy."

"Or secrecy either," Captain Brenner added. He gestured to a long, wheeled van that was parked nearby and they all got in.

It was a Senola vehicle, made mostly of wood, with benches on one side on which Anaviir and Meshatham sat straddled, and with Humanform seats on the other side for the rest of them.

"What about survivors?" Polski asked as the Senola driver turned the van toward the town.

"We'll see them first," Brenner said. "We've kept twenty some odd in the hospital here. The others—about half the population this time—have been sent to wherever we could find room."

"That's better than on Dorflyn," Polski told Rikard and Darcy. "There were only fifty survivors there altogether. Half the population was missing, the other half dead."

The short ride to the hospital was eerie at first, then disturbing. For the first few blocks the town was simply deserted.

"Lots of survivors here," Brenner explained.

But soon, through the transparent walls, they could see the bodies of Senola, adults and children, lying almost anywhere, but mostly indoors, in living rooms, or offices, or shops.

"We've commandeered every stasis unit we could," Brenner said. The squat beige boxes were set in the middle of each building, sometimes two or more in the larger areas. The number of bodies increased as they neared the hospital and, for the first time, Rikard began to get a personal sense of horror at what had happened here.

Which was probably what Polski had intended. The colonel understood how much the Leaves of Ba'Gashi meant to Rikard and Darcy, how much they would mean to anyone, especially a Gesta, who could recover them and deliver them to the Compassionate Brothers of the Capital on Seltique. Rikard respected and admired Polski, and would have been more than glad to help him, even on a job like this, if it weren't for the Leaves.

As it was, if he and Darcy agreed to become Polski's agents, they might miss forever the opportunity to pull off a stunt that would not only benefit them, but the rest of the Federation as well. If penetrating the raiders' base took very long, as it was likely to do, someone else might find where the Reliquiture had been hidden for the last millennium or so, and reap the benefits of the trade with Djentsin. Or worse, Djentsin might discover the significance of the Leaves, and take them to Seltique himself. Rikard was determined to turn Polski down.

But that resolve was shaken when they got to the hospital. The place was a nightmare. The patients lying dead in their beds were not so bad, it was the visitors in the lobby, the staff in the corridors, all having fallen where they stood, that brought home the reality of massive slaughter, though none bore any wounds.

The stasis generators had been set so that the visitors had no difficulty getting from the main entrance to the ward where the selected survivors were being kept. Only along this route had the bodies been removed. On either side, plainly visible through the glass walls, where there were walls at all, the corpses remained where they had been found, preserved from decay by the stasis fields that reduced all biological activity by a factor of about a thousand. Even the wards adjacent to the one where the survivors were being kept, under the care of three doctors, or this culture's equivalent, had not been cleared.

There were twenty-three survivors in all. They lay in their low beds, covered by sheets, and seemed unharmed except for being in a state of severe shock. Those who were awake stared vacantly at the ceiling or walls, some of them babbling softly to themselves.

"These are the best of them," Captain Anaviir said. "At least they respond to outside stimuli. All the others are just lumps."

One of the survivors, four beds down, seemed a little more alert than the others. At least, his—her?—eyes were open and watching the visitors. Rikard went to the bed, curiosity and revulsion struggling within him. "How are you?" he asked.

The victim looked at him with mingled terror and hilarity. "The skies are so greasy," he said, "so greasy. I can't see through them. But the lightning, it comes, you know, so black in the light, in the night, in the sky, the greasy sky." Then he broke down into a fit of giggling that seemed to go on for a long time but that actually lasted just seconds. Then he was quiet again, and stared at Rikard with huge purple eyes.

Rikard could only stare back. He wasn't sure he had understood the victim's words correctly—his dialect was very much local and backcountry, unlike Anaviir's or Meshatham's—but his intonation, his agitation carried a freight of meaning of their own.

"Did he really say 'greasy sky'?" Rikard asked Meshatham.

"Yes, he did. A few of the others, when they speak at all, have mentioned the same thing. We have no idea what it means."

"So many people in an empty house," the victim muttered, almost to himself. His gaze wandered from side to side, then came back to Rikard. "It's empty, I tell you. So many, many. . . ."

Anaviir went around the other side of the bed and pushed a button set into the wall over it. A section of the wall lit up, displaying information on the patient, written in the local typography, which Rikard couldn't read. "His name's Savathorn," Anaviir read. "No internal damage, neurology pretty scrambled, brain function peaking randomly—at least, that's what it says."

"Where was he found?" Rikard asked as Darcy came up to stand beside him.

Anaviir touched the button again. "In his home, with his family—two other adults and three children. They were all alive, but completely mindless."

"They keep throwing," Savathorn said, "like glass on my teeth, the tangled whips of my insides. I can't feel them, they knot and Oh dash I the whips keep tangling. Why? Can't you see them? But the house is empty."

"We've recorded everything anybody has said," Meshatham told them, "and we've had linguists and psychologists working on the transcriptions and tapes, but I don't think they're getting very far."

"Most of what they say," Anaviir said, "is just sounds, swearing, babble, noises without words. The few phrases and words they do use, however, all seem to involve this bizarre imagery."

The others were all standing around the bed by now, and Savathorn was looking from one to the other. He seemed most curious about the Humans, as if he had little or no experience with them. Then his eyes got very large, and he half sat up, and started shouting, barks and yelps, with only an occasional word—"nightmare," then babble, "light too bright, much too bright," then more shouts, a groan, "paint the walls," he said, "paint out the nightmare." Then, just as Anaviir started to turn away for help, Savathorn fell back on the bed, utterly calm.

But his outcry had been heard. Two Senola doctors came quickly into the ward and administered a sedative. "It gets worse," one of them said, "if you don't calm them immediately. Vashagrim over there"—he nodded toward a farther bed on the far side of the ward—"eventually threw himself onto the floor and broke two legs and an arm."

Savathorn did not resist the ministrations and, after a very brief moment, closed his eyes.

Polski, his face grim and determined, was looking at Rikard pointedly. Rikard stared back. They had come here only so Rikard would be convinced to join Polski's investigation. As much as Rikard sympathized with the plight of these people, he resented the pressure his old friend was putting on him. Of course, had their roles been reversed, he would have done the same.

"We've recorded extensive interviews," Chiang said, "with each of these people, even those who could not speak, observing their reactions to questions, key words, and the kind of imagery they use themselves. The tapes also include expert analysis, sometimes contradictory, of each response." She looked directly at Rikard. "Would you like to see them?"

Not only Polski and Chiang but the others were looking at him as well, including the doctors. Even Darcy was watching him, though her face was expressionless. "That won't be necessary," he said.

"What are their chances for recovery?" Polski asked without taking his eyes from Rikard.

"Not very good," Meshatham said. A doctor nodded. "Savathorn seemed to show some improvement at first, but not during the last few days, and now he's regressing again."

Rikard turned away from the staring eyes, to give himself a chance to think, and to calm down, but all he could see, through the glass wall in front of him, were the bodies in the other wards—patients, doctors, visitors. It was terrible. But what about the Leaves? He rubbed his hands over his eyes. "Let's get out of here," he said at last.

There were no objections, and no further comment as they left the hospital and got back in the van. But instead of going to the police's temporary headquarters, they went to the place that Forensics had tentatively identified as the site of the first attack, near the center of town, in an office complex.

Rikard kept to himself during the ride, and tried to dissociate himself from what he could see outside. He thought he should feel flattered that Polski valued his possible assistance so highly that he would go to the trouble to put on this display, but Rikard wasn't sure he was really the right person for the job. There were other Gestae who had far more experience than he. All Rikard had was his gun, which had limited utility, after all. Had Polski's concept of him gotten romantically enlarged since their last meeting on Seltique?

He felt Darcy's hand on his arm. Her eyes were bleak, but she said nothing. He wanted to ask her what to do, but the decision was his. He turned away from her, but the scene outside the window was too depressing—a playground or park, with children lying where they had fallen. He closed his eyes, and tried yet again to sort things out in his mind.

He was surprised, when the van stopped, to discover that he had fallen asleep. Not so much, he thought, from real fatigue as from emotional overload. He glanced around half guiltily at the others as they prepared to get out of the vehicle. Darcy had moved to sit next to Polski. Rikard looked at them for a long moment, half afraid of what that implied. He followed them out to the street, and looked at the building that was their destination, at least six stories tall, and set back from the street by broad, shallow steps.

"As far as we can tell," Captain Brenner was saying, "about seventy percent of the people in this building are missing. Another twenty percent are still here but dead, and the other ten percent, the survivors, have been removed to hospitals elsewhere. We don't know the exact number of people who worked here during the day, but records give us an estimate, and it's those ratios that indicate that this was the site of the first attack —more people missing than elsewhere, and of the dead, most but not all have been, ah, damaged."

They went up the steps and through the broad glass doors of the main entrance into what Rikard assumed was the lobby. There were very few interior partitions here, and those were of glass. Rather, the boundaries between "rooms" were marked by slightly raised strips of a lighter wood than the rest of the floor. Furniture did more to define interior spaces than did walls.

Captain Brenner showed them three bodies: one behind a large desk, two others on an overstuffed bench. All three had had their skulls opened, as if with the finest surgical tools. All three skulls were empty, and when Rikard bent down to look inside the hollow brain pan of one of those on the bench, he saw that the spinal cord, too, was missing.

Then Captain Anaviir led them on to several other "rooms" where they found more of the same, then up broad interior stairs to the second floor, as seemingly partitionless as the main floor below, and to an office at one side where a Senola corpse, under a sheet, was stretched out on two desks that had been pushed together end to end. Anaviir reached out a long arm and pulled the sheet aside.

Rikard had not seen an autopsy subject before, and though this one was not Human he still felt a twinge. The victim was lying on its face, its internal organs set out beside it. Its spine had been opened along its whole length to show that its spinal cord was missing. Other incisions, along the lines of major nerves, showed that every nerve fiber larger than a millimeter had also been removed.

"Was the body intact before the autopsy?" Rikard asked.

"Except for the skull being opened," Brenner said.

"How in the hell could they pull out the nerves, then?"

"We don't know. We've taken a few samples of the nerve sheath up to one of our medical ships, and sent others back to Corydon."

"They've got the best forensic facilities in the Federation there," Polski explained. "Any partials?"

"Thirty-one," Captain Anaviir said as he drew the sheet back over the body. "We've sent them to Corydon, too. But I saw one as it was being bagged. Skull open, brain half out. The doctors said the spinal cord was loose for about half its length."

"We caught them right in the act," Brenner said. His face, calm until now to the point of blandness, wore a mask of frustration and anger. "Except that we didn't catch anybody! The first crew down found the town pretty much as you see it now. No raiders, no suspects—and no ships either. Colonel, they have to have had a ship. But if they did, it left before we got here. But some of the bodies were still warm. We had scanners aimed on the site when we were still ten hours out. No shuttles left here during those ten hours. No starships. Nothing. No reports of strange craft in orbit, or at the jump-slot, or landing or taking off any time before we arrived. I don't care how they got the brains out, I want to know how they got their God damn ship out!"

Polski stared at Brenner for a long moment, then turned to Chiang. "Any ideas?"

"A Patrol craft," she said, "or a courier could land and take off here without being detected. We're far enough from major cities, and there's no reason to keep a watch. A shuttle might be picked up by regular air traffic control, if there's any normal air traffic in the area."

"But we had our long-range scanners centered on the town," Brenner said, "just as soon as we were near enough, and we kept our surveillance up until we landed. The most recently killed were less than an hour dead when we got here. These God damned raiders left while we were watching, and we didn't detect anything. That scares the shit out of me, Major."

Chiang stared at him tight-lipped, as if she wanted to say that was impossible, or that he must have been mistaken, but all she said was, "I'll check into it as soon as I get a chance. The fact that they were able to do that may actually be a clue."

"How about the town itself," Polski asked, "any damage?"

"Eight buildings trashed," Brenner said. He made an effort to regain control of himself.

"Let's see one," Polski suggested.

They left the building, but as they went down the broad, shallow steps toward the van parked at the curb, they saw, about a block away, a solitary figure walking down the middle of the street toward them.

It was humanoid, but so garbed in loose-fitting gray that its species could not be determined. It walked toward them with a calm deliberation, as if it owned the street, and with a strange combination of fluid grace and spastic clumsiness. Its face was covered, with goggles over its eyes, and what looked like a vocalizer over its mouth and nose. Anaviir and Brenner stepped forward to intercept the figure as it neared the van.

It reminded Rikard of the Circularians, a cult whose religious beliefs forbade them to show any part of themselves in public. Except that Circularians were strictly Human, and this person's movements could not have been made by Human physiology.

The figure stopped when it was a pace or two from the two captains.

"What are you doing here?" Brenner asked.

"My name is Grayshard," the figure said. Its mechanical voice was low-pitched, implying a masculine gender. "I wish to speak with Colonel Leonid Polski."

Maybe, Rikard thought, it was just so ugly, in Human terms, that it had decided to conceal itself in order to avoid causing dismay. The Ratorshya were like that, mammalian and human-oid, but they looked more like something long dead than alive, and in many places they had to remain covered by law. But they had four arms and were only a meter and a half tall. This stranger stood nearly two meters from the soles of its boots to the turbanlike wrappings around its head.

Polski hesitated only a moment, then joined the two captains. "I'm Polski," he said to the stranger. "What is your business here?"

"My credentials," Grayshard said. He reached slowly and carefully into the folds of his loose jacket. His voice did not lack intonation, but it was completely artificial, as if he did not have a typical vocal apparatus at all. He drew out a card and handed it to Polski.

Polski looked at it, touched a spot on its face and read what the card displayed. He took longer than he should have, and for a moment Rikard wondered if the card might have had an effect on him the way a dragongem would. But at last Polski handed the card back. "Very good, Msr. Grayshard," he said. "What can we do for you?"

"I am to participate in your investigation of these atrocities."

"Impossible," Sukiro said as she strode forward. "I know every species in the Federation, starfaring and otherwise, and you're not from here."

"It is true," Grayshard said, "still, I will participate."

"By whose authority?" Sukiro demanded.

"The Secretary of State," Polski answered dryly.

"The—what? I don't believe it."

Grayshard took the card out again and handed it to Sukiro. She activated it and read it, for far longer than Polski had. Even from where Rikard stood, he could see her face coloring. At last she handed the card back, turned abruptly away, and went to get in the van. Rikard couldn't help but chuckle at her discomfiture.

"Looks like she got her own back," Darcy said to him, smiling softly. But nobody else was amused.

Polski took a deep breath. "Let's go then," he said, and everybody else got in the van too, Grayshard last of all.

Sukiro was sitting way in the back, her arms folded across her chest, staring out the window. When Grayshard got in he hesitated a moment, then took a seat up near the front, away from the others, as if he respected their dislike or distrust of his presence. The driver started the van and drove off toward the far side of town.

The site of the damage was a house. Alone among its neighbors, it had been thoroughly destroyed, the window-walls broken out, the furniture knocked over, broken, and scattered, a corner of the roof half caved in. There were no bodies here.

Rikard got out of the van with the others. The sun was far too bright here. It glinted, almost painfully, off the all but invisible glass walls of the nearby houses. He squinted to shut out the glare and followed the others toward the ruined structure.

"In this neighborhood," Brenner said, "only one person in ten was found dead, and none of them were debrained. None were taken away, either, which is why we think this is at the limit of the raiders' activities. And an interesting point, this is where we found Savathorn."

They went inside, and had to step carefully over all the broken glass.

There were too many people here, Rikard thought. It made him feel very uncomfortable, and he wanted to drop back as they went from room to room, but he was in the middle of the crowd and couldn't get away without pushing somebody aside, and physical contact was the last thing he wanted right now. Occasionally they stopped to look at some particular piece of violence, but Rikard didn't pay much attention. He didn't want to be here, there was no need for this further demonstration, he just wanted to get away, from the house, the city, the planet, just go and get back to his quest. The Leaves were too important. He was not going to let Polski talk him into this.

They did not stay in the house very long. There wasn't much to see, after all, and nothing different from the other seven sites of destruction. But when they left the house Rikard's relief at not feeling so crowded was countered by his unease at being out in the open again. And everybody was looking at him as if expecting some reaction.

"Why did they do it?" was the only thing he could think of to say.

"We have no idea," Polski said. "Damage like this always occurs in isolated instances, and not in every town. It's another of those complicating factors that may or may not mean anything."

Rikard started to go back to the dark haven of the van, but the others—too many people, far too many—were going around the house toward the backyard. Reluctantly, Rikard followed. He felt uncomfortable with no ceiling over his head.

Darcy was looking at him with a concerned expression. "Are you all right?" she asked.

He stared at her for an instant. "Sure," he said, almost snapped. "Of course I am."

She said no more, but went to walk beside Polski as Rikard followed along behind the others.

There was a series of police flag-stakes making a line across the back of the backyard, and along the backyards on either side. On the left the line angled through the far side of the next lot over back to the street, where the van was parked, and on the right it cut through the next yard farther on to the next street over. Rikard hung back as the others neared the line.

"We occasionally find marks like these," Brenner said, pointing to something on the ground. "They might be footprints, it's hard to tell in the lawn." The grass had been lightly pressed down, but there was no shape to the mark, and each mark was a different size. "They're not made by Senola, their hoofprints are quite distinctive, and there are no such marks on the other side of this line of stakes, which is why we think the raiders stopped short just here. In other places, the line is not so clear."

Rikard didn't think the line was clear even here. He looked up from the gently bruised grass and stared at the stakes. The scar on the palm of his right hand itched. He groped for his gun, but it was still with his luggage somewhere. He scratched his palm with the first two fingers of his left hand, and saw the momentary, half-visible concentric rings of his built-in ranging device.

"No casualties on the other side of the line?" Sukiro was asking.

"No bodies at all," Brenner said, "except for a few who seemed to have died in accidents caused by their sudden loss of consciousness—falls, cars out of control, drowning in bath-tubs, and so on."

Rikard didn't want to be with these people. Their voices were too loud, they were moving around too much. He caught Darcy glancing at him with a strange expression on her face but couldn't meet her eyes. The only person who seemed to be acting normally was Grayshard, whom he'd almost forgotten about, and who was also keeping apart from the group, and from Rikard too.

He wanted to go back to the van, but the others went on across the boundary into the next yard. *I'll just wait there*, he thought, but as he looked around he saw the desolate town, heard the breeze through the trees, felt the oppressive emptiness of the sky—without even cloud cover—and in a half panic pushed on to keep up with them.

He passed between two flag-stakes. This is insane, he thought. He—they—were so vulnerable out here. No place to hide in a town like this, no way to get away from prying eyes. The sun was much too bright. Every minute reflection from glass walls, near and far, was painful in his eyes. People were scurrying around uselessly, burning up precious energy, moving too fast, talking too loud—he didn't know what they were say-ing, Brenner or Polski or Anaviir, and he didn't care. It was all he could do to keep up with them, to get even within twenty meters of them, to walk fast enough not to be left behind. He wouldn't have minded that if there had been someplace he could have waited. He looked over his shoulder at the van, its interior dark, comfortably enclosed, and wished he could go back there.

The group, with Brenner and Chiang in the lead, came to the far street and turned to the right. Rikard didn't know whether to follow them or go around the back of the house. He did the latter.

He could see the others through the transparent walls well enough, but he was afraid he would get lost, and that would be worse than being too close to these oppressive people. The line of flag-stakes came up the yard beside the house and crossed the street. The group crossed back over the boundary, and looked at him curiously as they did so. What business was it of theirs?

"Are you coming?" Polski called to him. The colonel's voice was harsh and grating.

"Be right with you," Rikard called back, and was shocked to

hear that his own voice sounded as unpleasant, more so even as it resonated inside his head. Reluctantly, he passed back across the boundary.

It was like waking up out of a nightmare. Much of the dream-feeling was still with him, the sky was too high, the light too bright, the people, even at this distance, too near. But his thoughts were much clearer now and curiously, just as an experiment, he stepped back across the boundary again.

As soon as he did the oppression closed in on him, half terrifying, half welcome. That ambivalence contributed to the nightmarishness of the feeling, and for a moment he was confused. Then he heard Darcy calling to him—they were coming back toward him, back toward the demolished house—and he quelled his momentary panic at their nearing and stepped back across the boundary one more time. The oppression faded again. It did not disappear altogether but was reduced enough so that he knew where he was, who he was, and remembered why he was here. He forced himself to rejoin the group.

"What's the matter?" Darcy asked. "You don't look well."

"I'm not," Rikard said. "Let's get back to the van."

"What's the matter," Sukiro repeated sarcastically, "this place getting to you?"

Rikard ignored her, and turned to Polski instead. "Leonid, do you feel anything strange about this place?"

"Aside from the obvious?"

"Yes. Like maybe the residue of some kind of psychic field."

"No," Polski said uncertainly. He turned a questioning glance to Brenner.

"Nobody's reported anything to me," the captain said.

"It's not as strong here," Rikard said, "but just beyond that row of flags it was fierce."

"I didn't feel anything," Darcy said. "What was it like?"

"Tathas," Rikard said, and watched with some satisfaction as both Polski and Darcy registered surprise.

By now they were back at the van. Rikard got in and they all followed. "It feels better in here," he said. "Enclosed. Not so much light. Too many people, but I can bear it."

"Well aren't you the tough guy," Sukiro sneered.

"That's enough, Orin," Polski said without looking at her. "Are you sure it's Tathas?" he asked Rikard.

"It's not exactly the same, but so much like it—"

"What are tathas?" Chiang asked.

"A degenerate fungoid race," Rikard told her, "found only on Kohltri, as far as we know. They'd been isolated and living underground for thousands of years. They're not intelligent anymore, but they're mildly telepathic. They project their thoughts and feelings, unconsciously. They're insane, want to be left alone, resent any intrusion, live on the memories of what their world used to be like before they started regressing. They leave a physical residue that has much the same effect, making intruders see the world as the Tathas see it, not as it is. They're hungry, fear light, hate to move too fast, and though they cluster together, hate company."

"I've never heard of them," Sukiro said.

"But how could they get here?" Darcy asked.

"I have no idea," Rikard said, "but I think we ought to go back to that house, with whatever detectors we can, and find out more."

"We haven't got time for that," Sukiro said impatiently.

"Wrong," Polski told her, with something like excitement in his voice. "That just might be the clue we've been looking for—if we can figure out what it means."

But before he could issue any orders, a call came on the van's radio for him. He took the message, then turned to the others. "The statistical report has just come in," he said, "at headquarters.

"We'll look into this later, Rikard," he went on, "but right now I want to see that report." He gave the driver instructions, and they drove back to the town's police station. As they went, Rikard noticed Grayshard watching him.

3

The police station, near the center of town, was only three floors tall and occupied less than half a block. Like all the other buildings, it was walled almost completely in glass. If there were cells, they had to be underground.

The main room was dominated by a large comcon screen, which had been temporarily set up against a side wall. This screen would normally be used to display orders of the day, progress reports, messages, and so on, but now it showed an enlarged view of the report's title—"Statistical Analysis of Belligerent Activities"—addressed to Colonel Leonid Polski, and with Federal and Police symbols, signatures, and other front matter.

The com sergeant, who would run the report display, was waiting for them at a smaller screen, from which she could control the larger one. When everybody was inside and seated in every available chair, Polski gave the word and the sergeant started tapping buttons.

The first image was a simulated 3D map of the stars of the Federation, those with inhabited systems shown as small disks, those without as rings. After a moment the uninhabited stars winked out, and those star systems where the raiders had not struck were reduced from disks to points. The victim systems formed an irregular clump, filling about a quarter of the volume of the Federation.

A legend appeared at the bottom of the large screen, a scale of colors from yellow through red to purple and then blue, divided into twenty-four shades, each color representing a different time period, from one year ago for palest yellow to dark blue, which covered the last fifteen standard days. The victim systems changed color to correspond to the scale.

"This is the data we've been working with," the sergeant said. She was reading text on her smaller screen. "As you can see, the earlier victim systems are nearer the center, the later ones toward the edge, though there's quite a bit of apparent variability."

It was not easy to see even that much pattern. There were white points representing untouched systems scattered throughout the colored region, and all the violet and blue stars were concentrated more or less on one side, though the yellow and orange systems were more toward the other side.

"Some of this distribution," the sergeant went on, "may be due to where potential victims were located, rather than to any plan on the part of the raiders."

"There are two kinds of victims," Polski said. "Those where there was occasional severe damage, as here . . ." About half of the colored stars now had small rings around them. ". . . and those where there was no appreciable damage."

"Natimarie is right here," the sergeant said, and one of the ringed blue stars flickered for a moment. "From what we understand, there were other variables besides damage, but nowhere near as consistent or as widespread, and nothing could be determined from them. But the damage implies the existence of two different raiding parties, one of which exhibited occasional fits of violence.

"The analysts still can find no pattern in the type of species taken, except that they're all intelligent and from small towns. But if they assume two raiding parties instead of one, the first thing is that we no longer have to seriously consider the possibility that their ships are faster than ours. The time between each raid of each party is more than sufficient for them to get back to a base somewhere within the area of activity and out again to their next target.

"If that assumption is made, and correlated with the dates of each raid, then a pattern does emerge—at least to the statisticians."

A transparent sphere was superimposed around the volume of victim systems, then another, smaller one was drawn inside that and more or less concentric with the first, then another deeper within, and at last a small sphere at the very center. "But as you can see," the sergeant went on, "there are no stars or systems at the middle."

Then the uninhabited stars returned to the display, little diamonds of green. None were within the innermost sphere, or even near it.

"But there is *something* there," the sergeant said, and the center sphere of the display enlarged until it filled the entire screen and beyond. A moment later a small dot appeared at the center of the still enlarging sphere. The image steadied for a moment, then there was a jump in magnification to show what might have been a small moon, craterless but not smooth, and very dark.

"What the hell is that?" Polski demanded.

"Preliminary probes," the sergeant said, "indicate that it's an artificial world of some kind." The lower left quadrant of the screen was replaced with a set of bar-charts. "The mass of the object is only a fraction of what one would expect if it were solid rock, or even ice, and the elemental survey indicates that it is in fact ninety percent metal, so we have to assume a hollow sphere." That data could be read from the charts, by those who understood them. "It is most dense at the center, which may mean that's where the main power plant is, but there are no indications of power of any kind." A new set of charts replaced the first.

"How big is it?" somebody asked.

"About three times the radius of any planetary station we have," the sergeant answered.

"This is fantastic," Darcy said. "Even if this isn't the raiders' base, we'll have to look into it sooner or later."

Rikard recognized an eager hunger in her voice, if only because he felt the same hunger in himself.

"And," the sergeant went on, "since there's no noticeable energy output, even in infrared, we have to assume that this station is a derelict, and has been for quite some time."

"Where did it come from?" somebody asked.

The sergeant turned to look at the speaker. "You've got to be kidding," she said. "This thing was discovered only three standard days ago. Your guess is as good as anybody else's."

Polski got up and went to stand in front of the screen. "This is important," he said. It was almost as if he were speaking to himself. He stared at the enigmatic object on the screen for a long moment, then turned and looked around the room. "I think it's worth investigating," he went on.

There was a general murmur of consensus. Rikard glanced sidelong at Darcy, saw her grin slightly. "Not the job we were asked to do," he said softly.

"He doesn't need us," she whispered back. "But damn, I wish we could get into that place before he does."

"We can always pay a visit after we get the Leaves. You think they'd let us?"

"Maybe we shouldn't ask," Darcy said with a self-satisfied smile.

"Major Sukiro," Polski was saying, "I want you to take charge of an expedition to check out that thing."

"And miss out on all the fun here? Let Major Chiang go."

"You're the best qualified for the job," Polski said tiredly. "You'll have a gunship and two platoons of goons."

"You think that might actually be the raiders' base?"

"I think it's possible, and if it is, I want you there to deal with it."

"And who's going to do my work here?"

"Major Chiang. You'll leave as soon as the goons are equipped and on the gunship." He turned to the com sergeant, who nodded and started making arrangements. Then Polski came over to where Rikard and Darcy were seated. There was a glint in his eye that Rikard didn't like.

"I suppose we can go on about our business now," Rikard said hopefully.

"I want you to go along with Sukiro," Polski told him.

"But why? You don't need a secret agent now."

"That's true, but you've had experience with entering and exploring mysterious structures, you can figure out what to do and where to go. The police just charge in with guns blazing. That might not be appropriate."

Rikard would have thought he was joking if it weren't for the intensity and seriousness of his voice. "All Sukiro has to do," he said, "is take her time. Look around. Put herself in the place of the people who built it."

"Easy for you to say," Polski said, and he was not joking at all. "We're not explorers, kid, we don't have the right mindset. And besides, if what you felt at that house was correct, then there are Tathas to deal with. You're the only person I know who has dealt with the Tathas and survived."

"There have to be others on Kholtri, who'd jump at the chance to help out if it would mean their freedom—or a reward."

"And who could I trust, if I could find them on short notice? No, Rik, I need you now, more than before."

"You don't know that."

"All right, then, how about going for its own sake. You'd love to get into that place before the authorities do, wouldn't you? And you will, if you help me now, without having to sneak, and who knows—I certainly don't—what you might be able to bring out—maybe even with the Federation's blessing."

Rikard tried to think of a demurer but couldn't.

"Isn't this just exactly the kind of thing you're looking for?" Polski went on.

"It is that," Darcy almost whispered.

"You think about it," Polski said. "Now I've got things to do." He left them and went to talk with Brenner and Anaviir.

Rikard and Darcy sat there for a moment, doing, in spite of themselves, just what Polski had told them to.

"So what are we going to do?" Darcy said at last. "That derelict sure is tempting, but. . . ." She got to her feet. "Let's get out of here."

They went out the front door but sat down on the step just outside.

"We don't really have to do this," Darcy said. "Just tell Leo no, then let's take the next ship out."

Rikard didn't answer. He looked around at the desolate city. Where the light was right he couldn't see the glass walls at all, just the floors, connecting stairs, and supporting columns, with here and there an enclosed sanitary. He could look through building after building, until even this fine glass's cumulative refraction eventually grayed out his vision, maybe three or four blocks away.

"The thing that bothers me most," Rikard said at last, "is being pushed. I hate being pushed."

"My sentiments exactly," Darcy said. "Leo doesn't need us especially. How about Kevin St. James? He doesn't know anything about the Tathas, but he could do almost everything else Leo wants."

"Sure he could. He's about the slickest Gesta I've ever met."

"Then there's Vashnia ka'Gorolshir."

"Who?"

"She's an Atreef on Kholtri. I'll bet she knows a lot about Tathas."

"Would she take the job?"

"Probably not. Maybe Silver MacReedy. What she doesn't know she can learn the first time out."

"I've heard of her," Rikard said. "Isn't she a little bit cautious?" Meaning she hardly ever took chances.

"I guess so," Darcy admitted. "But she *could* do it."

"Better one of them than me. Except for one thing."

"The Tathas."

"Exactly. Except possibly for Vashnia ka'Gorolshir, I'm the only person I know who's had any experience with them, and Vashnia's on Kholtri, and I wouldn't bet that any Atreef would leave there—not this generation at least."

"Then let Sukiro deal with them the best she can."

"You don't know what you're saying, Darcy. I've been *with* them, I've been touched by them, I've felt the full force of their psychic projections. And I've felt them here."

"I still don't see how they could possibly figure into this."

"What if somebody on Kholtri found out about them, found out a way to shield themselves from their psychic emanations —the way the miners protect themselves from balktapline ore —and has gathered up a bunch of them and is using them to subdue the towns they want to raid. Something like that."

"But Tathas are mindless, or at least so insane it makes no difference. How could anybody get them to cooperate?"

"Force them. Bring them out in cans, they'd feel safe in cans. Then expose them to sunlight and open sky. They panic, broadcast their agony all over the place, everybody feels it and falls down in shock. Or maybe use the Tathas effluvia some-how, find the active compound, distill it, spray it around, and use it to open the victims' minds to their own telepathic com-mands, even if they aren't naturally telepathic. However they do it, if Sukiro goes in there unprotected, and the raiders *are* there, and they *are* using the Tathas in some way, then they just do it again and Sukiro's force is knocked unconscious in less than a second. She won't even know what happened."

"Are you saying that you *want* to go along?"

"No, but I sure as hell feel guilty about turning Polski down."

"You almost make it sound like, if you don't go with her, she won't come back."

"That's exactly what I'm afraid of," he said. He stood up and went inside. She followed him a moment later.

Polski was talking with Major Chiang and several of her sub-ordinates. Rikard went up to him and said, "I'm going along."

Polski turned a broad smile on him. "That's great."

"But I've got to have some say in things."

"That's exactly what I want."

"Sukiro won't like it," Chiang said.

"She'll have plenty to do keeping the goons under control," Polski told her, "but as far as I'm concerned, Rikard and Darcy will be in charge of the operation—until they find the raiders, if they do."

"Not me," Darcy said, "I don't know anything about leading expeditions."

Rikard looked at her, not as surprised as he thought he should be. "You want to stay behind," he said, "and bring off the deal with Djentsin yourself?"

"It's a sure thing, Rikard. It's important." But her eyes flick-ered to Polski as she spoke. Rikard's stomach sank.

He turned away from her and looked at Polski. "The main problem," he went on, "is the Tathas. Somebody from Kholtri has to be behind that. The raiders must have learned how to use them if they can put a whole town to sleep all at once. That's what happens when you come under their influence, you slow down, shut down, look for a dark hole to hide in. If the feeling is too strong, and there's no place to hide, you find that hole in your mind, and then you go crazy.

"Some of what Savathorn said begins to make sense now. The Tathas make you feel that the light is too bright. The sky looks like black gun-grease to a Tathas. Tangled whips sort of describes what Tathas look like, with their tendrils and fibers all waving about. Black lightning, I don't know what that is, but it feels like Tathas talk to me.

"Who knows how many tame Tathas these raiders have in their control? Sukiro won't know if they're being used on her until it's too late. And then the raiders will take their brains."

"You don't have to convince me," Polski said with a wry grin. "You're leaving the day after tomorrow."

Rikard glanced at Darcy. She wouldn't meet his eyes. "What about our peculiar friend?" he asked Polski, to cover his dismay. He looked past the colonel to where Grayshard was seated in the far corner of the headquarters.

"He's got the credentials, and he's determined on going along. Orin doesn't like that, but too bad."

"Part of that," Darcy said, "is because Grayshard is pulling strings on her the way she did with Korijian on Nowarth." Her voice did not sound at all as if she had just brought a three-year romance to an abrupt end.

"Very likely," Polski said, "but she's also pretty tight about doing things by the book. Look, I'm going to be busy for the rest of the day, so you'll have to look out for yourselves, but I can let you have a driver and I'll fill you in on the details later on tonight, okay?"

"Fine," Rikard said, though, under the circumstances, things could hardly be fine again.

PART
THREE

PART
THREE

like taking orders from him but was too good an officer to make any trouble over it—especially since Polski had given her her instructions personally.

"Unless you can think of another way," Rikard said.

As it turned out, the goons didn't need most of the special equipment they had brought with them for just this purpose. Their two-meter prybars proved adequate to the job. But when the first seam was cracked, a cloud of gas escaped from the chamber within, momentarily frosting the helmets of the privates who were working the bars. Sladen and Petorska held the valve as it was until the gas stopped coming, then let Colder and Yansen take over while they cleaned off their face plates. The valve sections rotated like an iris, into the edges of the bulge, moving at last so quickly that Colder and Yansen would have fallen into the opening had there been any gravity to speak of.

The second squad was ready for this, and moved in at once, their light blasters drawn and set on full. They shone bright lights into the opening, but there was no movement within, and their lights showed only a circular chamber, its arching walls of ribbed steel, with a broad walkway surrounding a steep ramp sloping down below surface level.

Corporal Nelross sent a private in to circle around the walkway to the back, where there was an irregularity in the curving wall. This proved to be some kind of control panel, though Gospodin could make no sense of its buttons and dials. She came back around the other way.

Sergeant Denny called her goons in from their positions, and they formed up at the top of the ramp, ready to go in. Sukiro told the shuttle crew to keep tuned, then Denny's goons led the way. When everybody was inside, at the head of the long ramp, Falyn's goons closed the outer portal again, and pasted on a temporary seal, so that if there was air pressure farther in, it wouldn't bleed out when they opened internal doors.

The ramp, broad enough for five to march abreast, began to spiral counterclockwise after a run of about ninety meters and a descent of thirty meters or so, and as they went deeper they could feel the pull of artificial gravity, lighter than normal, but plenty enough to make movement easy. The gravity enhancers in their suits reduced power automatically in compensation.

The floor here was smooth steel, dusty and unmarked. The ceiling was also steel, with nothing that might have been light

fixtures. The walls were ribbed as in the hatchway above. Aside
from that, the ramp, which continued to spiral as it descended,
had no features whatsoever. But after one full turn all the goons
came to a sudden halt.

"What's the matter?" Rikard asked.

"We've lost contact with the shuttle," Sukiro told him.

One of the specialties of the goon forces was their built-in
communications linkage system, but it worked only between a
goon and a larger transmitter-receiver, on a Police craft or space
station, not between goons directly. The goons depended on
their com-links to provide them with the location and condition
of their fellows, communications with their officers, and other
status information. They could operate without the system, but
with much reduced efficiency.

It was Sukiro's decision, however, to go on. She went back
up the ramp until she regained contact, and told the shuttle crew
what had happened and that they would be continuing down in
spite of this.

After two full turns the floor became a level passage, which
continued for a short way before ending at a large, slightly oval
door with an iris valve, like the inner door of an airlock. There
were panels on either side of the iris, which might have been
manual controls, but instead of trying to figure them out, Sladen and Petorska just went to work with their prybars. When
the valves were open just the barest crack air whistled into the
evacuated chamber. It stopped after a moment, then the goons
forced the doors open the rest of the way.

The large chamber beyond was a kind of vestibule, with another doorway at the opposite end, and half-meter-high platforms at either side on which sat two rather large complicated
objects which, by their presence, might have been space cars
though, from their shapes, could have been almost anything. In
the steel-ribbed walls above the platforms were dark blue
panels, six on either side, taller than broad, outlined in white,
each with a silvery button in the middle. Rikard was eager to go
in and explore, but Corporal Falyn put out a restraining hand,
and they all waited while Jasime tested the air.

It took the private only a moment. The atmosphere inside the
derelict station proved to be an oxygen-nitrogen-CO_2 mix, with
a few other gases, but otherwise quite breathable—nothing
toxic, very low organic component, and not very dusty. On
Jasime's okay the goons opened their face-plates, and Rikard

and Grayshard shed their encumbering vac-suits and stowed them into small backpacks, though they kept on their light-weight helmets with the built-in headlamps. Rikard let his gloved right hand rest lightly on the butt of his .75, and felt a lot better about this whole business. The vac-suit glove didn't let the circuit close between him and the gun, but now he was in control again.

Denny took over the lead and they all moved cautiously into the vestibule. The ceiling here was not steel but plastic, amber in color, and transparent, though they could see nothing embedded within the six centimeters or so of its depth.

Rikard went at once to one of the machines parked on a side platform, half a meter above the floor. In general form it looked like a cross between a bobsled and an apple peeler, with parts that reminded him of a naked power generator, or maybe a torsion exercise cycle. There were no coverings or enclosures of any kind. He reached out for what could have been either control buttons or ornamentation on a pedestal near the middle of the device.

"Don't touch that," Denny said.

Rikard glanced at her, then took his hands away, and contemplated instead the silvery button in the center of the nearest blue panel.

"We have no time for that now," Denny said. She went to the door at the far end of the vestibule, dark blue and outlined in white, oval like the one by which they had come in, taller than broad, and sealed with an iris, at the center of which was what could have been a touch-plate latch.

Rikard stared at the sergeant's back for a moment, then touched the panel button anyway. There was a soft click as it swung open a centimeter or two.

Denny heard the sound and turned to stare back at him. "Leave those things alone," she snapped. "You'll have plenty of time to explore after we get rid of the raiders."

"Denny's right," Sukiro said. "Penetrate first, we may have very little time."

Rikard nodded reluctant agreement, and went to stand beside Denny as she examined the silver disk at the center of the door iris. "Seems simple enough," he said.

She glared at him, then reached out and pressed the plate. The iris, touch-plate and all, twisted open, then closed again with a snap, so quickly that all they saw was the movement.

Denny belatedly jerked her hand away, rubbed her gauntleted palms together, looked over her shoulder as if to summon a goon to do this experiment for her, then reached out and touched the plate again. Once again the iris snapped open and shut in a fraction of a second. She turned to Petorska. "Let me have your prybar," she said.

But while her back was turned Rikard just put out his hand and pressed the plate, hard enough so that, when the iris opened, his hand went through. And this time, with his arm extended to the elbow in the place where the iris had been, the door stayed open. Denny, with the prybar, turned back to see him wiggling his fingers in the blackness beyond.

"Damn fool thing to do," she said. Her voice was anxious, as if she had expected to see his arm cut off at the elbow. Rikard pulled his arm back, and when his hand was clear the valve immediately snapped shut.

"It's got a sensor," he said. "I think." He pushed the plate again, and again, for as long as he held his hand in the doorway, the iris stayed open, and snapped shut as soon as he took his hand away. He looked at Denny, grinned, then opened the iris one more time and stepped through into the darkness. The iris snapped shut behind him.

He played his headlamp around the room. It was different from the vestibule. It had the same amber, transparent ceiling, but the floor was milky white and the walls were pale blue, with two triple stripes of dark blue, the same color as the doors, running around them at waist and shoulder height from the floor. But before he could make out any details the iris opened again.

Sergeant Denny stepped halfway through the opening and to one side, legs astride the threshold, to keep the valve open while the rest of her squad entered the room as quickly as possible.

"Let's move it," she said, and the other goons followed at once, with Grayshard and Sukiro bringing up the rear.

It wasn't a very large room, and they had to crowd around a square table in the center to all fit in. The table had a matte black surface, and stood on a single pedestal leg. There were no chairs.

There was a counter, also matte black and about one meter high, over cabinets that ran along one side wall except where another door cut through it. There was a third door in the far wall, and on the other side wall what looked like a viewscreen with a control panel of some kind beneath it.

Rikard went to the side door and touched the latch-plate in the center of the iris. The door snapped open and shut, as quickly and as startlingly as the first had done.

Denny finally left her post astride the doorjamb. The iris snapped closed, she touched the plate, and they watched it snap again. "Just making sure we could get out," she said.

"It can't be purely mechanical," Rikard said, "or it wouldn't work so fast. That means there has to be power in here."

"Can't be," Denny said. "This derelict has to be at least ten thousand years old."

"But the doors do open and close," Corporal Falyn said. "And besides, how do you account for the artificial gravity?"

While the two noncoms were arguing, Rikard opened one of the dark blue cabinet doors under the counter. Inside were shelves filled with what looked like containers, made of card or metal foil or plastic, in neutral colors, but all of strange sizes, shapes, and proportions.

"Don't open any of those," Denny said, but she came over to look too. "The air may be good," she went on, "but we don't know what kind of volatile substances might be inside those things."

Rikard was, in fact, just about to break open the corner of a rusty gray box like a cube, except that none of the angles were square, but thought perhaps he wouldn't after all, and carefully put it down on the counter.

"We've got to get moving," Sukiro said. "The longer we delay, the more likely the raiders will find out we're here, and we'll lose our surprise." She looked at Rikard. "Which way do we go?"

"Which way's the hatch we want to get to?" Rikard asked back.

"Majorbank?" Denny queried.

The private glanced at the screen on the top surface of his hand-held mapping pad, then touched a button on one side. "We entered facing the other hatch," he said, "and made two full circles coming down. If we keep on going straight ahead, we should get to the area under the raiders' hatch eventually."

"Then let's get on with it," Sukiro said.

Denny went to the far door, pressed against the latch-plate, and stepped into the threshold when it opened. Like the well-trained troops they were, her squad was the first through, without further orders.

The room beyond was somewhat larger than the first, with counters along both side walls this time, and three other doors. There was a black-topped table in the middle, and a "viewscreen," on the opposite wall. Denny went to the far door and pushed the latch-plate. She stood in the doorway while her goons went through, then signaled the others to follow.

Beyond was a short transverse corridor, with five doors on either side and one at either end. They'd come in from the second iris from the left. The doors here, like the others they'd seen, were dark blue, outlined in white, and as before there were two rows of triple blue stripes that went around the walls.

Rikard looked at the place where the stripes intersected the white door outline. There was a set of slightly raised diagonal ridges, right where the blue lines ended. They were uncolored, and Rikard couldn't remember whether he'd seen them next to the other doors or not. There was a similar set on the other side of the iris.

"We'll take the door straight across," Denny said. "You got this mapped?" she asked Majorbank.

"No problem," the goon answered. He entered the information on his pad using the trackball at the base of its screen.

Then Rikard touched the ridges beside the door and the ceiling lit up, filling the corridor with a warm amber light. The goons all crouched, their guns aimed at the ceiling, which now glowed uniformly over its whole surface, without any indication of illuminating elements inside.

"Sorry," Rikard said. He touched the ridges again, a slightly downward stroke, and the light dimmed to deep amber. Grayshard was watching him, the only one there, besides himself, who had not been surprised. Rikard stroked the ridges upward a bit. The light brightened. Then he turned his headlamp off.

"Don't do things like that without warning," Denny snapped. She took a deep breath, opened the door opposite the one by which they had come in, stood in the iris and reached around to grope for the dimmer switch on the other side. Her goons were through the door even as the light came on.

Falyn hesitated by the door. She reached out a finger and delicately played with the ridges of the dimmer switch. "Touch just one," she said, "and nothing happens, but touch two or more . . ." She did as she spoke, the light in the corridor became almost blindingly bright. She dimmed the switch again. "I sure would like to know what's providing power," she said to Rikard as they followed the others at last.

The next three rooms were more or less the same, of varying sizes and unfurnished except for the central table and the occasional counter with cabinets beneath. The fourth room had only one other door, on the right, and they had no choice but to change direction. The room after that had no door in the direction they wanted to go either, so they went on to the next, which did, and beyond that they entered the end of another short corridor.

The room at the far end of this corridor was quite a bit larger than any they had been in so far, and Sukiro called a halt so they could rest a moment and take their bearings. Majorbank figured they'd come less than a quarter of the way to their objective and had come off to the right about twenty meters.

Sukiro and Falyn decided to investigate one of the viewscreens set in the wall. Every room had had at least one, which made sense, though some had had two, which did not. This screen was like all the others, about fifty centimeters square, set flush with the pale blue wall about one and a half meters from the floor. It was framed by dark blue stripes, which formed a larger square around it, and below it was a white enamel panel, with two rows of square, silver buttons, eight in each row, each with a different symbol in matte black. The speaker grill was immediately to the right of the buttons.

Sukiro and Falyn looked at the device closely, didn't dare touch it. After a moment Rikard went over to join them. "Just push some buttons," Rikard said, "and see what happens."

"What if we accidentally turn it on?" Sukiro said.

"Maybe it's already on," Rikard said, "and the raiders are watching us."

"You'd see it if it were on," Sukiro started to say.

"Not necessarily," Falyn interrupted. "If the camera were behind the screen, it could see us even with the screen dark."

"I don't think anything's on," Rikard said. He reached out to push one of the top buttons.

"Keep your hands away," Falyn said. She hesitated a moment. "Let me do it."

One by one she pushed the buttons on the top row. Nothing happened. Then she started pushing buttons on the bottom row.

When she got to the rightmost button the screen started to glow with a soft amber light, the same shade as the ceiling but paler.

"Now what?" Falyn asked. She was breathing heavily.

"If the on-off switch is on the bottom," Rikard said, "I'd guess the top buttons are for dialing other stations."

"What the hell are you doing?" Denny demanded. They hadn't heard her come up behind them.

"Just finding out how this works," Rikard said.

"Later, Msr. Braeth, later."

Rikard glared at her, jabbed the rightmost button, and the screen went dark. "After you," he said.

"Damn straight," Denny said, and strode to the door opposite the one by which they'd come in.

The room beyond was completely different. It was just big enough to hold them all, the rest of the space being taken up by stacks of shelves along all four walls and freestanding in four rows up the middle. There weren't many things on the shelves, but even Denny couldn't restrain her curiosity this time, with everything in view. Rikard, and even Grayshard, took the opportunity to look some of the objects over.

A few of the things looked like rounded-cornered cases or canisters, thirty to forty centimeters long and fifteen to twenty centimeters high and deep. Try as they could, they could not figure out how any of them opened. Each one weighed two to three kilograms, but no two weighed the same, and some of them rattled.

Most of the objects were far more complex, and mystifying, wrapped in a fine, transparent foil. They were all irregularly shaped, and either soft or flexible. They varied from the size of a fist to a few that were larger than the canisters. There were no seams on the wrappings, but Rikard did manage to tear one open.

The thing inside looked like a bunch of yellow rubber crab legs, organically hinged together in two places, where they were green. The "legs" folded out and back rather stiffly. There were lots of similar packages on the shelves, scattered here and there. After a moment the "crab legs" began to stink and Rikard decided not to open any of the other packages.

They could see what was inside well enough, and could make no sense of them in any case. Some of the objects looked like thick noodles, or wads of wet grass, or discus shapes with rubbery spines along the edge. On one shelf was a series of six similar objects, each one a variation on the next, like a combination between a loaf of bread and a jackknife, with thick rubbery "blades" opening on all sides of the quarter-meter "loaf," except that the whole thing was made of what looked like soft plastic. The blades could be opened even inside the wrapping, but they didn't stay open, and some of them folded into themselves as well as into the loaf, and one or two of them telescoped.

The three rooms beyond that were more typical, then they came to another transverse corridor, and in the second room beyond that Yansen discovered a semi-oval membrane set into one wall, the flat side against the floor. It was about a meter high and wide, and the covering membrane was quite flexible, with a puckered ring at the center. Yansen prodded at this and the membrane dilated. He put his hand in and the membrane closed around his wrist.

"What the hell are you doing?" Denny asked.

"Look at this," Yansen told her. Using both hands he easily stretched the membrane wide enough so that he could shine his helmet flash inside. The space beyond was about two meters deep, and the floor, instead of being milky white, was textured gray. Denny peered in over Yansen's shoulder as he reached in to touch the gray floor with his armored fingers.

"Feels funny," he said, then looked at his fingertips. The hardened steel was polished flat. "Holy shit." He held his hand up so that Denny, and Rikard and Sukiro, who were right behind her, could see.

"Kind of a dangerous thing," Sukiro said. She took a prybar from Colder and, while Yansen on one side and Denny on the other held the membrane open as far as it would go, reached in with it and probed at the gray floor. The end of the prybar seemed to sink into the flooring. When she took the prybar out they saw that the end had been cut off and polished smooth.

"Save it for later," Sukiro said. She handed the prybar back to Colder. "Sorry about that," she said.

"I'll keep it as a souvenir."

After that they all kept their hands off things.

It was shortly after passing what Majorbank estimated was the halfway point that Rikard began to feel more cheerful. He couldn't remember feeling sad, but there was no denying that he was happier now than he had been. Falyn must have noticed a change in his behavior, because she glanced at him and cocked an eyebrow in question.

Rikard shrugged. "I just feel good."

"All of a sudden? Just like that?"

"I guess so." He thought about it as they went from one pale blue room to another. "It *is* kind of odd," he said.

"How did you feel before?"

"I'm trying to remember. Closed in? No, that's not it—"

"You ought to feel closed in, in a place like this."

"That wasn't it. Too many people." And even as he spoke, he felt shivers run up his back, and he looked over his shoulder the way they had come. "Like in that town on Natimarie." He stopped where he was. "Very faint, but that was it. I didn't recognize it—being closed in was 'good,' the people were 'bad,' and they sort of canceled out. But now. . . ."

"Let's tell the major," Falyn said, and they hurried to catch up with the others, who hadn't noticed them falling behind. The platoon was crossing a room far larger than usual and Sukiro was in the middle of the group.

"Major," Rikard called as he hurried up to her. "Wait a minute." Sukiro stopped and turned around, but the rest of the platoon went on. "I felt the Tathas."

"Good," Sukiro said, "that means we're getting close."

"No, back there."

"Somebody out exploring. Come on, we don't want to get too far behind." She walked away.

"But the trace was back there."

"We'll check it out when we come back," Sukiro said. "If we can. We've got to locate the base first."

"But I don't feel it here," Rikard insisted as they rejoined the goons. They were now crossing a transverse corridor. Denny was waiting for them.

"You get lost in here," she said to Rikard, "and we'll just leave you."

"No we won't," Sukiro said. "But keep up with us," she said to Rikard. "The closer we get to that other hatch, the more dangerous it's going to be."

Rikard didn't say anything more. Sukiro was probably right. But the feeling he'd had—it wasn't like a Tathas had actually been there, but more like being near it, a room or two away. And now the Tathas were behind them—or had been, at least.

As they neared their objective the group moved both more

quickly and more carefully. Denny kept her goons moving through door after door and they no longer hesitated to look at anything. Nelross had his squad right behind, ready at the first sign of trouble to take cover and blow away doors if they had to. The rest of the platoon brought up the rear, with Sukiro, Rikard, and Grayshard out of harm's way should there be any shooting.

Then at one door the first two goons to pass through stopped short, then hurriedly backed out, guns leveled. Denny had reached in and turned on the light, but she stepped out of the iris and it snapped shut.

"Somebody's been in there," Sladen said. "There's footprints all over the floor."

Nelross came to stand by the iris, opposite Denny, and their goons took up a formation, weapons drawn, ready for a fight. Denny palmed the switch, she and Nelross stepped into the threshold, the goons charged in through the gap in the counter, fanned out, squatted down, and covered the area with their blasters.

There was nobody there. It was a small room, with no place to hide. But the dust on the floor had been churned up over almost the whole area. The rest of the goons moved in while several of the first to enter went to the other two doors, which were set into blank walls.

Rikard followed as quickly as he could and looked around. "Look here," he said. He pointed to an object on the counter, right beside the door, a rusty gray box like a cube, except that none of the angles were square.

Falyn, who was standing beside him, turned to look at the object. Sukiro came in right behind her and looked too. "So what?" she said.

Denny, standing ready at one side door, looked back at the boxlike object on the counter. Her face registered dawning surprise, and her gaze turned to Rikard. "Is that . . . ?" she started to ask.

Rikard picked up the box and turned it over in his hands. "Here's where I tried to break it open," he said, pointing out a slightly crushed corner.

"What are you talking about?" Sukiro demanded. She reached out to take the box from him.

Rikard looked at Denny, their eyes locked. "That door," Rikard said to the sergeant, "leads to the vestibule."

Denny grimaced, then opened the door, reached around the jamb, and turned on the light. Sure enough, there was the vestibule, exactly as they had found it before.

"We've come full circle," Rikard said.

"Impossible," Majorbank snapped. He held out the mapping pad. "We've followed a straight line, more or less, from where we came in."

"Then how did we get back here?"

"We're not *back* here, we're somewhere else. All this—it's just a coincidence."

"I don't believe it. Maybe somebody found this box where I left it and brought it here? Why would they do that?"

Nobody had an answer.

"Check the square of the room," Rikard suggested on sudden impulse. Denny glanced at Hornower and nodded.

The goon took a device from his belt, a box with a pistol grip set diagonally under it. He went to a corner, and stopped about two paces from it. The other goons nearby made room. He aimed the corner of the box at the corner of the room, pressed a trigger on the grip, then twisted a dial on the top, and read out a number on a small screen by the knob. "Eighty-five degrees," he said. He went to another corner. "Same here." Another. "Ninety-five." The fourth. "Ninety-five. This room isn't square."

"None of them are," Rikard said. "They all make up a geodesic surface. Add it up, how many rooms would it take, shaped like this one, to turn us around one hundred eighty degrees or so?"

Hornower calculated on his device a moment. "About as many as we've been through," he said. "Given a good margin for error."

"So when we thought we were going in a straight line," Denny said, "actually we were angling off by about five degrees, every time we went from one room to another."

"Looks like it." Majorbank was embarrassed. "We should have measured."

"You had no reason to," Sukiro said. Then she turned to Rikard. "And you felt that Tathas trace at about the halfway point."

"That's right," Rikard said. "They weren't there, but they were near, or had been."

"There's got to be some mistake," Nelross insisted.

"There was," Denny said, "just like we figured out."

"When did you first feel these Tathas," Grayshard asked Rikard. It was the first time he'd spoken since they'd entered the derelict.

"I don't know," Rikard said, "I just noticed it when the feeling stopped."

"All right, Msr. Braeth," Sukiro said, "you were right after all. Let's retrace our steps, and this time, tell us when you first feel the trace." They returned the way they had come, and when they got to the room where Rikard had become aware of feeling good again Sukiro let him take the lead.

He tried to be alert to the first sense of Tathas, but it didn't come at the next room, or the one after that. Then he became aware that he didn't like these goons pressing him so closely— they were only two or three meters from him—and he stopped. "I don't know when it started," he said, "but I can feel it now."

"Woadham," Denny said to one of her goons, "Colder, you stay right beside him."

"Don't mind me if I twitch," Rikard said to them. "It's part of the Tathas effect."

He followed the trace, every now and then taking a side door instead of the one directly opposite, in this way compensating for the forced change in angle of their progress. He went as quickly as he could, his two guardian goons beside and a little behind him, the others following, and as he went the Tathas sensation got subtly stronger. But it was only an indication of proximity until he opened a door that led, not into another room or a corridor, but into a narrow tube, spiraling down.

He stopped at the top of the tube and looked down the corkscrew ramp. There were four sets of footprints in the dust, one pair coming up, the other going back down again. The feeling was very strong here, but he was able to suppress most of its effects.

"Do Tathas wear boots?" Sukiro had come up beside him and was looking down at the footprints.

"No, but whoever made those prints was carrying a Tathas. Not recently, maybe eight or ten days ago."

"How can you tell?"

"There's something about the feel of it. I can't quite describe it. It's not the weakness of the trace, but sort of like . . . granular? Stretched? It's not fresh, in any event."

Colder and Woadham led the way down. The spiraling tube

ramp was so narrow that they had to descend single file, and Denny wanted trained goons to meet whatever they might find at the bottom. The spiral turned twice, then ended at an iris door that opened into a room, similar to those above, with three other doors.

Rikard paused in the middle of the room. Sukiro was right behind him. She was still suspicious of his ability to sense the Tathas, but he had no patience with her. He chose the door on the left because it somehow felt more "recent," and the others followed him through, to another room, then to another, then into a corridor. The door at the far end opened onto the top of another spiral ramp, which led them down again, one more level.

When they left the ramp this time they found themselves at the side of another corridor. It was at least ten meters wide and extended in both directions into the darkness. The switch by the iris caused only one section of the high, amber ceiling to be illuminated.

The decor here was the same as above, pale blue walls with two triple dark blue stripes, and milky white floors below the amber ceiling. There were several other doors visible, those on the near side of the corridor not opposite those on the far side. All were dark blue and outlined in white.

Other than that the corridor was empty, but all could see the marks in the dust on the floor, where someone had walked before them. There were enough tracks this time, going both ways and toward some of the doors, so that they could not just follow the set from the ramp, but needed Rikard's further guidance.

He stepped out into the middle of the corridor, looked one way, then the other, then closed his eyes and felt the subtle Tathas trace. It was everywhere, very faint, rather old.

"All the marks look like they were made by boots or shoes," Sladen said.

"That's right," Rikard agreed, "they'd be carrying the Tathas in containers of some kind."

"But they'd have to be shielded, wouldn't they?"

"The carriers, yes, but not the containers. If they had been, I couldn't feel the residual effects of their presence here."

He closed his eyes again, looking for the kinds of images he'd felt and seen in the caverns under the Tower of Fives on Kohltri, but nothing like that came. Just a feeling of—grayness? Discomfort? Some slight madness, surely. It was stronger . . . "That way," he said, pointing to the right.

Quickly and cautiously, they moved off up the corridor, toward the darkness beyond the light.

2

They went up to the corridor to the right. As they neared the shadowed portion the ceiling ahead turned on automatically, and the section behind went dark.

This happened at the next section, and when the one after that lit up they could see that the corridor came to a T intersection. There the footprints went in both directions, but Rikard led them to the left.

There was a dark hole in the middle of the next section of corridor, the head of a ramp leading down. As they neared it an iris behind them snapped. But when they stopped, startled, to look behind them, all the irises they could see were closed.

They went on to the head of the ramp. The footprints led down, and so they followed, descending eight meters or so to another corridor parallel to the one they had just left.

One line of footprints went on ahead, but most of the tracks doubled back around the side of the ramp, and this was the trail Rikard followed. As they came to the end of the lit section of corridor and the lights in the next section came on they heard two irises snapping, at the far end of the newly lit corridor, one right after another, one on either side.

The goons froze in a crouch, ready to fire at anything that showed itself. Grayshard nearly flattened himself to the floor. They could not tell which irises had opened, and there was nobody in sight. After a pause they went on, but when they got to where the sounds had come from they could see a trail in the dust, crossing the corridor. It was not footprints, but a mark as if someone had blown or swept the dust aside, from one iris to another.

Beyond this disturbance most of the footprints led on down the corridor, but a single trail angled off to a side door. Rikard started to lead them that way when an iris behind them snapped open and shut. Sladen, who was in the rear, lurched forward and fell to his hands and knees as if he had been knocked down from behind, and even over the sound of his fall and curses they could hear another iris snapping.

Longarth and Raebuck went to Sladen's aid, and even as they helped him to his feet Longarth called out, "There's another swipe across the dust here. It comes in, crosses where Sladen was standing, and goes on in an arc and back out the same iris again."

"What the hell is going on?" Falyn demanded.

"Does that have anything to do with the Tathas effect?" Sukiro asked Rikard.

"Not as far as I know," he said. When they had recovered themselves he led them through the side door into a large room. The floor was a half meter below the corridor level but without any steps. There were two strange objects set between the ubiquitous pedestal-footed table and the wall. Both were roughly rectilinear, but with complex surfaces. There was no dust on either of them.

The larger object, on the right, was a meter long, half a meter high and wide, light red on top shading to dark red near the floor. The visible faces had randomly placed pyramidal concavities of a much lighter red, ten centimeters square and as deep, and from the near side projected a cylinder that angled upward, also about ten centimeters long, and of a much darker red. The smaller object, on the left, was an orange cube, thirty centimeters on a side, lighter above than below. Each face had a square recess, off center, about five centimeters deep. The two objects and the table left little room for the group to move through, and several of the goons tried to move the smaller thing out of the way, but it wouldn't budge.

There were three other doors in the room, and Rikard led them to the far one. On the counter beside it was a much smaller object, composed of three steel-colored spheres in a row, connected by short black rods, about twenty centimeters long altogether. Jasime picked it up in passing, and found that it weighed hardly anything at all.

The next room was larger than the first, with columns supporting the ceiling. Here were several more of the rectilinear objects standing on the floor. Rikard led them to the far door, but as he did so the iris by which they had entered snapped. Sladen and Brisabane, the two goons nearest the door, fell on their faces as if struck from behind. The rest of the platoon spun around, weapons drawn, to face the now silent iris. There was nothing to aim or fire at.

Brisabane, on the floor, was lying on his back, almost under the central table. He called out, "There are things under here," and Sladen looked up at the underside of the table too.

"What are they?" Rikard asked as he went to see.

"There's another one of those three-sphere things," Brisabane said, "and two boxes, about as big as my hand, with lids. They look like they're made of wood." He reached up, touched one of the boxes. It fell into his hand, which startled him, and he dropped it.

Sladen reached down and gingerly picked it up. "What was holding it up?" he asked.

"I don't know." Brisabane took the box back, and put it up against the underside of the table again. "It's just sticking there now." He took it down again and crawled out from under the table. "It didn't feel like magnetism," he said as he turned it over and over.

"Leave that there," Denny told him.

Brisabane was almost glad to put it down on the table, but as he did so the hinged cover opened. He reached out to close the lid again, then decided not to.

Rikard looked into the box. It was empty, except for a collection of tiny rods sticking up from the bottom.

He left it there and went back to the iris where the vague Tathas trace was strongest and led the platoon through into another transverse corridor. Then he turned to the left and as they went on, a section of the corridor, two hundred meters ahead, lit up briefly. The ceiling light was on for only an instant, and nobody saw anything that might have tripped the automatic switch.

With growing apprehension they went on into the next section of corridor, then through a door on the left side, into an L-shaped room. The central square of the L was half a meter below the end by which they had entered, and the far leg of the L was half a meter higher again. There were two irises in each of the long walls, and one in each of the other six walls.

Each section of the L had its own black-topped table. In the first part of the room were two orange cubes like those they found before. In the center section, on one side, was a different kind of greenish rectangular object. In the last section, into which Rikard led them, was yet another object, one that looked like a rust-colored couch with arms and back, and about that size, light on top and shading darker toward the floor. But one half of the "seat" had a half-cube recess, the other had a half-cube projection, and the back was covered with a seemingly random set of projecting pale orange square rods, each five or six centimeters across and from one to ten centimeters long.

Suddenly all the irises snapped rapidly several times in succession. The goons nearest the doors fired but succeeded only in damaging the walls and irises.

"God damn it," Sukiro shouted to the noncoms, "keep your people under control."

Falyn had fired her own blaster. She put it away, half-angry, half-guilty.

The noncoms ordered the goons to each of the doors. They opened them all at once, ready to fire if there was any movement. But behind each door were only marks on the floor where the dust had been swept or blown away.

"Something *was* here," Nelross said. He was getting as jumpy as his goons.

"Let's keep moving," Sukiro said, so Rikard led them out a side door in the far leg of the L, into a smaller room, furnished with two red rectilinear objects. As they passed through, *something* moved through the room in the opposite direction, so fast that they could not see what it was. Everyone in its path was either knocked down or jostled to one side.

It took a moment to restore order after it had gone, and then the only evidence of its passage was a trail on the floor where the dust had been swept aside, and a lot of dust now hanging in the air. The noncoms had a hard time getting the goons back under control, indeed, were having a hard time keeping from getting hysterical themsleves.

"Are you sure that's not the Tathas doing that?" Sukiro asked Rikard.

"Absolutely," Rikard said, "there's no new Tathas scent here, and besides, Tathas move very slowly."

But he, too, was beginning to feel frightened. Without further hesitation he led them on into another corridor. They went along it for three sections until they came to a ramp, in the middle of the corridor, which went both up and down. They went down, then along another section of corridor to where it opened onto the ground floor of a two-level arcade. The level above them was surrounded by balconies. There were more doors there, reached by spiral ramps recessed into the corners of the arcade and into the centers of its long sides, where a catwalk crossed the arcade at balcony level.

Rikard had to pause in this large space, to find the direction of the now very faint Tathas trace. "I think it's coming from over there," he said at last, "on the second level, and down toward that end."

They had crossed half the distance to the side ramp when all the irises on both levels snapped in rapid succession, several of them more than once. Plumes of dust rose into the air, behind things moving so fast that they could not really be seen.

Nobody had time to react before the dust-devil streaks caromed through the outer edges of the group, knocking several people down. The dust-devils raced away, and there was not even a hesitation at the irises as they worked the latch-plates. Before those goons who had fallen could get to their feet, there was another attack.

Rikard pulled his gun, felt the slowdown of his time senses, then something brushed him very lightly but with great force. His gun flew from his hand as he was spun around.

When he stopped moving the dust-devils were gone again. His gun was a few meters away. As he went to retrieve it he shouted, "Everybody, backs together in the middle of the room!"

There was a moment's hesitation then, as Rikard got to his weapon, the noncoms repeated the order. Then the dust-devils came again. Most of them knocked against the goons on the outside of the group, but some passed through the center.

Rikard gripped his gun, time started to slow, the air was filled with dust. Goons jostled against him as they tried to move together and were hit by the dust-devils. Falyn backed sharply into Rikard, knocking him off his feet backward.

With his time perception slowed he almost seemed to float down through the air toward the deck. Even as he fell he saw *things* passing on the edges of his sight. He tried to turn his eyes to look at one of them, but his eyes could move no faster than normal. Only his perceptions were speeded up, and before he could focus on one of the dust-devils, it was gone again.

He struggled to his feet, ready for another attack. The goons around him were organizing as quickly as they could, forming a ring with himself and Grayshard in the center. Rikard eased his grip on his gun for a moment, and time returned to normal. They waited.

But no attack came.

"Where's Sukiro?" Nelross suddenly asked.

"She was right here," Yansen started to say, and then they took count. Besides Sukiro, six other goons were missing: Gospodin, Hornower, Tamura, Longarth, Saydee, and Brisabane.

"What the hell is going on!" Jasime demanded.

"The raiders are onto us," Sladen suggested.

"There was nothing like this in the briefing," Majorbank complained.

"We've seen the raiders' tracks," Rikard said, "they're human. This is something else."

"There's no time to argue about it," Nelross said. "We've got six goons missing—and the major. We've got to go after them."

"But which way did they go?" Denny asked helplessly.

"Check the doors," Rikard said. "Look for unusual tracks."

The noncoms gave orders to do so.

"Maybe it's the people who built this place," Raebuck suggested.

"Don't be silly," Falyn said, "this station has been derelict for ten thousand years."

Judging by the marks in the dust, most of the attackers had come through ground-level doors, and one in particular, at the far end, seemed most promising as their probable exit.

"I think they went out this way," Colder said when Rikard came to her summons. "See, it looks like they were dragging something."

"I think you're right," Rikard said. "In any event, it's our best bet." He called the others and they went out.

In the room beyond the iris was a new kind of object, sitting over to one side. It was a pink quadrilateral the size of a desk, but with very rounded corners and edges and without a kneehole. The surface was pebbled instead of smooth, and covered with a random pattern of brown stripes except where the top surface was sunken. From the center of the recess a round spike projected upward to a point—the only point in the room—ringed at odd angles with navy.

Rikard gave the object only a cursory glance, but while he and Denny paused to determine which way the tracks led, Raebuck prodded at the desklike thing, and once tried to move it.

"I think this was their rallying point," Denny said, tracing the marks from door to door. "It looks like they split up here and went to other entrances, so as to attack us from all sides at once."

They went through the far door, from which most of the tracks seemed to come, into another room. There was no central table in this room, nor counters, nor stand-alone "furniture," just an object that floated in the middle of the room, at about head height.

It was roughly octahedral, about fifty centimeters across, of an amber color the same as the ceiling except that it was opaque. On each face were panels, of the same shape as the face, made of what looked like milk-glass. There were no projections or recesses, no controls or knobs.

It was a startling object. Woadham reached out to touch it even as Falyn snapped, "Leave it alone!"

Beyond the far iris was another transverse corridor that ran parallel to the arcade. It was completely dark, but off toward the left they could see light coming up from a descending ramp, and the dust trail headed in that direction.

"Robots could move that fast," Falyn muttered to Denny.

"They can," she said, "but they'd have to be controlled, and the controller's reactions couldn't be that fast."

"Not telefactors," Falyn said, "robots, completely autonomous."

"Then they're soft robots," Sladen said. "When I was hit it was something soft, it was just moving so fast that it knocked me around. If it had been a robot it would have taken my arm off."

Then the light in the ramp went out. "Headlamps," Denny ordered.

Rikard found a switch by an iris, but it didn't work. They went on, using their headlamps. They came to the ramp, started to descend, and halfway down the light in the section of corridor below came on.

At the bottom of the ramp was another corridor parallel to the one above. The dust marks along the floor were perfectly evident.

"Maybe the attacks are made by some kind of energy field," Raebuck suggested, "you know, set as sentry against intruders."

"On a station like this," Petorska said, "who would expect intruders."

"Besides," Yansen said, "the attackers didn't act like fields."

"Of course," Raebuck said, "you're right."

"No," Falyn said, "it could be possible. If the walls contained a grid, a field could move in three dimensions and be of small size."

"But we could almost see something moving," Yansen said, "and fields would be invisible."

"If they could use fields that way," Nelross said, "why not just crush us between a pair?"

"We know nothing about their psychology," Petorska said, "don't make assumptions."

"Whatever it was," Colder said, "they left drag-marks." She pointed to the trail on the floor.

They went down three sections of corridor to a side door, which opened onto a descending spiral ramp. It was twice as wide as the others they had been in, and was swept clean of dust. It went down a long way.

"No life form we know can move as fast as our attackers," Denny said as they descended. "If we discount robots and energy fields, maybe it's some kind of energy *being*, a life form sort of like the Taarshome."

"It's not the Taarshome," Rikard said. "They don't behave that way, and besides, if a Taarshome touches you, you just turn into a cinder."

"Well, not them, then, but something like them."

"I suppose it would be possible, but then how come they haven't attacked the raiders in the year or so they've been here?"

They went down at least four "levels," as far as they could judge. When they came to the bottom they found themselves at the head of a T of three corridors, each ten meters wide and about twelve meters tall. There were intersecting corridors and Ls in all three directions.

The trail led them to the left, through an iris to a balcony at the top of a four-level room. There were four tables on the floor below, and an open spiral ramp in the corner leading down to it. There the trail split into a number of smaller trails, but the drag-marks became more pronounced, as fewer of the attackers were left to carry each victim.

They went out the far door into a two-level corridor. There the trail turned left past a four-way intersection and on to a T, then turned left again to another T almost immediately. There they turned right and went to the third door on the right, and into a three-level room. It was empty except for another floating device.

This one was a dark green dodecahedron, with pale lavender spikes projecting from all but the top and bottom faces. Each spike ended in a cube of milk glass. As soon as Raebuck saw it, she stopped, transfixed. The others crossed the room, following the obvious trail over a waist-high rail between the first section and the next, which was three meters lower. There was a ramp at one side leading down, broad enough for only one person at a time. But Rikard lagged behind with Raebuck. "What's the matter?" he asked her.

"Nothing," she said, but her attention was fixed on the floating object.

"Come on," Rikard said, "we've got to go."

She turned to follow him but kept looking back over her shoulder as they went into the lower, center section and up the ramp in the middle of the two-meter rise to the far side of the room.

They went through an iris into the side of a corridor. They followed the dust trail to the right to a four-way intersection. There the trail led them left to where a ramp, occupying the right half of the corridor, went down.

"At least we're not being attacked anymore," Dyson said.

"Maybe they're local," Sladen answered.

"Except that we're following their tracks."

"Maybe they got what they wanted," Yansen said.

"Maybe they were just hungry?" Jasime suggested.

"I suppose they could be vermin of some kind," Dyson said, "surviving somehow and mutated."

"How could they survive," Sladen said, "without goons to feed on?"

The ramp ended in a door that opened into the side of another corridor. From there the trail led them left, past a three-way intersection to a T, then left again to a four-way, and right again to an iris on the right side of the corridor. This opened onto a balcony at the room's second level.

As they went around the balcony they passed an open panel, in which were shelves containing objects like those they had investigated before, things like rubber crab legs, jackknife bread loaves, and other small things wrapped in transparent foil.

At the corner the trail went down an open ramp to the floor of the room, which was split into two levels, the second a meter higher than the first, with a rail between but no ramp connecting. On the floor were two round-cornered, round-edged rectilinear objects.

The first of these was yellow, twice the size of a desk, with random narrow stripes of deep red shading to maroon. There were round-edged holes going all the way through from one side to the other, and another hole at the front that went only to the transverse hole. Each hole was lined with round knobs of dark green.

The second object was light blue, and rather small, a meter high and seventy centimeters from side to side both ways. It had narrow half-tori projecting from three sides, all of which were navy or black, and had a half dome on the top, of a paler blue, which extended down over the fourth side, and was marked with ugly olive green streaks and smears.

The trail led over the rail to a door on the right side and out into another corridor. From there they went left past a three-way intersection, to another like it where they turned left again, on past a four-way to an iris on the right, which opened onto a balcony at the third level of a large room.

There was another floating object here, larger than the first two, a pale gray twisted bipolar pentagonal prism. The far side of the floor was half a meter higher than the near side, with no railing between, and around the walls were counters. The trail led down the corner spiral to the main floor.

The faces of the floating object that were visible from the near side of the room were blank, but the four contiguous faces on the far side were deeply recessed. Within each recess was a series of hexagonal crystal lights, and around the equatorial juncture between the two pyramidal prisms was a series of levers or rods, projecting into the recesses in the faces.

This stopped Raebuck dead in her tracks. After a pause, in spite of the goons moving past her, she went to the floating object, and reached out to touch one of the rods in one of the upper recesses.

When she did so, the rod sank down into the body of the shape, and a series of hexagonal lights in that recess went on, shining white, and one light in each of the other three recesses also went on, shining blue.

Nelross came around the floater just then, and watched as Raebuck touched another rod, a silver one in the other upper recess. A string of lights in that recess lit red, and one light in each of the other recesses lit yellow.

Rikard was watching her too, and he went to stand beside her just as the whole object turned from pale gray to pale blue-white. Raebuck did not seem surprised by this but reached out for another rod, a black one, which she pressed to the right. All the unlit lights in that recess lit green, and two of the lights in each of the other recesses went pink.

Rikard could hear a faint hum coming from the object. The goons who were still nearby hesitated to half watch as Raebuck turned the machine on. Rikard said, "What is that thing?"

She had not heard him approach, and jumped. "I don't know," she said. But she reached out and touched a flat plate at the back of the upper left recess. All the lights went out, and the floating device returned to pale gray.

"Then how did you learn how to turn it on?" Nelross asked.

"Sorry," Raebuck said, and hurried away.

Rikard and Nelross exchanged glances, then went to catch up with the others, who were going out the door at the far side of the room. Beyond the iris was a corridor. The trail went to another iris directly opposite, and they went inside.

The seven missing people were lying scattered on the floor of the room. Hornower, Gospodin, Tamura, and Brisabane were only unconscious, though badly bruised, but Saydee and Longarth were dead, apparently due solely to rough handling. Sukiro was alive, and began to come to even as the others were being revived.

Denny and the corporals questioned the survivors, but they could say nothing about what had happened, and didn't even know where they were. Sukiro was unable to help either.

The tracks of their attackers went off in all directions. Nelross wanted to pursue, but they had no idea which way to go.

"And besides," Sukiro said, "we still have the raiders to deal with."

"How can we be sure," Nelross asked, "that they aren't the same as whoever it was who brought you here?"

"Because it's totally out of character," Sukiro said.

"I think," Grayshard said, "that if it had been the raiders who have been attacking us, they would have just killed us, not have taken prisoners only to abandon them later."

"And even if it were the raiders," Sukiro went on, not exactly liking to agree with Grayshard, "then this whole business was just a ploy, to divert us from their base when we got too close. If we go off chasing after dust-devils now, we'll be doing exactly what they want. We've got to go back."

"What about Longarth and Saydee?" Falyn asked.

"We can't do anything for them," Sukiro said. "If we can come back for them later we will. Right now we've got other work to do."

3

Rikard kept his eye on Private Raebuck as they followed the broad trail in the dust, back the way they had come. She had known too well how to work that thing for it to have been just some lucky guesses. Where had she picked up that knowledge, and why wasn't she saying anything about it now?

They retraced their steps to the three-level room in which they had found the second floater—about half the distance back to the arcade. As they passed through, an iris snapped on one side of the room and another iris opposite snapped almost immediately after. The goons were tense, and three of them got off shots which merely put pockmarks in the wall. The only evidence of their invisible intruder was a cloud of dust hanging in the air, stirred up by the speed of its passage.

As the other two noncoms brought the goons back into line, Nelross told Sukiro that he wanted to try something.

One of the items of special equipment his goons were carrying was a vibracoil, a kind of energy weapon that was harmless to most objects but that literally cooked organic matter by disrupting any materials with high moisture content. It could also shake certain microcircuitry to powder. It was typically used when a criminal had blockaded himself in a place that couldn't be reached by regular weapons, or which was too valuable to destroy by blaster fire. It had the advantage that its energy could pass, with only minor attenuation, through rigid materials, such as metals, stone, and certain very stiff plastics, although it was thoroughly damped by wood, normal plastics, and any thickness—ten centimeters or more—of clothing or flesh. Armor was unaffected by the vibracoil, but its energy, passing through lighter grades of armor, could cause the wearer to boil in his suit, so rapidly that he exploded.

It was not a convenient weapon to use. Nelross had the goon carrying it set it up so that it could be activated. That done he carried it under his arm like some kind of bulky and clumsy rifle, and they left the room.

Irises snapped again in the corridor beyond, just what Nelross was waiting for. He aimed the clumsy vibracoil at the iris that had snapped last and triggered it. A tracking beam shone white on the iris, and there was a faint but disturbingly modulated hum that lasted for several seconds. Yansen and Dyson, the goons nearest the iris, waited until the white tracking beam went out, then opened the iris and looked into the room beyond.

"You got something," Dyson called back. There were smears on the ground, and a rancid smell in the air. But there was no body to tell whether the residue on the corridor floor was from the thing itself, its vehicle, its outer surface, or some other thing it had carried.

They returned to the trail. Nelross, with his vibracoil, was always the second to enter any room or corridor. But for a long time he had no reason to use it.

Even so he did not let down his guard, so that when, as they entered the L-shaped room, the iris on the far side, their intended exit, was just snapping, he was ready and fired a long beam from the vibracoil. On the other side they found ample evidence of the effectiveness of that particular weapon under these circumstances.

As far as they could tell from the mess on the floor, at least three of the invisible intruders had been hit. There were three distinct smears of goo; pieces of what might have been semitransparent leather; a couple of dozen objects that looked like insect legs, but that had been so shattered by the expanding, superheated fluids inside their owners' bodies that it was hard to be sure. There were no artifacts of any kind. The goons picked their way through the mess and went on. After that, there were no further attacks.

They neared the arcade and Rikard's concerns were replaced by others when he felt the first tingle of what he had so far interpreted as the Tathas effect. He hurried forward to tell Sukiro.

"Is it bad?" she asked.

"No, but it's there."

They entered the arcade. "Just what it is that you're feeling?" Sukiro asked.

"It's hard to describe," Rikard said. "It's not just psychic, not like communicating with the Taarshome. The Tathas exude a chemical substance, wherever they go, like a snail's trail. It corrodes almost anything except glass and some kinds of plastic, and even then it leaves a residue. The thicker the corrosion, or the residue, the stronger the feeling, and if there are Tathas present, you get a bit of their thoughts, too. I don't feel any thoughts, just the sensation of comfort at being closed in, discomfort at having so many people around me."

"But then why was it so strong on Natimarie? There was no residue there that we found."

"Stuff in the air," Rikard hazarded, "too thin to be seen or noticed without a specific chemical analysis. And there, the Tathas were being forced to release that stuff all over the place, so it would be strong enough to affect the people. When they're in their holes, where this stuff is thick, where there's been a lot of corrosion, and they've laid down a kind of shell, as it were, they resonate with it, and the feeings I get feel good to them. Here, the Tathas would be kept in dark confinement, which they find comfortable, instead of being exposed to bright sunlight and open air, as they probably were on Natimarie and at the other raided towns. For them, that would be the ultimate terror and torture."

Rikard followed the strongest traces across the arcade and into a large, rectangular room on the other side, with three of the sharp-angled, rectilinear objects they had seen before, set close around the central table. The corners of this room were obviously not square but sharply in conformation with the geodesic pattern that all the rooms obeyed.

Rikard followed the Tathas trace to another, even larger room, though with only two of the strange artifacts, and from there into a corridor, and to the room directly opposite. This room was rather small, with a few objects on the table and counters, but no floor-standing artifacts. There was an opening in one corner of the room, where a ramp went down. The trace led that way.

On Denny's command Colder and Woadham preceded Rikard from this point, until they came out at the bottom of the ramp, three levels lower, at an intersection of corridors. These were only one level high, but they went in all four directions, and were lit as far as they could see, with frequent crossings and intersections visible in the distance. Rikard closed his eyes, felt discomfort to right and left and behind, and so led them straight ahead.

They followed this corridor a long way, then took an L to the left, then the branch of a T to the right, which ended at last in another T, and from there went into the room opposite the end of the corridor.

The light was already on when they entered. There was an object of a kind they hadn't seen before, a stellated polyhedron, sitting in the middle of the floor on three of its points. It was three meters tall and two meters wide, metallic in part, transparent elsewhere. Each point was of a different size, shape, and angularity. It had what appeared to be functional knobs, switches, and levers, set into one surface or another, and some of the transparent spikes showed what looked like electronics inside, but not always connected to other parts or to surface elements.

In the next room beyond was another object, similar to the first but larger, with more points more acutely angled. Everybody had a hard time taking their eyes from it, but they were too near danger to pause now. The next room had two smaller, similar objects, differing in color as well as number and acuteness of points. Then they entered a transverse corridor, went to left and through the third door on the opposite side.

This room contained yet another of the stellated objects and besides that, from one wall projected a device that intersected the counter as if set into it. It was rectangular, with knobs and levers and panels and projections and hollows, all in metallic colors. It was about one meter high and half a meter long. That it was control equipment of some type was obvious, but what it controlled was a mystery. They did not stay to investigate, though there was a faint humming coming from the thing, but went on out the opposite door.

Here they found themselves in a corridor two levels high, with a ramp going down on one side, at the bottom of which was a door that opened onto a transverse corridor. They went along this a ways and then turned aside and through an iris into a room.

There were three of the stellated objects here, all very small, placed near the corners of the room. As they passed through Tamura, to avoid touching the pointed thing, jostled the table in the middle, and several small objects fell from its undersurface onto the floor.

She picked one of them up, a collection of pentagonal rods, each as big as a thumb and from ten to twenty centimeters long. The rods slid over and around each other, but they didn't come apart. She put it down on the table and went on with the others.

The next room was very large, with columns up to the ceiling though it was only two levels high. There were "control" devices projecting from all four walls. Some of these were actually blinking. The goons kept their distance as Rikard led them past.

They went into another corridor, along it for quite a ways, and turned at several intersections. They went through a room with one huge stellated object, on into another corridor, along it to a ramp that led down to the end of another corridor, and from there into an empty room on one side, where once again the lights were already on.

But Sukiro looked around the room with a strange expression on her face. "You know," she said, "if I stop to think about it, I wonder if I'm not feeling something odd too. Like—feeling the walls."

"That's it," Rikard said.

"Which way do we go?"

"I don't know, it's—too generalized. I don't get any sense of direction at all."

"We should go up," Majorbank said. "Hornower's been feeding me data on room angularity, and I calculate we should be almost directly under the raiders' hatch."

"All right, then," Sukiro said. "Sergeant Denny, you're in charge."

There were three other doors in the room, but Denny led them through the one opposite their entrance. The room beyond was also lit. Stacked to one side were plastic containers of typical Federation design.

They had been going on suspicion until now, but the contents of this storeroom confirmed that this was, indeed, the raiders' base. They didn't bother to investigate any of the containers but went out the opposite door into a corridor, the ceiling of which was lit for its whole length.

"Here's what we're going to do," Sukiro said as they went up the hall. "We're going to just cross their entire base at this level, until we come to the other side. That will give us some idea of the area they have under their control. Then, assuming we've not run into trouble, we'll go straight up as near to their perimeter as we can, until we come to an inhabited area. At that point we'll try to find out how many of them there are, how they're armed, and what kind of force it would take to take them."

"Should we spread out?" Nelross asked.

"Let's keep together," Sukiro said, "until we have a better idea of the layout. It won't do for any of us to get separated."

"What if we come on someone by surprise?" Denny asked.

"Back off if you can," Sukiro said, "but if you can't, try to take prisoners."

"What if we get to the top and don't find anybody?" Falyn asked.

"In that case we start cleaning up. Any more questions? Then let's go."

They entered the room at the end of the corridor. Here shelves had been built along the walls and in freestanding rows down the middle of the room. Each shelf held a Human body.

All were nude, all were dead, held in stasis by devices, attached to each of the shelves, of a design totally unfamiliar to Sukiro or Falyn. Each body had had its skull opened.

Petorska brought out a small, emergency stasis-anti-stasis generator, and turned it on the body of a middle-aged, slightly overweight man, then Jasime and Dyson examined the corpse. They found no other damage than that the brain pan was empty.

The chamber to their left was also filled with Human bodies.

They did no more than look inside. The room on the right was different—it was filled with Senola corpses.

"The victims from Natimarie," Sukiro said with a long sigh. "Or at least some of them. I don't think there are more than a thousand bodies here."

They went through the fourth door of the first chamber, and in the room beyond found the bodies of a different race, the Aaliir. They had spherical bodies covered with thick fur, mostly black, but some mahogony, or a dark brick color, and one or two pale terra-cotta with amber shading. They had four dog-legs radiating from the lower quarter, each with two large, massively clawed toes. They had two long and muscular arms just above the middle of their bodies, with two fingers and one thumb, also strongly clawed. They had no heads, their dome-eyes were set into the fur on the top of the body and the mouth was a slash just below these.

The rooms on either side of this one contained more Humans on the left, more Senola on the right. The fourth led into a corridor. They crossed it and went into the room opposite.

Here were the bodies of yet another race, the Neugar. They were humanoid, tall, slender, fair, handsome with a vaguely feline cast to their faces. Their hair shaded from white to gold or silver-gray. Their large eyes were open, in shades of blue or startling black.

The room beyond that held more of the same, then they came to another corridor. The next two rooms held Grelsh.

These were an arthropoid species, pseudo-humanoid, their exoskeletons reduced to form external "bones." Otherwise they had a hard "skin" of a semi-glossy light brown. They had four legs in pairs set very closely together, and were functionally bipedal. They had only two arms but each had an extra joint. Their hands were composed of two central thumbs and two pairs of opposing fingers. Their faces were round and flat, with a mouth like that of a grasshopper, four small eyes, and no feelers or visible ears.

What they had seen so far represented only a tiny fraction of all the victims taken from any one world, let alone from all the worlds the raiders had visited. The thought of all the levels of the base filled with bodies in storage like this was overwhelming.

But they still had no idea of the force they were likely to run up against. Given the equipment they'd seen, a custodial crew would need to be no more than twenty strong, even at the rate that new bodies were being brought in—assuming that all missing victims actually got here and were not jettisoned in transit. Such a base crew would be able to do nothing other than stack bodies, of course. It was more likely that there would be many more than twenty, maybe as many as a hundred.

"We don't have to go any further," Sukiro said. "If they've made room for half a million bodies or more, it could take us a week just to go across. And it wouldn't tell us anything about the raiders stationed here, or those who actually bring the victims in. Let's start up at the next ramp we come to."

But the first doors they checked only led into more storage rooms, with their hundreds and thousands of stacked bodies— Human, humanoid, centauroid, and other forms. Aside from the bodies, the stasis shelves, and all the lights being on, there was no sign of whoever was working here. At last they found an ascending ramp and went up to another level.

The first room they entered here was four times the size of the ones below, and its contents were even more appalling. Shelves lined the walls and filled the room in a huge maze of aisles. All were filled with tanks, and each tank contained not a body but a brain, still alive, connected by tubes and wires to life-support devices that stood in the middle of each stand of shelves.

There were brains of all varieties, matching the variety of the bodies in storage below. Each tank bore a label, with an alpha-numeric code above another code written in an alphabet never seen in the Federation. Some of the shelves held additional equipment, the purpose of which was not clear. None of the aisles between the shelves ran the full length of the room.

If there was another way up it had to be on the far side of the room. The goons went in and spread out, passing through the maze of shelves, looking at the brains, forgetting for a moment their purpose here.

Grayshard, for the first time, began to show some animation. He went from tank to tank, looking at the brains within. At first he seemed to pulse, as if with excitement or indignation, but when he realized that he was being watched he forced himself to become rigid.

He threaded his way, with the others, from aisle to aisle, but at last he stopped, turned to see Rikard and Sukiro still watching him, and said, "I have seen what I need. There may be hope

for these yet. Do what you must, there must be an end to this."
His voice, as usual, was expressionless, yet there was an intensity to it in spite of its mechanical production.

"You were expecting something like this," Sukiro said.

"I was hoping not, yet I knew it would be. I—"

But before he could say anything more, Fresno, near a door in the right-side wall, called out softly. "I heard an iris snap, just outside."

"We can't fight them in here," Sukiro said, "not if these brains are still alive."

"Now I hear footsteps," Fresno said, "somebody's coming."

"Everybody take cover," Denny ordered.

4

Now that there was an enemy the goons could understand their training took over, and if Rikard hadn't been in their midst he wouldn't have known anyone was there. In spite of their armor the goons could be almost totally silent if they chose to be, if they had to be, and they found hiding places quickly. But Rikard, taken by surprise by the rapidity of the action, stood where he was until he felt hands on his shoulders, pushing him down. He accepted the suggestion without protest.

From where he crouched he could just see the edge of the iris, through the stacks of containers on several rows of shelves, and saw it snap open, then stay open as four people, humanoids of some sort, came shuffling in. Two of them turned to the racks of brains against the wall to the right of the door, and thus remained within his limited view, while the other two attended to the racks on the left, moving out of his sight.

There was something wrong about these people. Their movements were slow and clumsy, and at first Rikard thought that was because, though humanoid, they were not actually Human but some other race with which he was not familiar. But more than that, their clothes were dirty and torn, and their movements were not just alien but unpracticed, an eerie shamble and fumble, almost as if they were moving in their sleep.

The two technicians who Rikard could see went from container to container, tapping each, sometimes adjusting switches and dials. They worked side by side, starting with the top shelf and working downward, moving methodically along the wall until they were concealed by intervening shelves.

The goons near Rikard seemed agitated, and then he noticed that they were signaling to each other with complex but subtle hand gestures. Without the com-link to the shuttle or gunship to coordinate their wired-in communications system, they couldn't talk with each other. But they were not confused. They had been trained to deal with situations such as this, however infrequently they might occur, and their sign language was highly effective.

Rikard was fascinated by this interplay, and as he watched he saw that Sukiro had gotten one aisle over from him without his noticing. She tapped Falyn on the shoulder and, when the corporal turned, made a gesture. Falyn acknowledged silently, then drew her jolter—a paralyzing neuronic whip—stood up and quietly and quickly walked up the aisles toward the technician nearest her, now separated from his companion who was working his way farther down the wall. Rikard craned to look around a shelf full of equipment and watched as Falyn touched the technician with the tip of her jolter, just below the base of the skull.

The technician staggered but did not fall, and Falyn, expecting to grab the man and drag him back out of sight, lurched off balance for an instant. Before she could conceal herself again the technician turned. His face was expressionless, even when he saw Falyn and the others behind her down that aisle. It took only an instant, Falyn was already reaching out with the jolter, but the technician was faster, and without a sound turned quickly away and lurched toward the iris. In unison the other technicians stopped what they were doing and did the same.

The goons, surprised by this turn of events, hesitated just an instant, afraid to use their blasters for fear of damaging the brains. This was enough time for the jolted technician to get out the door. The goons nearest the iris jumped forward to try to stop the three others, but they were in too tight a space and the two technicians nearest the iris escaped.

The fourth technician might have escaped too, in spite of the quickness of the goons. Though he had shambled somnambulantly before, he was moving quickly now and not confused by his surroundings. But while he was still some three meters from the iris there came the soft snapping of a single unitron round being fired. The technician staggered, then lurched away. The goons nearest him all ducked back. Rikard looked in the direction from which the sound had come, and saw Sukiro standing clear and taking careful aim with her gun.

She fired again, a burst this time. The five 10mm rounds made just a little noise. The technician was hit all five times, and staggered again, but kept going in spite of his body wounds.

Sukiro pushed the goons near her aside—and other goons in the line of fire backed off, recognizing their commander's prerogative—then aimed a longer burst at the technician's legs. The humanoid went down as the shattered bones folded, and flopped out of sight behind a rack of supplies.

Rikard hurried toward the door, ignoring the goons around him, who were now coming out of cover. The noncoms were snapping orders: "You three get out into the hall," "Hold your fire," "Form up and hold steady." Too much control, he thought, let them get the technicians before they get away.

He came up to Sukiro just as she reached the place where the wounded humanoid had fallen. There was no body, but there was a trail of blood on the floor. Falyn came up quickly as Sukiro, after an instant's consternation, stepped over the blood and strode along the crimson trail in search of the fallen man.

Falyn did not break stride but went off after Sukiro, and Rikard went along with her. "There doesn't seem to be enough blood for the wounds that guy took," Falyn said.

Denny, still standing by the iris, called out. "Shall we give chase to the others?" Stupid, Rikard thought. Nelross was bringing his goons forward in an orderly fashion.

Rikard and Falyn followed Sukiro, around one end of an aisle and up another. Sukiro called back to Denny, "I'll be with you in a minute." Then they came around a section of shelving filled with equipment instead of brain containers. There was the technician, lying facedown, arms and legs sprawled out. And the top of his head was lying beside him.

"There's no brain," Sukiro said, dumbfounded.

"How could he possibly have moved?" Falyn asked.

"No wonder he didn't bleed much," Rikard said dryly.

Then Grayshard came hurrying up to join them. He didn't even look at the corpse. "The others," he said, "you must shoot in the head."

"But it's empty," Sukiro said.

"It is now."

They all looked at their mysterious colleague, but Denny, still by the iris, called out. "They're getting away."

"Then go!" Sukiro snapped, irritated, and they all turned to hurry after the goons as, at last, they went out the iris in pursuit.

Rikard came out into the corridor just behind Sukiro, with Falyn right behind him. The goons on the right had started up an empty hallway, but those on the left dropped into a crouch to fire their blasters at the three zombie technicians, now a good two hundred meters away. One of the zombies was hit and his head exploded. A second was hit in the back, and folded at its new waist and crumbled to the deck. But the third zombie jerked unharmed into a side passage while blaster shots pocked the walls beside it and sang on down the corridor beyond.

"Full power," Denny snapped, "go get him." The two goons in the lead straightened for an instant. Rikard could hear the click as their armor became fully activated. Then they raced down the corridor, accelerating as they went, in pursuit of the escapee.

Before Rikard and the others could get to the fallen zombies the pursuing goons reached the corner, jumped around it, and fired two or three times each. "We got him," one called back.

But Rikard's attention, and that of those with him, was focused on the zombies now at their feet. The one hit in the head was as one would have expected, completely still, but the one shot in the back was moving, though Rikard could see the deck through the hole in its body. There was, in spite of this, very little blood. And not, Rikard suspected, just because of the cauterizing effect of the blaster shot. There was a rank smell in the air.

While the others stared, Rikard knelt down beside the zombie and turned it over on its back. There was an incision just under the hairline on its forehead.

"Kill it," Grayshard called out as he came running up.

"Not just yet," Rikard said. He grabbed the top of the zombie's skull and tried to lift it off, but it was fastened securely. Private Ming dropped down onto her knees by the zombie's feet and grabbed its legs. Rikard took another hold of its hair and pulled again.

This time the skull came off, and inside, twisting and coiling, was a mass of pale, creamy white tendrils. It seemed to be trying to compress itself into the lower portion of the skull.

Rikard rocked back on his heels, disgusted. It looked just like a Tathas, though very small and not the same color as those on Kohltri. But he didn't feel any Tathas effect.

Gospodin and Brisabane, too, were disgusted at the sight of the thing. Several of the other goons were having a hard time keeping their stomachs down. The body wound was not the issue, it was the coiling mass of white fibers where a brain should have been—a parasite, a monster. Private Petorska couldn't stand it. He pushed Rikard aside, drew his blaster, and fired at the zombie's skull. Rikard was knocked backward by the shock. Bits of tendril and splots of fluid spattered his face and chest.

Falyn grabbed Petorska and jerked him to one side. "Get control of yourself! You could have hurt someone!"

"God, I—" Petorska gasped. A cloud of vapor and smoke rose around them. It stank.

"And now how are we going to interrogate it?"

"I—" He swallowed hard. "Yes, sir." He turned away and holstered his weapon.

Rikard wiped slime and bits of tendril off his face, took a deep breath, then reached down into the brain case. His stomach nearly turned over, but he pulled out what was left of the creature inside. A thick bundle of tendrils went down through the hollow spinal cord. Rikard kept on pulling, until he had withdrawn nearly two meters of the creature from the man who had been dead long ago.

Sukiro stared down at the thing. "There must have been one of those in the man I shot in the brain room," she said. Her voice was flat and even.

"There was," Grayshard said.

Falyn turned to Gospodin and Brisabane. "Check out that one down the hall," she ordered. They went. "And kill it!" she shouted after them.

"But the one in the brain room," Rikard said, "it's still alive." He looked at Grayshard. "Could it call for help?"

"It could," Grayshard said.

"You, you, you," Sukiro said to Colder, Dyson, and Char-

ney, "come with me. The rest of you keep watch here." Then
she started back toward the brain room. Rikard got to his feet to
go with her.

But there was no sign of the brain creature when they got
back to the body. Sukiro directed her three goons to search the
floor nearby, to look for any signs that such a creature might
have made. "It can't move very fast," she said to Rikard, "it's
got to be hiding somewhere in here."

They looked behind canisters, boxes, electronic equipment.
They looked under shelves, on top of shelves, circling out from
the body on the floor. They found no monster, they found no
trail.

"It could be almost anywhere," Rikard said. "We don't have
time to open every box. I think it went for the first exit and got
out."

"Could it operate an iris?" Sukiro asked.

"I think it could. Tathas can stretch themselves up very tall,
and it doesn't take much pressure to trip the touch-plate."

"Then it's as good as gone."

"But the damn thing is," Rikard went on, "I get no Tathas
sense in here at all—except for what was already here."

"So then that thing really wasn't a Tathas."

"It sure as hell looked like one. And there *have* been Tathas
here."

Charney suddenly turned toward the door, and the others
looked too. Grayshard stood in the open iris, watching them.
They waited for him to speak, but he did not.

"Or something related to Tathas, perhaps," Rikard went on,
looking straight at Grayshard's vision receptors. Grayshard just
stood there.

"Parallel evolution?" Sukiro suggested.

"Not very likely, but one time the Tathas had starflight, or
their ancestors did, and this race could be descended from
those."

"But you didn't get any of that Tathas effect from the one in
the hall."

Rikard looked down at his hand. There was a slight sheen of
pearly white here and there, the juices of the dead creature he'd
pulled from the skull. "No corrosive effect either." He wiped
his hand on his pants.

"A different race?" Sukiro suggested. "A subspecies?
Workers and administrators and so on?"

Grayshard's goggles could not reveal which of them he was actually looking at. He said nothing.

"We can speculate later," Sukiro went on. "Now we have to assume that the alarm has been given. We've got to move, before the rest of the raiders here escape, or hide somewhere—or launch an attack."

"And," Rikard said, "if they can produce a Tathas-like effect, then we could be in big trouble."

"We've got to find their headquarters," Sukiro went on, "as soon as we can, while we only have a custodial force to deal with."

"There's an up-ramp over here," said Dyson, pointing to an iris in a far corner.

"Then let's take it."

Sukiro called in the rest of the goons and the noncoms got them organized. Denny took the lead as they went up the ramp in the corner. Everybody was ready for trouble.

The ramp led them up to a room like the one below, filled with racks of brains and life-support equipment. The brains were visibly of different types, large and small, with varying arrangements of lobes and ganglia and "spinal" cords. One of the other doors in the room opened onto a hall that had a ramp going up the side. They took this up through the center of the floor of another arcade.

There were several objects here, of the kind they had seen before, round or sharp cornered, of various sizes and degrees of complexity. And there were spiral ramps, set into the corners of the arcade, which led up to the second-level balcony. But even as the goons spread out to check out the numerous exits and find the best way to go up again, all the irises around the balcony opened, and dozens of people poured out to spread along the balcony and take up combat positions.

They were partially armored, and without helmets. Most of them were Humans, but a fair number were of another race— humanoid except for a turtlelike beak instead of a mouth, crab-stalk eyes, a high stiff crest of hair from the brow to the top of the spine, and unshod feet that could grasp as well as hands could.

The ambushers started firing before they were well set in place. The goons returned fire at once, then tried to take cover. But the raiders were shooting down, and the artifacts on the floor of the arcade, even the largest of them, provided protection from only one side, and the goons were surrounded.

The goons were equipped with only the lightest blasters, and it seemed that the raiders were no better armed. Their aim was atrocious, but their volume of fire increased as more and more came out of the second-level irises and moved around the balcony, many to lie on the floor and fire down over the edge.

It was inevitable that some of their shots would hit, but goon armor, semiflexible titalumin, seemed proof against these weak blaster bolts. Even though they were exposed, the police were not as careful as they might have been, and became overconfident when, receiving a hit, they suffered no more damage than to be knocked aside.

The raiders did not fare so well. The goons aimed carefully, and though the raiders' armor was, itself, more than proof against these light police blasters, it was not a complete protection. Eight or ten of the raiders were hit with devastating effect before the rest of them learned to lie facedown and shoot over the edge of the balcony.

There were shouted commands from the surrounding raiders, in a language nobody knew, and they coordinated their fire, up to ten of them picking one goon as a target. Sladen, hit by concentrated fire, fell with his right arm half blown away. Then Choi was hit, and the titalumin on his legs flew off. Gospodin went down when her helmet cracked open. And Maturska, who jumped to Gospodin's aid, was hit by seven near simultaneous shots, her body armor was blown away, and she was knocked back, a broken mass.

Rikard and Grayshard were at a complete disadvantage. They crouched behind a large divan-shaped thing and several goons formed a wall between them and the raiders on the other side. But it was not enough. A stray shot passed between the protective goons, hit the object beside Grayshard, and the back-flash took off his left arm.

These casualties seemed to galvanize the goons who, though they had been taken by surprise and were still at a positional disadvantage, were much better fighters. They, too, changed tactics, and teams of two or three picked common targets, aiming just at the edge of the balconies where only a gun or the top of a head was exposed. One by one they began to pick off the raiders, in spite of the massed blaster fire crashing around them.

And any raider who got frightened and tried to run was hit even before he could get to his feet.

It began to look like the police were going to win this fight after all, in spite of better than four to one odds, especially when the raiders started a general retreat out the nearest doors. The goons eased their fire, having no desire to kill frightened people who had given up. But then Rikard began to feel a strong Tathas effect. The goons' shots began to miss, and several of them threw themselves facedown on the deck.

Then an iris on the ground floor opened and the Tathas effect became stronger. Most of the goons stopped shooting and the raiders on the balcony held their fire as well. Rikard wanted to crawl under the object behind which he' was crouching but forced himself to turn toward the iris, and so saw, coming from beyond the open portal, two of the shambling humanoid zombies, wearing a kind of harness sling between them, in which hung, as if in state, a very large Tathas-like creature. It was bigger than any Tathas Rikard had ever seen, massive, creamy in color with shades of almost orange, each of its tendrils tipped in red. It was this that was broadcasting the devastating psychic weapons, the same, Rikard knew, that had been used at all the towns the raiders had depopulated.

Rikard's panic was almost overwhelming. He knew all too well the kind of madness those alien thoughts could engender, the horror of being touched by one of those degenerate things, being dissolved and eaten while still alive. He fought to control his fear, fumbled for his gun which, till now, had been forgotten, so sudden and intense had been the ambush. His hand found the grip of the .75, his fingers closed around it, the concentric circles danced in his eyes, and his time sense began to slow, but even as he pulled the gun his vision blurred, not from his built-in ranging system but from the now overwhelming effects of the Tathas' psychic attack. On either side goons sat slumped, or fell, or crawled headfirst into the edge of an artifact or the body of one of their fellows. Many of them seemed able to resist the assault, as if their armor were at least some protection from it, but it was not enough. The monster Tathas was far too strong, and determined, and one by one the goons fell and lay still.

The ceiling was too high and far, far too bright. There were too many people, beside him, above him, they pressed in on his senses like sandpaper on raw skin. The smoke of blaster-fire was almost sweet, the sounds of groaning an itch under his skin. Gray stones, the thought came from nowhere, gray stones, and he tried to reach under his shirt for the dragongem, the one thing which, once long ago, had helped him against this evil, but he couldn't get his hand to work. There was a gun in it. It went off, under his body. His leather clothes and mesh-mail just barely protected him from the flash of the shell. He let the gun go, tried to raise his head, saw raiders with glistening hair plastered on their heads and necks coming out of balcony irises, down ramps, across the floor from first-level entrances. The Tathas-thing loomed large, though it was so far away, its carrier zombies striding, clumsy but purposeful, toward him.

He concentrated all his energy on retaining awareness. He could not reach the dragongem, but he could think about it. It helped. A bit. He watched as the raiders, new raiders, moved among the goons, taking weapons, removing the helmets from those who still struggled. Their shining hair wasn't hair, he saw, but some kind of skintight cap that protected them from the Tathas' attack.

The effort was too much. Rikard gave up trying to watch and just thought about the dragongem pressing against his chest. It was right against his skin, and warm, generating its own psychic field. If he could have looked at it, could have closed the circuit between his skin, the gem, and his sight, he might have been able to resist the psychic assault.

He started to make the effort, to pull his hand under his chest so that he could reach into his shirt but stopped before he had moved an inch. The raiders paid too much attention to the moving victims, those who stayed still they more or less ignored. If they saw his effort, they'd wait to find out what he was trying to do—and then they'd find the dragongem. He couldn't allow that.

He made himself relax. All he could do was *think* about the gem, *remember* how it felt to look into its glowing depths, the feeling of warmth, of joy, of health. It wasn't as much help as he wanted, but it kept him awake.

His concentration on the dragongem did not prevent him from becoming aware that the Tathas-thing, the sentient fungus, was in charge. It rode in the harness between its zombies, going here and there, flanked by two of the strange humanoids with turtle beaks and crab-stalk eyes. It wasn't really coming toward him, it was just going to the center of the arcade floor where it could oversee all that happened. There was no way to tell where its attention was directed except by the way its carriers were facing, but it seemed to scan the place and occasionally one of the turtle-beak humanoids by its side gave an order.

And then it came over to him after all. After all, Rikard and Grayshard were ringers here, without armor, different from the rest. Richard looked up at the creamy orange thing with bright red tendril-tips. One of the turtle-beaks said something, the other made a gesture, he felt a crush of black greasy sky, and passed out.

It seemed but a moment before he woke up. Had he been dreaming? He was lying on his back on the hard deck, and beside him were others. He did not turn to look. Through slitted eyes he saw raiders moving nearby, heard others more distant. Some of the raiders were carrying pieces of police armor. His own clothing, he realized after a moment's introspection, was intact. There were clanks and chunks. The entire police force was being disarmored.

He thought about the dragongem still pressing against his chest. He thought about Tathas, and thought that there was something subtly different about this psychic influence. He lay perfectly still, listening as the raiders picked up the police goons, one by one, and carried them off. His turn came and he was lifted up by two Humans, a man and a woman, and dragged across the arcade floor. He could see, from the corners of his eyes, other police, now dressed only in their underclothing, being similarly dragged, some by Human raiders, others by pairs of zombies.

Other zombies were picking up armfuls of armor, and weapons, and other police equipment. All together, they were being carried away. His personal carriers came to the iris and went out into a corridor. The raiders beside him were carrying one of their own, or at least the upper half of him.

They were carried along a series of corridors. Rikard couldn't keep track of the turns and branches, but at last all of them, even the dead raiders, were dropped on the floor of a large empty room. Their captors left them.

When he was sure that all the raiders had gone Rikard struggled to sit up. When his vision cleared he looked around the small room. It was filled with bodies, live and dead together. The surviving goons were twitching, groaning. He hoped that their minds hadn't been permanently scrambled.

Several of the goons started crying. The psychic violation of the Tathas-creature's psychic attack was hard to bear. Rikard crawled to each of these, regaining his strength as he did so, to comfort them as best he could. It wasn't easy, but they did respond, at least enough to let him know they had not permanently lost their minds.

Sukiro was sitting up now, on the other side of the room. Her face was white and strained. Rikard, having done what he could, got unsteadily to his feet and went to the single iris door, stepping over living and dead to get there. He touched the latch-plate, but nothing happened. He pushed on it, and the iris itself, but it remained closed. They were locked in.

Denny was sitting up now. "What's going to happen to us?" she asked. Her voice was a croak.

"My guess," Rikard said, "is that we'll wind up like those brains downstairs."

PART
<u>FOUR</u>

PART
FOUR

1

They separated the wounded from the dead, and the police from the enemy. Some of the goons wanted to kill the still-living raiders, but the noncoms wouldn't permit it. The implications of the wounded and dead raiders being piled in with the police was bad enough, they didn't have to descend to the level of their enemies.

Sladen was in very bad shape. Automatic seals had closed off and cauterized the stump of his arm, near the shoulder, but he was in shock, had lost a lot of blood, and without proper attention would soon die. All they could do was try to make him comfortable. Choi, who's leg-armor had been blown off, was in a lot of pain and had burns and lacerations, but was able to walk with assistance. Gospodin, who had lost her helmet, was unconscious but breathing regularly. Maturska was dead, of course. The six wounded raiders watched the police administer to their own, and did not ask for help, though two of them sorely needed it, one missing a leg below the knee, another with a severe burn along her left side that exposed her ribs.

When the police casualties were attended to as well as could be under the circumstances, the noncoms turned their attention to the raiders. "You seem to have been abandoned," Nelross said to the woman with the side wound. "Why don't you tell us what you know, and maybe we can get you out of here alive."

But the woman just turned her face away, and none of the other raiders who could talk would say anything.

It wasn't very long before the iris opened and their captors returned. Three of them were Human, but two were of that other species, their crab-stalk eyes waving above turtle-beak mouths. They all were carrying blasters. They took up positions on either side of the iris, weapons aimed, eyes wary.

A moment later a pair of zombies came in, carrying in the elaborate harness slung between them one of the Tathas-like beings, a huge mass of wiry tendrils, nearly pure white except for the ends of its tendrils, which shaded to pale blue. In spite of the size of the creature, bulking more than a Human if one could judge by the effort of the zombies to stand upright, Rikard could feel only the faintest trace of the Tathas effect emanating from it.

One of the turtle-beaks spoke, in its own language. The three Human raiders holstered their weapons and went over to where the dead were lying and started to drag them out, one by one, into the corridor where two or three other Humans and a number of zombies were waiting to take them away.

"What are you going to do with her?" Sukiro asked as the raiders started to drag Maturska's remains out too.

"Nothing," one of the turtle-beaks said, and the raiders dropped the body. "It is too badly damaged to serve as a replacement for the *manuals* whose bodies you destroyed, and has been dead too long for its brain to be of any use."

The last of the dead was Grayshard, but when two of the raiders went to pick him up his body was as limp as empty rags, and after a glance at one of the turtle-beaks, they let it drop too.

Then the turtle-beak spoke again in his own language, and the three Human raiders started carrying out their wounded. When that was done, they picked up Sladen.

"Now wait a minute!" Sukiro said. "What are you going to do with him?" She started to step forward, but the turtle-beaks warned her back with little gestures of their weapons.

"Your turn will come soon enough," one of them said.

The Human captors left with their last burden. The zombies carrying the Tathas-thing turned and went out. The turtle-beaks, still brandishing their blasters, backed through the iris, which closed behind them. Sukiro strode to the door, but it was locked again.

"I can still feel Tathas," Rikard said. The sensation was not coming from the now closed iris, but from where the bodies had lain. The only ones left were Maturska, a bloody mess, and Grayshard, folded up on himself in a way impossible for anyone with bones. There was a bit of pale, pearly ooze on the deck beside him. Sukiro stared at Grayshard's body too. Rikard felt his skin crawl. The goons nearest the corpse backed off.

The body moved. Slowly, fluidly, Grayshard straightened himself out so that he was no longer bent double at the chest, so that his remaining arm and legs no longer seemed to have three or four knees and elbows. One foot untwisted out from under him as he slowly sat up. His whole body, inside his clothes, rippled as if he were a bundle of worms. The slick pearly ooze was thick on the shoulder of his jacket where his arm had been blown off.

"It's one of them," Majorbank said in a choked voice.

Grayshard lifted his "head." "You are right," he said. His mechanical voice sounded even flatter than usual. "I, too, am a Vaashka." With his remaining arm he undid his mask and the upper part of his jacket. What made it horrible was that it looked as though this one hand were being assisted by other arms inside his clothes. The seams opened, the fabric came away as he lifted the mask over his face, leaving only his vocalizer.

Inside the clothes was a mass of creamy tendrils, tipped in red. More tendrils appeared at the shoulder, some of them charred off short.

"Vaashka," Rikard said. "And a warrior."

The disguise fell partially away, revealing a complicated system of supports inside, of braces, straps, baskets, in which Grayshard rested.

"Of sorts," Grayshard said as he struggled to his "feet."

"Kill it," Petorska said.

"We've been betrayed," Nelross rasped.

Several goons started toward the thing they'd known as Grayshard, but as they did so he began to project the numbing psycho-chemical effect. "Don't make me defend myself," he said.

"Back off," Sukiro snapped. "If you jump him, he'll just blast us all, and then where will we be?"

"I am not your enemy," Grayshard said.

"The hell you're not," Falyn said, "you're one of them."

"I am a Vaashka. Are you a pirate, because you are Human? Most of your enemies are Human, so you must be just as bad as they."

It was the right thing to say, it gave them pause. There were still murmurs of "Don't trust him," "He's a spy," and "All Tathas are evil," but the goons did not attack, and the psychic assault faded to an almost unnoticeable background.

"How dare you judge my race by the actions of these criminals?" Grayshard said. "Shall I judge all Humans by the likes of Rikard Braeth? I am not a Tathas, I am a Vaashka. We may have had a common ancestor, millennia ago. Are you monkeys?"

"In some ways we are," Sukiro said. Her tone was apologetic, her voice was tired. "But let us not behave like our forebears or collaterals." She addressed the goons. "Grayshard has been wounded too, and he could have shown himself to our captors had he really been on their side."

"But I am not," Grayshard said. "It was all I could do to keep the Human pirates from revealing my true nature to the *administrator*. I was afraid s'he would detect me, even so, from the *fluid* that was leaking from me."

"I take it," Rikard said, "that they wouldn't have welcomed you with open arms—as it were."

"Not these *predators*. Slow torture would have been my fate, instead of a quick and painless death, as your wounded companion will receive—and you, too, if we do not escape before they come back."

"You've got the right idea," Sukiro said, "but we need some explanations. What are you doing here anyway?"

"The same as you," Grayshard replied, "trying to put a stop to this evil business. What happens to the people these *predators* take is worse than slavery, and those who buy neuromass are as addicted to its use as the most debased of your drug users. There is slavery in the Federation, and drug addiction, and your government does not condone it, does everything it can to stamp it out. Neuro-slavery and the use of high-order natural bodies are equally despised by my government, my people—except for those who are addicted to it, and those debased people who supply the addicts' needs."

"So you're a cop, then," Denny said. She seemed—provisionally at least—to accept this explanation.

"In your terms, yes, very much like you. By breeding, rather than by preference. I was grown as a member of the fighting class, to be a *warrior*, as our recent visitor was grown to be an *administrator*, and those who inhabit the bodies you call zombies were made to be simple laborers—though they had to have been kept 'pruned back' to keep them so small and docile. That is another evil practice. There are others of us who have been given other specialties though most Vaashka are more generalized. Most do not have the ability to affect the neuro-psyche of so-called higher order life forms. And I was not fit to be a part of our regular security forces. I'm not as powerful as those *warriors* who attacked us. This is not uncommon."

"If you're substandard," Charney said sarcastically, "then how come you were sent on this mission instead of someone better qualified?"

Grayshard was silent for a moment. "You have a saying," he said at last. "'Set a thief to catch a thief.' In the 'Wrinkly' stars, I am considered to be somewhat as Rikard Braeth is considered here in the Federation. We Vaashka, too, have our equivalent of your Gestae. I am not fond of my home government, but for reasons you may not be able to comprehend, until now I have preferred to stay there.

"Perhaps I was wrong. My government is not popular elsewhere, it is more oppressive than it should be, though it is in the 'Wrinkly' stars that neuro-slavery and body-riding are most prevalent. When it was found that much of this illegal trade was being transacted within our star nation, *administrators* from my government decided to put an end to it, primarily for political reasons, and to that end found means to persuade me to participate.

"We do not have 'families' as you do. We do not reproduce the same way, but by buds and spores. It is a complex form of genesis. Still, we have strong affection for those individuals who grew from pieces of ourselves, and those others who grow from our freely released genetic material. I have six bud-siblings and thirteen spore-children, and their welfare is important to me. These are my 'family,' in your terms, and they are being held hostage against the successful completion of my mission.

"Perhaps I should have abandoned them long ago, when first I felt the urging to disregard the petty regulations that bind so much of our lives. Had I done so, my 'family' would not now be in danger. There are other star nations, after all, where my chosen style of life would not have been so frowned upon. But I misjudged the vengefulness of certain of my fellows, and especially of those equivalent to your police and courts. So I am here, seeking to find the source of illegal traffic in neuromass and riding-bodies. I will rather die than go back as a failure. But if I should succeed, I will not return even then, but find some other place to go."

The tension in the room eased, and Grayshard no longer felt he had to keep up his guard, though some goons were still dubious. Grayshard adjusted his supporting disguise, and took a

tentative step toward Rikard, but as he neared, Rikard felt an
increase in his awareness of the subtle "Tathas" effect and
turned away, and was surprised when his legs gave way and he
had to sit down.

"Forgive me," Grayshard said. He wrapped his jacket around
himself, closed the seams, brought the goggled mask down over
his "face." "You have been hurt," he said, "by the *projection* of
the *warriors*. The armor your police wear offers them some
protection, else they would not have recovered so quickly, but
you have received the full force of the attack, and how you are
able to function is a mystery to me. You must let me help you if
you are to recover fully."

"Stay away from me," Rikard said over his shoulder.

"I can help you," Grayshard insisted. "I must."

"Just leave him alone," Denny said, "he'll recover in time."

"Perhaps," Grayshard said, "in days or weeks."

"I think you'd better do what you can," Sukiro told him.

"No!" Rikard insisted. The thought of Grayshard coming
anywhere near him made him want to scream. He knew his
reaction was largely irrational, but he couldn't help but shudder
when he saw Grayshard extend a bundle of fibers from the torn
shoulder of his jacket.

He felt a subtle increase in the "Tathas" effect—but it was
different this time, calming and soothing, not filled with anxiety
and terror. Still he started to turn away, his revulsion almost
overpowering.

Sukiro caught him before he had gone more than a few steps
and held him. He struggled for a moment, then got hold of
himself, though the idea revolted him. "All right," he said. "Do
your worst."

Grayshard came toward him, moving with that odd kind of
grace he had always shown and which now was fully explained.
Rikard flinched when the fibers came out of Grayshard's sleeve
toward his face and head, but he held himself steady, felt the
delicate touch, like a feather, as the Vaashka's filaments laced
through his hair. He felt the telepathic intrusion as the tendrils
conformed to the shape of his skull, the back of his neck—but
it was not what he expected. The sensation was bright and clear
and euphoric. It was more like the Taarshome communication
than the nightmarish feeling of the Tathas effect. He seemed to
be floating in a prismatic pastel soap bubble.

Then the bubble popped and he opened his eyes. The sense

of oppression was gone. There was still a trace of the "Tathas" effect, but now it felt good, not evil.

"It's not as easy to reverse the effect," Grayshard said, "as to cause it."

Rikard's eyes focused on the lenses of Grayshard's goggles. Then Grayshard reached out with his good false hand and carefully folded the tatters of his left jacket sleeve over the torn-off place, and as he did so, the last traces of the psychic effect faded.

"You were very careful to conceal yourself," Rikard said. In spite of the good feeling he now experienced, he was still suspicious.

"It had to be done," Grayshard said. "My garments are a shield designed to keep any psychic or chemical trace of myself from leaking. This damaged shoulder will be a problem. We know the effect our *effluvia* has on chordate animals and people, especially the so-called mammals. We—that is, the agents of my government—were also unsure about the effect our appearance would have on you. Those humanoid soldiers with the *administrator*, they are Srenim, a species we have had long contact with. They are used to us now, but we find ourselves a minority among the stars, and most intelligent species do not like our appearance. So it was decided to provide me with a disguise, as you see, which would serve not only to conceal my nature from you, but from the other pirates, who have become sensitized to our mode of communication by long association, and from those of my own species, the *predators*, who could detect me by means most normal to ourselves.

"The price has been high. I could not in turn detect their presence, as you have been able to do. I had wished many times to speak out, but dared not. This thing you call the Tathas effect is simply an exaggeration of our normal mode of communication. Since I donned this apparel, I have been muted."

"Seems like your government went to an awful lot of trouble," Sukiro said.

"And hasn't yours done the same? The 'Wrinkly' stars sent out only me, your government sent all these police to the same end."

Woadham was sitting beside Gospodin and Choi. "Can you help them?" she called out to Grayshard.

The Vaashka looked over at her. "What is the matter?"

"They're bleeding to death."

"I am not sure." He "walked" over to where the two wounded goons lay, bent down, and looked at them. "I have not been trained as a healer," he said, "and I know very little about the mammalian life forms."

"But you healed Braeth."

"Those were psychic wounds, and the healing, as you call it, merely entailed a reversal of the offensive forms. This is different. Still, let me try." He extruded a thick cable of tendrils from the torn-off shoulder of his jacket and played it over Choi's bruised and burned legs.

"Does that psychic attack work against other Vaashka?" Rikard asked.

"It does," Grayshard said. "Why else would we have developed it?"

"As a weapon," Denny said, "against other species."

Grayshard did not pause in his probing. Fibers caressed lacerations, wove nets over massive bruises. Choi lay there, too weak to protest. "Your weapons work against other species too," Grayshard said at last. "Did you develop them for that purpose?"

Denny stifled a protest. Grayshard continued to feel the hurt man's legs. "There are mammals on many of our worlds," he said. "Even on our home world, so I am told, there are life forms which you consider higher than, ah, fungi. We are well aware of our uniqueness, as a sentient life form among the stars, and have considerable experience in dealing with biologies different from ours."

"Where is your home world?" Sukiro asked.

Grayshard paused to do—something—and Choi began to relax and gingerly flex his legs. Grayshard muttered, "There has been much subcutaneous bleeding, no bones are broken, and severe infection is the greatest danger. All I can do here is cauterize the major blood vessels. He will still need attention from your own doctors if he is to be able to walk again." Then he moved to Gospodin. "This one is not so badly damaged," he said. Only when he had spread a fine network of his filaments over the woman's scalp and temples did he respond to Sukiro's question.

"My home world," he said, "is not the home world of my species. I come from 'Thickness,' one of over one hundred inhabited planets in the 'Wrinkly' stars. Not as large as your

Federation, perhaps, but in some ways more technologically advanced. We do not, unfortunately, share our culture with other sentient races, which are rare. But other star nations nearby, the Cone, Greech, and Ten-Walker nations, are blessed with other sentient, and sometimes highly technological cultures, as your Federation is.

"But that is not your question. You wish to know, are we near to you. No, we are not. All the Vaashka nations are a very long way off. So then, why have our *predators* come such a long way for their neuromass? Quite simply, the better to avoid detection from my government and other Vaashka governments."

He withdrew his fibers from Gospodin's head. "She will heal in her own time," he said, then drew his tendrils back into his jacket. "But this is taking far too long." He stood on his artificial legs and turned to face the crowd of goons surrounding him. "Our enemies will be back soon, to take each of you off, for your brains and bodies. We must be out of here before then."

"The iris is locked," Sukiro said.

"So we'll wait until they're inside," Denny said, "and then jump them. We'll take casualties, but we'll get their weapons."

"One blast from that Vaashka riding on the zombies," Rikard said, "and we'll all be helpless."

"The *administrator* cannot attack you that way," Grayshard told them, "but there may be *warriors* waiting outside. No, we must be away from here before they come."

He went to the door and once again extended a bundle of tendrils, this time toward the touch-plate in the center of the iris.

Rikard came up to watch. The ivory white tendrils, some of them finer than a Human hair, probed around the interface between the touch-plate and the surface of the iris.

"If our captors had known who I was," Grayshard said, "they would not have left me here with a trivial mechanism like this." The iris clicked, and slowly—not a snap—dilated open.

The corridor outside was empty at the moment. Choi and Gospodin were helped to their feet, half-comatose, and carried out with the others. There was no ceiling in this corridor, just darkness above their heads.

"We've got to get to the hull," Denny said. "If we can get

close enough to the surface for our com-links to work we can call for help."

"We get our weapons first," Sukiro told her. "I've got tracers on mine." She looked one way, then another. "It's around back," she said, and led them to the corner. The walls on either side went up just one level, with only open space above. She turned left and led them up the hall to a door on the right.

The iris was not locked. They went in and found all their armor and weapons, dumped on tables, spilling onto the floor. The goons quickly identified their own armor and put it on. They gathered up their weapons, except for the vibracoil, which was damaged beyond repair. Gospodin and Choi were armored, too, so that they could move on their own. And Rikard was especially relieved to find not only his .75, but also his gloves, without which his gun wouldn't provide him with his special advantage.

"Now let's go get them," Denny said.

"You think we can?" Rikard asked her. "It will be just like the last time, they don't even have to shoot at us."

"If two or more *warriors project*," Grayshard said, "the effect will be even stronger."

"I hate to say it," Sukiro said, "but now is not the time to fight. The best thing to do is to get away, find another hatch, and call for help."

"I've never called for help," Denny said.

"Neither have I," Sukiro told her. "I guess there's a first time for everything."

They left the room and looked for a way down, intending to go as deep as they could before going to one side and then up again, they hoped far away from the raiders' base. But when Denny asked Majorbank for some idea of their position, the goon just held out his map-corder ruefully. "This thing doesn't work anymore," he said. "They must have dropped it."

"Let's take the easy way," Sukiro said, and led them up the corridor to the iris at the end. They went through it and stepped out onto a balcony, overlooking a huge space, with what looked like a collection of child's blocks, arrayed in a rectangular pattern, on the floor far below them.

Private Raebuck tensed as she looked over the rail. At first Rikard thought she was just reacting to their height above the deck, maybe ten levels below them. But after a moment she said, reluctantly, "I think I can find our way out."

2

Sukiro was surprised by Raebuck's statement, but Rikard had been expecting something like this.

"How could you possibly know anything about this place?" Sukiro asked.

Raebuck pointed down to the deck below, where the pale blue rooms were arranged like blocks, separated by corridors with no ceilings. "See that peculiar cluster there toward the middle?" she said. "Where the blocks are arranged sort of like a cross? I've seen that before, on videotapes."

"And when did you see these videotapes?"

"When I was in college." She cast Rikard a sidelong glance. "I took an archeology course that dealt in vanished starfaring races, and this was one that we studied."

"Are you sure?" Sukiro asked her.

"I am now," she said. "When we found those big square objects, sitting on the deck like furniture, they sort of looked familiar. And then there were those other round-edged desklike things. I was sure I'd seen something like that before, but I couldn't remember where. And then when we found that stellated object, I remembered."

"How about that thing you turned on," Rikard asked, "did those tapes show you how to do that?"

"No, but in some of the tapes we saw the Tschagan, the people who built this place, working with some of their devices —just background action I think."

"What the hell are you talking about?" Sukiro asked. Rikard

told her about what Raebuck had done while they had been following the trail of Sukiro's captors.

"I see," Sukiro said when he'd finished, then turned back to Raebuck. "And now you think you know where we are."

"Yes," Raebuck said, "but the tape showed this place from a different angle. If I'm right, there ought to be an outside door on the main deck, right about there"—she pointed—"that opens onto the top of a broad ramp."

"Let's go check it out," Rikard suggested.

They went along the balcony to a ramp that led them down to the next level. "How were those tapes made?" Rikard asked. "Previous explorers?"

"No," Raebuck said, "they were recorded from broadcasts the Tschagan made. They were a nasty people, and tried to dominate the League that existed then, before the Federation, before Humans came to space. They broadcast a lot of propaganda, threats and intimidations, footage of their military victories, and so on. The League outnumbered them greatly, but the Tschagan had a well-established home cluster, some technology the other peoples didn't have, and absolutely no compunction about doing horrible things to get their way and increase their power."

As Raebuck spoke they continued to descend, level by level, along one wall on balconies, then along the second wall to the main deck. By the time they came to the second corner they could see that there was a door where she had said it would be, and they hurried to it. Rikard was the first one there and pressed the latch-plate. The iris opened and, sure enough, there was the head of a broad ramp, at right angles to the wall, descending into the darkness.

Falyn reached around the edge of the iris to turn on the lights. The ceiling illumined only the first fifty meters of the ramp. The noncoms formed up the goons and they started to descend.

"Why didn't you tell us about this before?" Sukiro asked Raebuck.

"I wasn't sure until now that I was right, and I didn't want to say anything out of place."

They got to the bottom of the ramp, which ended in an iris door, which in turn opened onto a balcony. Falyn palmed the ridges of the light switch beside the iris, and parts—not all—of the ceiling glowed amber. They were halfway up the wall of another huge chamber, again overlooking self-contained rooms like an irregular chess board, or a huge set of children's blocks.

Raebuck looked around from the railing. She pointed to an arch in a balcony one level lower on the other side of the huge chamber. "That looks right," she said.

"Where are we going?" Sukiro asked as they all went along the balcony to the nearest ramp down to the next level.

"There's a kind of well," Raebuck said, "where we can go down as far as we want. It should be through that arch."

"Was this place just abandoned?" Rikard asked.

"Not 'just.' Something over ten thousand years ago the people of the League finally got tired of being intimidated, and a race called the Vengatti, pretty much black sheep themselves, led an uprising. All the Tschagan establishments in the League were destroyed—many by the Tschagan themselves when the 'rebels' pressed too close—and their home system was invaded."

"I've never heard of the Vengatti," Sukiro said.

"They died out about two thousand years later, about the time the first Federation was being formed."

They reached the arch, which opened onto a broad corridor, which penetrated deeply into the space beyond, with no surface features of any kind. There were no lights here so they had to switch on their headlamps which, bright as they were, did not reach the far end of the corridor. "This is right," Raebuck said.

"So what happened to the Tschagan home worlds?" Sukiro asked as they started down the corridor.

"Destroyed, the home world itself and three or four others, and every base on the other thirty or so worlds they controlled. They were slavers, genocides, and there wasn't much left of the sentient species who had grown up on the worlds under their direct dominion."

"And yet this place still exists," Rikard said as their headlamps at last showed another arch at the far end of the corridor.

"Everybody assumed," Raebuck said, "that their home world was their capital. But all their broadcasts came from the same place, and this was it. This was their capital, not a world but a giant space station, and nobody knew it even existed, until now."

"What worries me," Rikard said, "is how their capital came to be here."

They came to the end of the corridor, beyond which was a larger space, completely dark. About fifty meters beyond the

arch was a rail, picked out in their headlights, and beyond that
was nothing, not even the reflection of a floor.

"That's the well," Raebuck said.

They all went to the rail. Their lights could not reach across
the huge empty space, but, judging by the curve of the railing,
it must have been over three hundred meters across. They shone
their lights down into the well and could see, marked clearly in
the pale blue wall, the edges of level after level below them—
some with openings, some with balconies—dropping far down
into the heart of the station. There was no sign of the bottom.

Rikard looked up into the space over their heads. Maybe
twenty floors above was a domed ceiling.

"Why don't we go up that way?" Sukiro asked.

"We're still too close to the raiders' base," Majorbank said.
Though his map-corder was broken he had been keeping track
of their movements in his head.

"So how do we get down?" Sukiro then asked.

"I don't know," Raebuck said, "their cameras just went out
into the middle of this space and descended, on floaters obviously."

"Maybe not," Falyn said. "The gravity here is artificial,
maybe it's turned off in the shaft."

Majorbank looked at his broken map-corder, then tossed it
out into the well. Its arc was nearly flat, and it dropped only
two floors by the time it was too far away to be seen in their
headlamps.

"Looks good to me," Denny said. She stepped up onto the
rail, then turned around and stepped off backward, a careful
step so she would not drift too far away. For a moment she hung
suspended, then slowly began to descend. When her shoulders
came even with the rail she reached out and stopped herself
with one finger. "Come on in," she said, "the gravity's fine."

Following Denny's lead the others spread out along the rail
on either side of her, climbed over, and linked arms with each
other, with Denny in the middle of the chain, and let go. For a
long moment they just hung suspended, and then began slowly
to descend.

"We'll never get anywhere like this," Denny said as they
dropped centimeter by centimeter. She gave commands to her
goons, and in midair they re-formed into several groups of
three, with two on either side of a third goon, holding this one
so that his or her hands were now free. At the same time other

goons grabbed hold of those groups, and kept hold of the wounded, Rikard, and Grayshard. Then the middle member of each group of three pushed up at the wall in front of them, accelerating their drop.

They passed a long stretch of unbroken wall, and marked their progress by the passing of the triple dark blue stripes, which were painted at every level. Then they came to another balcony recess, and as they got within reach of the ceiling the goons pushed up against it, gaining them more speed. There was another recess immediately below, and they accelerated again. Then there was more blank wall, then another balcony, and down they went, faster and faster.

After maybe ten minutes, Sukiro asked, "How far do we go?"

"To the bottom," Raebuck said.

"How long will that take?"

"Hard to tell, maybe half an hour, maybe more."

They fell in silence for another five minutes or so, then Rikard said, "So tell us more about these Tschagan."

"I'm trying to remember. They dominated the various species of the League for over a thousand years, and in spite of their inferior numbers they kept on adding worlds to their own nation. No other race we studied was so brutal or so violent, and there were certain secrets about their nature which gave them an advantage, and which no one was ever able to discover. They were greatly outnumbered, but in spite of that they controlled most of the League, by intimidation, threat, and frequently actual violence. They broadcast films of their victories, made demands, and sent out thousands of hours of propaganda. Originally they were from outside the League, but that area is now fully within the Federation.

"There were other races in their home systems, but they were all slaves. The Tschagan had been in power at home for at least fifteen thousand years before they were put down. They had made war on every world they found, and had 'joined' the League only because the League was more powerful than they. But the Tschagan were well on their way to total dominance when the Vengatti and others rose up. They had been like bullies among a crowd of pacifists, and the Vengatti, once not thought well of, became the core of the vigilantes that threw them out."

The trip down the well lasted a lot longer than Raebuck's

story. The character of the wall down which they were now falling at a considerable rate remained much the same—triple blue stripes at each level when there was no balcony or recess to mark the various floors. Occasionally they passed a silver plate set into the surface of the wall, on which were inscribed flat black characters similar to those they'd seen on the controls of the com-cons.

Sukiro began to get worried about hitting the bottom, and had Ming and Dyson keep a lookout below. They were going fairly fast by now, and if they didn't have enough time to slow down, Rikard and Grayshard would be injured when they did hit.

"I think there's quite a way to go yet," Raebuck told her. "We'll pass some projections and deep bays before we get near the bottom."

"We'll keep a watch anyway," Sukiro said.

Which turned out to be a good idea. The lookouts reported that a balcony, projecting into the shaft, was coming up below them. All who had free hands put them out to slow their fall, and they had come nearly to a full stop when they dropped down past the last floor above the balcony, and the artificial gravity took effect. It was not very strong, but still they dropped to the balcony floor in free-fall. This took them by surprise, and though nobody was hurt it was a moment before they could sort themselves out.

"That was one of the landmarks I was looking for," Raebuck said breathlessly. "The tapes didn't show the effects of gravity, of course. We're about halfway down, I think."

They stepped out into the well again, deployed as they had been before, accelerated downward, and after a while came to a place where the recess was far deeper than the others they had passed, and maybe fifteen levels high. There was no way to slow themselves down here, if they had a need to, and the goons prepared to cut on emergency antigrav if it should prove necessary.

It wasn't, and all were relieved when unbroken wall came up past them again. The goons' antigrav might not have been enough.

"What purpose do you suppose this well served?" Nelross asked Falyn.

"Possibly ventilation."

"Have you seen any signs of a ventilation system anywhere so far?" Sukiro asked.

"No," Falyn said, "no vents, no grills. But there has to be something."

"If there is," Denny said, "it's too sophisticated for a simple tube like this to be a part of it."

The wall continued here much as it had been above, sometimes blank, sometimes with open balconies that ran around the entire shaft—as far as they could tell—but after a while the balconies become just square openings in the wall, sometimes in front of them, sometimes to either side, and in some places there were windows instead of openings, either very wide or very small and square.

"This is all like I remember it," Raebuck said.

At last they passed a place where vertical ribs stood out from the wall, four levels high, each only a few centimeters wide and half a meter deep.

"That's another thing I was looking for," Raebuck said. "We should start to slow down now."

The goons in contact with the wall used their hands and feet to brake their fall and the group began to slow. Almost at once Ming and Dyson reported reflected light from below. They slowed more and almost came to a standstill. But not quite. They continued to descend cautiously until the gravity in the floor below them took hold and they dropped the last two levels. They turned on their antigravity, and the landing was easy.

From where they now stood they could see a large archway to their right, and another farther away to the left.

"Which way?" Sukiro asked.

Raebuck walked into the center of the floor. The others followed, spread out as they did so, and shone their helmet lights all around. From the middle of the bottom of the well their headlamps were bright enough to reach the entire surrounding wall, and now they could see seven exits, more or less equally spaced. Each was an arch, but each one was different—one had a semicircular top, another had a wide jamb, another was very low, another very broad.

Raebuck pointed to one that had two shallow steps leading up to it. "That one," she said.

"Are you sure?" Sukiro asked.

"Yes, it's the steps. That arch should be at the head of a flight of stairs."

"Stairs?" Denny asked, "in this place?"

"Well, it looked like stairs in the video."

The goons kept spread out and wary as they went toward the arch. There was no iris here, just an opening. Denny reached around inside and found a light switch. She brought the amber ceiling up full bright.

And sure enough, the floor beyond the arch did look like broad, shallow stairs, but in fact it was just a succession of ever-lower floors, each only three meters deep and only twenty-five or so centimeters below the other. The walls slowly fanned out as the floors descended, though the ceiling remained at a constant level and did not slant downward parallel to the floor. On each side of each of the step floors was an alcove, iris, or arch, or an object that looked like a cross between an advanced electronic game and a set of closet organizers. Raebuck ignored all this and just went straight down the broadening and descending corridor toward another arch set into the wall at the far end.

This opened into the side of a large hallway, fifty meters wide and high. As they stepped out into it the ceiling directly over them lit up, illuminating a section just fifty meters long. There were a few widely scattered artifacts of the kind they'd seen before, standing on the floor here and there, but not arranged in any way that made sense.

"Several of the tapes showed this," Raebuck said, "and this hallway should intersect with an even larger one, that way." She turned to the right.

They followed her lead. The section of ceiling ahead of them lit up automatically as they neared, and the section behind darkened as they left.

Every seventy to a hundred meters along the hallway was another of the Tschagan objects—now a large brick-colored thing like an oversize filing cabinet without drawers, then a smaller light blue thing with rounded corners and edges, with tori of dark navy projecting from three sides and a black half-dome smeared with olive on top. Each of the objects they passed was different from the previous one.

There were few doors here, and only an occasional darkened archway. They passed a deep alcove, thirty meters high and wide, with a broad spiral ramp descending into darkness. Much later they passed another one, on the other side of the hallway, only its ramp was going up.

"What are we looking for?" Sukiro asked. "Are you sure this is the way?"

"It's been a long time since I saw those tapes," Raebuck admitted, "but I'm pretty sure this is right. This hallway should end soon."

It was as she had predicted. The end of the hallway opened into the side of one even larger, one hundred meters square. To the left, at the edge of the lit area, was a cluster of rectangular objects. Some were similar to those they had seen before, but some of them were quite different, like psychotic soft sculptures. Raebuck led them in that direction.

"The Tschagan certainly had a peculiar life-style," Fresno muttered.

"They were insects," Petersin said.

"Warm-blooded arthropods," Raebuck corrected him.

"A bug is a bug."

There were many more of the floor-standing objects here, of all three types, sometimes in clusters. They passed these by without more than a glance. Raebuck strode purposefully forward until they came to where another fifty-meter hallway teed into the larger one.

Though Raebuck led them on past without hesitation, Rikard thought he could detect a hint of uncertainty in her movements. He watched her closely, saw that this uncertainty continued until, when the lights came on several hundred-meter sections farther on, they came to a huge object, a machine of some kind, twenty or more meters tall and half as broad, standing in the middle of the floor. It was rectilinear overall but highly complex, a combination of cubes and boxes, with rods of metal and crystal projecting and connecting, panels that might have glowed, and a delicate enclosing framework of ramps and platforms.

Raebuck sighed with relief. "Yes, this is just how I remember it."

There were fewer individual objects beyond this point, most of them, whatever their type, gathered in clusters. They went past another side hall, then to another hundred-meter hallway that crossed theirs, where an object thirty meters tall and almost as wide and deep stood, right in the middle of the intersection. This one was even more complex than the first, with half-domes, diagonal beams, and plates of what looked like crystal. Like the previous machine the upper portions were reached by spidery catwalks and ramps.

"This is right," Raebuck said. But again, as she looked at the machine, Rikard felt sure that she was not really that certain after all. He touched her arm. She glanced at him. "It has been a long time," she said, then went on past the object.

They passed another cluster of smaller artifacts, a smaller side hall, then came to a great intersection with another hundred-meter hallway, again with a huge, complex machine where the two corridors met.

"This is right," Raebuck said again at the machine. "See that chrome sphere there, behind the orange cube? There's a black shaft coming out the other side." They went around to look, and it was so.

Still she led them straight on, past clusters of small objects, another hundred-meter intersection with its giant machine, occasional smaller side hallways, and once or twice an alcove with a ramp rising or descending.

But after another twenty minutes or so Raebuck began to look uncertain again. "There should have been another major intersection," she said.

"Videos can be edited," Rikard said gently.

"At least," Sukiro said, "we're getting far from the raiders, and at some point we could just go up toward the skin and find another hatch."

"Yes," Raebuck said, "there's always that." But she did not seem to like the idea.

"What are you really looking for?" Sukiro asked her quietly.

Raebuck glanced from Rikard to the major. "I was hoping to find one of those places I saw on the tapes," she said, "like a museum. The Tschagan brought back lots of trophies."

Rikard could sympathize, but Sukiro had other concerns. "We'll have to save that for another time," she said. "We're far enough away from the raiders now, let's go up."

Then there was the sound of tearing air, and a streak of dust zipped past them, and Glaine, on the edge of the group, went crashing to the ground.

Everybody dropped to a full defensive posture. Rikard saw another cloud of dust, but it had gone by him knocking Yansen over as it did so, before he could fully register its movement. They waited, weapons drawn, staring around in all directions. But there were no further attacks.

"All right," Raebuck said at last, "we'll take the first way up."

They did not backtrack but went on, past an alcove with a

ramp leading down, until they came to a cross hall that was different from the others they'd passed—much smaller. Suddenly Raebuck was excited.

"This is the way!" she said.

A dust-streak zipped by behind them, and they all hurried into the side hall.

3

The smaller corridor was not very long, and quickly opened into a huge chamber, all but completely filled by a single, complex machine. There were balconies and ramps around the walls of the chamber and around the machine, and catwalks connecting the two.

Raebuck looked up at it. "This isn't right," she said. "The corridor is supposed to tee into a kind of gallery, with doors all along the far side."

"You've misremembered," Sukiro said, as she and the noncoms walked curiously around the gigantic machine.

"It doesn't seem to be turned on," Falyn observed.

"Or the tapes didn't show consecutive movement," Raebuck said. Ramps led up to catwalks, which led to other ramps and what looked like service stations, but what possibly could have been done at them was anybody's guess.

"Could there be other places like the one you saw in the tapes?" Sukiro asked, "and we just found the wrong one?" They came around the far side of the machine, where a closed archway offered the only other exit.

"That's the most likely," Rikard said. "If that well we came down does serve as a ventilation shaft, there could be hundreds similar to it all over this place."

They started to go back around the machine when two dust-devils came whizzing out from behind it, arced in front of them, knocked Jasime down, then whizzed out again. The goons who were in range fired but hit only the walls.

"Hold your fire, dammit!" Nelross yelled.

They proceeded more cautiously, weapons drawn, back toward the open arch, but more dust-devils whizzed out at them, barely grazing those in the lead, but moving so fast that even the lightest touch knocked the goons off balance. The party was forced back into the chamber.

Rikard drew his .75 in the hopes that his slowed time sense would give him a glimpse of whatever it was that was attacking, but the dust-devils were gone before he could get a grip solid enough to bring his internal mechanisms into play. By the time the concentric circles of his heads-up display came clear in his eyes, he could find no target. With his perceptions speeded up by a factor of ten to one, the dust in the air seemed to hang dead still, and the goons he could see were moving in ultraslow motion.

He heard a bass groan, relaxed the grip on his gun, and time returned to normal. The groan was Sukiro's slowed voice, asking Grayshard, ". . . are those things, something your brain pirates brought with them?"

"I know of nothing like that," Grayshard said.

"Could they have picked up some allies on their way here?" Nelross asked.

"How could they trust anybody they did bring?" Denny muttered.

Everybody watched the archway from which the dust-devils had come, but they did not reappear. Sukiro gave quick commands to the noncoms, who formed up their squads to make another try for the corridor.

But even though the goons were facing down the corridor, and could see the dust-devils as they entered at last, and fired at them as soon as they saw them, they hit nothing. The dust-devils swerved from side to side, easily dodging the blaster shots, for which there was time for only one or two. In an instant the dust-devils were among them, hitting them, pushing them back into the chamber. The goons fell back, tried to pick targets, but the dust-devils were gone as quickly as they had come.

"Robots could move that quickly," Falyn said, "dodge that quickly." She tried to catch her breath.

"Then someone's directing them," Sukiro said. "Their movement is too intelligent for them to be completely automatic. But if that were the case, the directors would have to be thinking at least as fast as the robots are moving. I don't think they're robots, I think they're alive."

"The only possibility," Raebuck said, "is survivors. But nothing I saw on the tapes suggested that they could move like that."

"How could anybody survive in here for ten thousand years?" Rikard asked. "I mean, if they had an ongoing culture, yes, but this has been a derelict."

"We haven't seen a fraction of a percent of this place yet," Falyn said. "Who knows what's going on in deeper levels, or on the other side."

"If they don't want *us* here," Denny said, "how come they haven't bothered the pirates?"

"*I* don't know," Raebuck said. "Maybe they do. Maybe the pirates keep them out with force screens."

"They first attacked us in the pirates' territory," Rikard commented.

"It really doesn't matter," Sukiro said. "The question is, how do we get up to the surface?"

"Let's go where they want us to go and look for a chance," Rikard suggested.

It seemed like the only reasonable thing to do, so they went back around the machine to the closed arch on the other side. The iris here was not typical. The opening was too large and flat-bottomed, and there was no touch-plate in the middle, which in any event was too high to be reached. But there were plates on either side of the iris, and when Rikard touched one the door opened. Without further discussion they went through a thick wall into another chamber.

This room was larger than the one before and the machine inside filled it from wall to wall and floor to ceiling, though it was less bulky, more spindly. Again there were ramps and balconies along the walls, with catwalks to platforms and balconies near the machine, some of them almost embedded within its struts, angling members, dangling plates, cables, and wires.

There was more space to the right of the machine, and they started to go that way, the better to defend themselves, but dust-devils appeared in front of them, swooped by without actually hitting any of them, but effectively driving them back around to the left.

"We're being herded," Sukiro said.

"I can't stand this," Denny half shouted. "We can't even fight!"

The dust-devils did not attack them as they went around the left side of the machine. In the wall on that side was a deep alcove. The interior was deeply shadowed, but there was an iris door at the back. On Denny's command, Fresno and Van Leet started to go past the alcove but stopped as soon as a swirl of dust appeared at the far end of the room.

"We're being herded all right," Denny said. "They want us to go in here."

"Have we any choice?" Nelross asked rhetorically.

"Not that I can see," Sukiro said.

They entered the alcove.

Dyson, on point, touched the latch-plate. The iris opened to reveal a short corridor that ended in another iris at the far end. It felt claustrophobic in there, with so many people in so small a space. The far iris opened into another chamber, smaller than the first of these they had entered, but almost completely filled with its machine, bulky, solid, and catwalks between it and the wall balconies just a few steps long. They were compressed in here, without space to fan out.

"Which way," Falyn asked, "right or left?"

Sukiro chose right. They met no resistance. And as they came around the machine they could see that some of its lights, dials, panels, and screens, some located in places that made no sense, were lit, or twitching, or humming.

Raebuck went toward one of the functioning panels near the floor, but a dust-devil suddenly came from behind, zipped between her and the machine, forced her back to the wall, then disappeared, all in an instant. Nobody shot. It was too close in there; the back-flash of the blasters would have hurt those who fired.

They went on in the way they were being forced to go, but whenever a goon got too close to the machine, another dust-devil would zip past, to keep him or her from it, and once even knocked Private Glaine against the wall so that he nearly hit Grayshard.

"Please be careful," Grayshard said, "if you hit me, you will crush me. I have no armor to protect me."

"Even armor isn't good enough," Petorska said. His chest-plate had been cracked in the first dust-devil attack.

"Then keep to the wall," Sukiro told him, "but keep some-body between the softies and the machine."

Rikard didn't like being referred to in that way but had to acknowledge the wisdom of the action. The few times a dust-devil had brushed against him had hurt enough, and those had been just love taps compared to what some of the goons had taken. Lakey and Delamar, as well as Petorska, had suffered damage to their armor.

They went around the second corner of the machine, from where they could see that the third wall was one huge, open archway, beyond which was a truly tremendous chamber, twice as big as the one before this one. But unlike the first three chambers, it was not filled with its machine.

The device here, as huge as it was, was dwarfed by the cubi-cal chamber in which it stood. The machine was standing, in the center of the floor, on a convoluted spindle, rising halfway to the ceiling, with above it a spike that continued up to just short of the ceiling. Ramps led up to balconies that encircled the chamber, with long catwalks that led to other balconies encir-cling the device itself, but there were no workstations at the spindle or spike. And this machine, too, seemed to be opera-tional.

They moved into the chamber, under the massive machine bulking over them. Besides the arch by which they entered there were two other doors in this wall, one on either side, and three doors in each of the other walls, and other doors at various levels of the balcony.

"I get a bad feeling about this," Rikard said.

And sure enough, as soon as everybody was well within the chamber, and fanned out to cover all directions, the dust-devils started their attack. They came in from all the iris doors and the arch, some even entered from balcony doors above and whizzed down the ramps. None of them moved in a straight line, each of them zigged and zagged, traveling not only at high speed but also at odd angles, zipping in to hit a goon now and then. The platoon drew closer together, keeping the vulnerable in the center, trying to get off a good shot when they could.

"These guys aren't armed," Rikard said with sudden realiza-tion.

Braced against the attack, and firing at impossible targets, the goons who were hit by the speeding dust-devils weren't as badly battered as when they had been taken by surprise before, but Gerandine was hit hard from behind by a dust-devil that managed to streak right through the clot of defenders. She smashed to the ground, the left arm of her armor half popped off, her helmet cracked hard on the deck.

The attack had come so quickly, and the goons had reacted so quickly and were pressed around him so tightly, that it was a long moment before Rikard was able to draw his gun. He did not try to aim it but just gripped the butt, and concentrated his attention on focusing on a passing dust-devil, even as he felt his time sense slow. The attackers were still moving so fast that it was hard for him to even keep his eyes on them, but he did manage to get a passing glance at one or two who were moving more or less directly away from him.

The creatures he saw were like huge caterpillars, the fore-parts of their bodies half raised up from the deck. The lower body, maybe four meters long, was slender and tapered, with stiff cilia instead of jointed legs. The upper portion was composed of four segments, each with a pair of four-jointed arms. Their heads were spherical, but he could not see their faces. They were dark gray in color, shading to pale gray at the ends of their bodies, except for their heads, which were almost black. At least, that was as much as he could see.

He tried to bring his gun to bear on the nearest of the receding creatures, but Dyson, beside him, was too close and hindered his movement—which, after all, was only two or three times faster than normal even though his perceptions were ten times normal—and by the time he got his gun up and saw the concentric rings in his eyes move to the general vicinity of the dust-devil, it had turned aside and sped away.

He carefully moved away from Dyson, to give his gun hand room to move, and tried to pick another target. The goons around him were shooting, not aiming now but laying down a general barrage of fire. Rikard was fascinated to see one of the dust-devils turn its hard, shiny head just as Colder shot. It seemed to watch the blast, which was traveling faster than any bullet, as it crossed three-quarters of the distance toward it. Then it jerked away so quickly that even Rikard's hyper senses couldn't see it as movement, and dodged the shot, which passed within centimeters and blew a chunk out of the wall behind it.

And then his chance came. He didn't take the time to think about it, he just acted. A dust-devil was charging straight at him, as if it knew that he was vulnerable. His gun was half aimed already. He pushed his arm toward the thing as hard as he could. The concentric rings of his built-in sight centered on the creature's chest. It continued to race toward him with frightening speed. It had six simple eyes, a mouth like that of a spider. Rikard watched as the spot in his eyes, indicating the point of the bullet's impact, moved into the center ring, even as he was pulling the trigger. The gun fired, he watched the bullet's flat arc, watched the devil twitch aside at the last instant, watched the bullet pock the wall as the dust-devil swerved aside, and hit Majorbank.

From the corner of his eye he saw another of the monsters finish its charge and arc away, leaving Valencis with his body armor dislocated. He wrenched his arm around, focused on the creature's back. The spot in his eyes moved painfully slowly as his hand came around and the creature zigged into Delamar, knocking off her helmet, and zagged into Lakey, breaking his shoulder armor.

It was hard to keep his eyes on the thing, even speeded up ten times, let alone bring his gun to bear. He started to pull the trigger even as the rings of his internal sight bore on the thing's back. The target spot entered the outer ring, the gun went off as the spot moved to the center ring, the creature started to zig again, the bullet flew and hit it in the side instead of the middle of its back. The dust-devil jerked forward but kept running in spite of its terrible wound, and Rikard watched as it zipped out a door.

And then all the other dust-devils aborted their charges and raced away out the doors nearest them. The attack was over. Rikard released his hold on the gun and time returned to normal.

The enemy's departure was so sudden that the goons fired one or two shots more before they realized that the attack was over. Rikard tried to ease the cramped muscles in his gun hand. Then the noncoms shouted orders, the goons regrouped and tried to catch their breaths. Woadham and Brisabane had been wounded by body blows, and Gospodin was now lying still and dead on the deck.

"I've seen our assailants," Rikard said in the silence.

"Impossible," Denny said.

"He can do it," Sukiro told her. "So what did they look like?" Everybody listened as Rikard described them. "And I was right," he finished, "none of them had any weapons. They were just hitting people with their shoulders or fists as they passed."

"What you've just described," Raebuck said, "sounds exactly like the Tschagan. But how could they move so fast? They moved just like normal people on those tapes I saw."

"They must have slowed the tapes down for broadcast," Sukiro said. "Did you ever see the Tschagan and other people together?"

Raebuck paused to think a moment. "A lot of the tapes showed other species," she said, "but I don't remember if they were with the Tschagan or not. They seemed to like to hog the stage."

"That's nice to know," Denny said sarcastically, "but how will that help us if they decide to attack again?"

"An awful lot of them went out that door," Rikard said, pointing to one of the irises on the side.

"Then let's see what's out there," Falyn suggested.

Under her command, the goons approached the iris, Colder with her prybar in hand. When the goons were ranked in front of the iris, all with weapons drawn, Colder reached out with the bar to touch the latch-plate. The iris snapped open, and all the goons fired at once. It snapped shut again, and only one or two of the blaster shots hit it.

Colder then stepped up to the iris, opened it with her hand, and stepped into the jamb to keep it open. Majorbank, Charney, and Van vleet, immediately behind her, quickly stepped through into the huge chamber beyond. There were no giant caterpillars. The rest of the force followed quickly.

This chamber was as big as the one they had just left, but its machine almost completely filled the space within. It had been hit a number of times by blaster-fire, though it showed little damage.

But in front of the machine, visible now that they were inside and the lights were on, were smears of organic matter. Rikard and Sukiro were the first to see them.

Most of it was unrecognizable, but there were several of the stiff, jointless appendages that served the Tschagan as legs, and over to one side was a fragment of an arm, with the four mutually opposed fingers of its hand intact. Aside from that, and a few fragments of skin, all the rest was just burned pulp, spread out over a two-meter radius.

"That's two down," Rikard said, "and I wounded one just before they broke off the attack."

"That's what made them quit," Denny said. "That doesn't seem like what you would expect from soldiers."

"Let's not just stand here and talk about it," Falyn said. "At their rate of movement, they could have completely reorganized by now and called in reinforcements. We've got to get out of here."

"I agree," Sukiro said. "They can wear us down faster than we can them, and who knows how many of them there are. If only one-tenth the potential population of this station still lives, the odds against us are at least a hundred thousand to one."

"No problem anywhere but here," Falyn said sardonically.

"Shall we go back the way we came?" Nelross asked.

"We should go on," Raebuck said. "We know they're behind us but they may not be ahead."

"Then let's start moving up," Sukiro said. "There's an iris at the top of that ramp, let's hope it leads to a way out."

They followed the ramps and catwalks built against the wall up to the highest balcony, and to the door there, and went into a low, broad hallway, many times wider than it was high. Even as they did so, Tschagan again zipped at them, but only from behind, and the goons by now had learned to not pick targets but just to set up a random area fire all around. They kept moving even as they fired, and one or two Tschagan were hit, immediately after which the attack stopped.

The way ahead was the only way to go, so they went, spread out along the broad, low corridor, looking for another door or ramp up. At last they found what they wanted, a ramp right in the middle of the corridor floor. It was three meters wide, and led straight up through the ceiling.

4

The broad ramp led them up through the middle of the floor above, into a rather large chamber, where the high ceiling was already lit. There were low, padded rails, like benches, scattered around the far walls, detached counters set between them, and several of the furniturelike objects they had come to know so well, set out in the middle area. There was an iris at the far end of the chamber, and three larger irises along the left side wall, but the right wall was composed almost completely of arches, with modified irises three times normal height and breadth, set into its surface.

As the last of them came to the top of the ramp, the iris in the wall behind them snapped open and a pair of dust-devils—Tschagan—came racing in, arced around the left wall, then went out the iris in the front wall.

Sukiro gave a command and the goons formed a ring, facing outward. Again the Tschagan came, from the end walls and the three arches on the left, moving in fast arcs at the defenders, who shot but hit nothing but the walls and some of the furniture. None of the Tschagan came between them and the wall of arches.

"Looks like they want us to go that way," Rikard said.

"All right then," Sukiro said. "The middle arch, at full run."

The defenders ran even as the Tschagan started another attack, but this time, instead of moving in evasive arcs, the Tschagan dithered around the place where the goons had been, and some even moved in direct pursuit for a few meters.

Majorbank was the first to reach the arch. He slammed the latch-plate, swung astride the jamb to keep the iris open, and the others raced through. He jumped free and the iris snapped shut.

They were in a much larger chamber, by far the largest they had seen so far, with a high vaulted ceiling and a floor that sloped down, away from them, toward what looked like a stage area, an elevated platform that ran not quite the whole width of the chamber, at the far back, maybe three hundred meters away. Halfway to the stage the floor was empty, but the rest of the way, in the wider part of the auditorium, were more of the padded rails like those they had seen outside, placed end-on to the stage, arranged in rows and columns.

The police moved in a loose group toward the stage, nervously waiting for another attack, but for the moment it seemed that they would be left alone.

"Funny thing about their behavior back there," Sukiro said. "If they can move so fast, how come it seemed like we surprised them?"

"Maybe they don't think as fast as they move," Denny suggested.

They reached the first row of rail benches without incident, and paused there a moment to reorganize.

"Do you know where we are?" Sukiro asked Raebuck, who was gazing around with tense and controlled interest.

"I think so," Raebuck said. "It looks like the place where they filmed most of their propaganda broadcasts."

"It looks like a theater to me," Fresno said.

"It is, if it's the same place. It looks the same, except there's nothing on the stage, no trophies or prisoners." She looked up at the ceiling, and pointed to a hemisphere hanging directly over their heads. "That's the camera pod. It comes down when they're filming. When it's fully extended it comes to within about five meters of the floor. But if this is the place I think it is, I have no idea where the museum is."

"But why did they bring us here?" Sukiro wondered.

"They're going to record their last attack," Raebuck told her, "so they can broadcast it when they let everybody know that they're back in business."

"But why didn't they do something like this with the raiders?" Nelross wanted to know.

Rikard looked at him and said, with sudden inspiration, "Because of the Vaashka." He turned to look at Grayshard. "How much do you want to bet that your warrior's psychic weapons work on Tschagan too?"

"That would make sense," Grayshard said. "The neuroslavers have been here a lot longer than we have, so it must have been they who aroused the Tschagan from whatever retreat they were in. The *projection* does not work on all life forms. Most who are affected are slowed, some just suffer from a clouded mind. But in either event, the Tschagan, I think, would hesitate to attack anyone who could do that to them."

"You're a warrior," Rikard said to him, "you can generate that kind of psychic attack."

"Yes," Grayshard admitted, "though I am not well trained."

"But if you do that," Brisabane said, "you'll affect us too."

"Seal up your suits," Rikard suggested. "If we keep out the chemical component, maybe the psychic component won't affect us so strongly."

"It's worth a try," Denny said, and gave commands.

"Perhaps," Grayshard said, "but my own clothing is a better defense. It was designed to be so. I can just open the, ah, front here, while Rikard, and those whose armor is no longer airtight, stand behind me. There should not be much leakage."

"We should keep our face-plates open," Sukiro said to Denny, "until Grayshard actually projects, so we can hear and give commands."

Falyn finished inspecting her squad and turned to face the arches at the narrow end of the auditorium. "What are they waiting for?" she asked no one in particular.

"Reinforcements," Nelross suggested. "Let's fall back to the stage; they'll have farther to travel and we'll have a better chance of hitting them, especially if they have to funnel down these aisles."

"Best idea I've heard so far," Denny said. "Let's move."

They fell back in an orderly manner toward the stage, though still keeping their attention fixed on the arches. And even as they started down the aisles between the rails, the arches opened and hundreds of Tschagan came pouring in across the sloping floor toward them.

The goons fired as rapidly as they could, but the Tschagan were moving so evasively that very few of that horde were hit. The wave of attackers finally broke halfway to the seats and raced back to the arches, which all snapped shut.

"They're not soldiers," Denny said.

Grayshard was twitching. "They'll destroy me if they hit me," he said as they continued their retreat toward the stage. Without needing orders, Petorska and Glaine took up positions on either side of him, between him and the arches, solely for his protection.

As they continued to back up a second wave of Tschagan came, even faster and more numerous than before. This time Grayshard, with a shouted warning, opened the front of his disguise. The police shut and sealed their helmets in an instant. Rikard, who was well back and directly behind Grayshard, felt a subtle tingle in his mind, a distaste for this huge open space, a dislike for the light everywhere. It was not a strong feeling.

But the Tschagan in front of Grayshard slowed, slowed enough to become visible. Those on the flanks broke in confusion and started to rush away. The goons, somewhat distracted by the intrusive images of Grayshard's psychic sending but otherwise unaffected, now could pick their targets, mostly those who had slowed the most though they were still moving very fast, and brought down a couple of dozen or more before the other Tschagan, accelerating as they got farther from Grayshard, could get away.

The goons hurried back through the aisles of rail benches toward the stage. After a moment there was another attack, the Tschagan streaming down both sides of the auditorium. Grayshard could face only one way or another without exposing his companions to his *projection*, and chose left. The Tschagan on the right got close enough—running over the rails, not between them—to hit several goons. Grayshard immediately turned in that direction. The Tschagan nearest him stopped abruptly, some of them actually fell. Those a bit farther slowed enough to be seen, and staggered. Those farthest just turned and raced away. The goons in the path of the projection faltered, but the rest took the opportunity and shot as many of the paralyzed and slowed Tschagan as they could.

Nelross grabbed Hornower and Dyson, put them in front of Rikard, and yelled to Grayshard, "Open up, cover the whole area."

Grayshard started to pull his disguise aside, then hesitated. Charney and Yansen joined Petorska and Glaine to help protect him. The group continued its retreat, but by the time the next wave of Tschagan came, repeating their earlier flanking maneuver, Grayshard was almost completely exposed, though barely able to move in his support clothes, and *projected* as hard as he could.

All the Tschagan within about thirty meters immediately succumbed to the effects of his psychic weapon, and the goons, though they too were affected, took a terrible toll.

At last their backs were against the front of the two-meter-high stage. The goons, with their powered armor, could easily jump up, even backward, and when they did the attack suddenly stopped. Rikard felt hands on him, then Hornower and Van Leet helped him up onto the stage while Charney and Petorska lifted Grayshard. The other goons blasted any Tschagan still slowed or paralyzed while the others raced away.

They waited on the stage for another attack, but after a full minute nothing was forthcoming. Falyn cracked her helmet, and with taps and hand signals, had the other goons do likewise. "Now that they've got us where they want us," she said, "why don't they finish us off?"

"Maybe they didn't expect us to get on the stage," Nelross suggested.

"You get the feeling they're not really very bright," Denny said. "What else would they expect us to do?"

Grayshard was having difficulty moving because so much of his supporting disguise had been removed. He wabbled several long tendrils at Rikard. "Take part of my clothing," he suggested, speaking through the vocalizer, which was now at the center of his mass. "Make a hood and cloak to protect your brain and spine from my *projection*. I may have to use it again."

"But how will you move?" Rikard asked. "You can't keep up with us without those clothes, especially if the goons use their powered armor."

"If someone will carry me," Grayshard said.

"I'll do that," Private Ming offered.

Grayshard removed the rest of his supporting apparel, part of which Rikard took to fashion a shield for himself as Grayshard had suggested. Ming did the same with the rest, discarding the rigid portions of its frame. Then Grayshard, moving in a kind of slithery crawl, naked and terribly fragile, slithered up onto the private's back, and wrapped himself around her shielded torso and head, careful to leave her face-plate and arms free. It was a grotesque sight. Rikard watched Ming's face, saw her trepidation and anxiety—and determination.

"So what do we do now?" Sukiro asked. She turned to Raebuck. "Do you know of any other way out of here?"

"None of the tapes I saw showed any," she said as the group moved toward the center of the stage. "There may be exits at either end."

Denny started to send pairs of goons to either side when one of the irises in the bank of arches at the back of the auditorium snapped. The goons all spun to face the sound, prepared for the next attack, but no Tschagan entered the place.

"They're afraid of us now," Glaine said.

"At least they're being cautious," Petersin answered.

"Do we just wait here?" Falyn asked.

"Maybe we can attack them," Nelross suggested, "if we've got Grayshard to slow them down."

"You mean," Falyn said, "just go out there?" She waved at the now silent arches.

"Not a good idea," Sukiro said. "They'd crush us by sheer force of numbers. Let's take advantage of the time we have and try to figure out a plan."

"How do we know," Denny asked, "that we aren't doing just what the Tschagan want us to do? After all, this is where they drove us, we're in a cul-de-sac, they could be calling in their regular troops, even as we wait."

"And if they've brought armed reinforcements," Rikard said, "then we're all sitting ducks."

PART
<u>FIVE</u>

1

Rikard wished he'd kept his mouth shut. He could almost feel the gloom of despair descending over the battered police force. Even Sukiro seemed to be at a loss. What could be done to get these people moving again? Why did Rikard feel that it was his responsibility? It was Raebuck who had led them into this trap. He turned to her, saw her staring at the back wall of the stage area. "We've got to do something," he said. He tried to keep his anger from showing.

"This isn't the way I remember it," Raebuck said, half to herself. "There should be a series of alcoves back there."

"Maybe this is a different auditorium," Denny suggested.

Raebuck walked slowly up to the back wall, but Sukiro said, "We've got to find a way out of here. We don't know when the next attack will be."

"The Tschagan all left when we got onstage," Dyson said. "maybe there won't be an attack."

"We're right where they want us," Sukiro said. She looked up at the camera module. "How can you tell that thing is on? Maybe they're filming us right now."

Rikard followed Raebuck toward the back wall. As he neared he saw that the panels there, separated from each other by narrow pilasters, were not the same as all the other walls they had seen. "No blue stripes," he said, "everywhere else there's blue stripes."

Sukiro turned to watch them. "Do you know what kind of weapons they had?" she asked Raebuck.

"I'm not sure," she answered distractedly, "projectile weapons and lasers, I think."

"How about blasters?"

"No, not that I know of." She turned to stare back at the major. "That's a much more recent development."

"That's the way I understood it, but the Tschagan were very

advanced for their time. Are you sure they had no energy weapons?"

"Except for lasers. Why, is it important?"

"They have not yet used any weapons against us. And they don't behave like soldiers."

"So what's the point?" Denny demanded.

"I see one of two things happening," Sukiro said. "Either the Tschagan won't attack again at all, now that they've seen how we can defend ourselves—or they've gone for soldiers who can hit us from a distance."

"That makes sense, but so what?"

"In either case, I think we may have some time. Soldiers could hardly be battle-ready. So instead of standing here glooming, or rushing around in a panic, let's take the time to figure things out, so we won't be taken by surprise."

Somehow these considered words had a calming effect on the police. Falyn sent several of her goons out to investigate the nearest of the Tschagan corpses. Nelross had his goons line up along the edge of the stage, seated, arms braced on knees, ready to fire. Denny sent pairs of goons to the far ends of the stage, to see if there were exits there.

"We may as well go out clean," Sukiro said.

Falyn's goons came back to report that they'd found no evidence of weapons of any kind among the Tschagan bodies they'd investigated, not even clubs. "They don't wear clothes either," Yansen said.

"That's right," Raebuck said, "not even jewelry. It makes sense, clothes and things would be subject to inertia, and make it hard for them to move as fast as they do."

"So what!" Denny shouted. "Save it until we get out of here."

"Easy," Sukiro told her, "get a hold of yourself. But I agree, we can get as academic as we like after we get home."

"Sukiro's right," Rikard said. "And since you're the one," he said to Raebuck, "who has studied this place, however vicariously, I think you should turn your attention to finding us a way out."

"All right," she said as she looked at the back of the stage. "But there's something I'm trying to remember about these panels." She turned and, in spite of protests from Denny and Sukiro, went to the nearest of them and ran her hands over it. Then she went to the pilaster separating it from the one to its right.

But before Sukiro and Denny, who had run out of patience, could get to her, Raebuck touched something on the pilaster and the panel in front of her started to rise up into the overhead. Behind it was an alcove, dark in spite of the light from the auditorium ceiling. Sukiro and Denny stopped just behind her and on either side, and stared into the revealed space.

Raebuck reached around inside the edge of the alcove for a light switch. "This is it," she said excitedly. "This is where they kept the trophies they used to brag about and show off on their propaganda broadcasts." She found the switch and the lights in the alcove came on.

It was a showcase. In the middle of the floor was a platform that looked as though it could be moved out onto the stage. In the middle of this was a knee-high table, on which stood a model of a building, at about one-hundredth scale. The original had been made of white plastic, with rounded edges, and with a short square tower at each corner. On either side of the table, on shoulder-high stands, were tiny jeweled statuettes, of centauroid beings with pyramidal bodies, four dog-legs, and four arms. The stand on the right held a full-sized spacesuit suitable for such a being. On the left was a brass-colored thing like a giant loving cup, unadorned except for a fancy lip and two graceful handles. Behind all this was a tapestry woven in brilliant, shimmering colors, an elaborate and subtly asymmetrical geometric pattern.

"Good God," Rikard whispered as he stared at the trophies. He had seen the originals of those statuettes. He and Raebuck went toward the table and Sukiro and Denny, as fascinated as they, followed behind them.

"That's Atreef," Raebuck said, "from before they dropped out of the Federation."

It was all Rikard could do to hold himself in check. "You're right," he said, "but we've got to move."

Raebuck wasn't listening. She went back to the pilaster and touched again the place that had caused the panel concealing the alcove to rise. This time the panel on the next alcove to the right went up. She reached in and found the light at once.

Another showcase was revealed, this one with an arc of seven stands, each bearing a crystalline object: a perfect sphere half a meter in diameter, shimmering prismatically; a spindle two meters tall on which were impaled five disks, the middle one half a meter across, those next above and below some hundred centimeters less, the top and bottom two only two hundred centimeters in diameter; three crystal squares set at right angles to each other and intersecting to form an octahedral shape; a three-hundred-centimeter lens that stood at forty-five degrees from one edge; something like an armillary globe, with another one nested inside, and a third inside that; a stellated polyhedron more than a meter across, of maybe forty or fifty points; and another spike, with tapered ends and a black greasy sphere in the middle.

"Aren't those Anchika scepters?" Raebuck exclaimed.

"I don't know," Rikard said.

"Sure they are." Raebuck went to the lens, pointed at the edge where it stood on the stand. "See, it really balances here."

To Rikard's surprise, Sukiro said, "By damn, I believe you're right."

The other goons, though fascinated, were nonplussed. Gray-shard, riding on Ming's shoulders, said softly, "If Vaashka *warriors* come looking for us, I won't be able to defend us."

"We've got to get moving," Rikard said. But though his anxiety was increasing moment by moment, he couldn't find it within himself to protest as Raebuck and Sukiro went to the next alcove to the right.

In the showcase revealed here they found two humanoid beings, sitting in chairs on either side of a miniature starship of unfamiliar design. The figures were short, stocky, dark, ugly, with a vaguely reptilian cast to their faces. Their hair was black, shading to gray on one and to blue on the other. They had four eyes, one pair above the other. Each hand had four mutually opposable thumbs. Both were naked, one male, the other female.

This time several of the other goons reacted. "Those are Teleref," Hornower said.

"Or statues of them," Raebuck said. But on closer inspection the figures proved to be not statues, but mummies, carefully preserved.

"I'd forgotten about that," Raebuck went on. "The Tschagan liked to mummify the leaders of anybody who resisted them, and put them on display along with their other trophies."

But while Hornower and Sukiro and even Falyn were wondering about this and about the miniature starship, Raebuck backed away from the display, halfway out to the center of the stage again, and looked at the opened panels and those on either side.

"We've got to go now," Rikard said. "We can come back later."

But Raebuck was too excited to listen. "Just one more," she said, and went across the open alcoves to the panel to the left of the first one she had opened and triggered the switch that raised it. The panel slid up, she turned on the light. "Ahaa!" she gasped.

Rikard was slow to follow her, and before he could come near enough to see inside, the irises at the top end of the auditorium started snapping. A horde of Tschagan poured in and raced down the sloping floor toward them. At the same time, Rikard saw the camera module at the top of the auditorium ceiling start to descend.

Whatever fascination the others had found in the treasures Raebuck had revealed, it was forgotten in the need of the moment. Everybody had heard the snapping of the irises, and they all turned toward the wall of arches, caught by surprise yet again, but they sealed their helmets against Grayshard's psychic sending and were ready to fight.

Ming stepped out toward the center of the stage and Grayshard started to *project* his mind-numbing attack. Rikard had to wrap his piece of Grayshard's clothing closer around his head to shield himself from the assault, and saw Ming stagger as the power of Grayshard's sending penetrated her helmet, wrapped as he was around the private's head.

The goons opened fire as the nearest of the Tschagan began to slow, and their aim was deadly. But they were not completely protected from Grayshard's effect, and there were too many of the enemy, those at the back pushing the nearer ones forward.

Then, from the top of the auditorium, came shots. Bullets struck the apron of the stage and the closed panels behind them, but none of the goons who were in front of open alcoves seemed to be targets.

Rikard drew his .75 and took aim at the Tschagan at the back, those who were firing, who had to pause momentarily to take aim themselves. He missed with his first two shots, but his third was good, and the Tschagan soldier's head splattered.

The goons quickly realized where safety lay, and those who were in front of closed panels moved so that they had the open alcoves behind them. They all blasted away at their attackers, with deadly effect.

Rikard missed his fourth shot, but hit another Tschagan soldier with the fifth. Then the attack broke, and the surviving Tschagan raced back out through the arches. The goons stopped firing at once. Blasters were good for a long fight, but they would run out of energy eventually.

Rikard popped the clip out of his .75, even though it had one shell left, stuck it in his belt, and put a new clip in. His ammunition was far more limited than that of the police. He turned around to see how everyone was faring. Majorbank, Van Leet, and Tamura had fallen.

"Let's get out of here!" he yelled.

"Not yet!" Raebuck yelled back defiantly.

He turned toward her, and saw her striding into the last alcove she'd opened. In the middle of the showcase display was a huge figure, like a giant serpent with a humanoid torso, but with four arms. It's head was wolflike and snakelike at the same time, with domed eyes, small bat ears, and fangs projecting below its lower jaw. It was sitting on a massive and strangely shaped throne thing.

Raebuck looked over her shoulder at Rikard. There was an ecstatic expression on her face. "It's the crown," she said. Her voice was a shouted whisper.

Rikard couldn't help but stare at the figure on the throne. He walked into the alcove behind Raebuck, who was now standing at the very edge of the platform on which the throne sat. Behind him Sukiro was almost yelling. "Let's get out of here, dammit! where's Braeth?"

"I'm in here," Rikard called back, and went to stand beside Raebuck.

The serpent sat coiled on its throne, bronze and green and deep blue, its "waist" higher than Rikard's head, its arms folded across its deep chest. And now Rikard saw the thing to which Raebuck had referred, very much indeed like a crown, a circlet of black metal on the serpent's head, with a curved spike on either side just in front of its tall, pointed ears.

"What are you doing?" Sukiro demanded angrily as she came up behind Rikard. "We've got no time for—" Then she saw the figure on the throne. Rikard didn't pay any attention. His gaze was riveted on the serpent-being's face.

"That's quite some statue," Sukiro said at last. Rikard glanced at her. Ming, with Grayshard riding on her head and shoulders, was right behind her. Grayshard was waving dozens of tendrils at the four-armed serpent.

"It's not the statue," Raebuck said, "it's the crown."

"We've got three dead," Denny said. "If you don't know a way out of here, then we'll have to find one for ourselves, or go out there and fight our way through."

"It's the Ahmear," Grayshard said.

"It is indeed," Raebuck murmured.

"Or at least," Grayshard went on, "a representation of one."

"What the hell is an Ahmear?" Ming asked. She tilted her head back for a moment, as if by doing so she could get a better view of the Vaashka wrapped around her helmet.

"The Ahmear," Raebuck said, "were among the first of the starfaring peoples. They left our limb of the galaxy very long ago. All they left behind were stories among the younger races, some of whom were advanced enough at the time to have made recordings. That crown on its head is the only known Ahmear artifact; they took everything else with them. Why or how that thing was left behind, nobody knows for sure. The earliest record of it is for over fifty thousand years ago, when a people called the Reneth showed it in a film about pre-Reneth ruins on one of their outer planets. The ruins had nothing to do with the Ahmear, the crown was just found there. It was kept in various places by various peoples until it was lost when the Tschagan sacked Tromarn, early in their career. It's the oldest artificial object in the known universe."

"We have records," Grayshard said, "of contact with the Ahmear back when our history began. They had been starfaring for at least a hundred thousand years before that."

"That's just great," Denny said, "but we're dying in here. We've got to go."

"That crown," Raebuck said, "is worth more than the whole of this station—and we're going to take it."

"You're damn straight we are," Sukiro said, to everyone's surprise. "That's not just a crown, it's a machine. Nobody has been able to figure out its technology before, but maybe we can now, and if we can, brain pirates won't matter a whiz. To hell with them; getting the crown back to civilization is the most important thing we can do right now, even if we have to die trying."

"Well and good," Denny said, "but the operative concept is getting back to civilization. It won't do us any good if we all die here."

"Okay, Raebuck," Rikard said, "let's get that thing, but by God we've got to get out!"

By now the rest of the goons had come into the alcove, and were staring at the enthroned figure. "You want us to move that whole thing?" Petersin asked incredulously.

"No," Raebuck said, "the statue is just for looks, all we need is the crown."

"Then let's do it," Denny said. She stepped up onto the supporting platform and reached out to climb up on the lower coils of the figure, but jerked her hand back even as she touched it. "That's no statue," she said, "that's real skin and scales."

"Impossible," Sukiro said, and went to touch it herself. "Holy shit! you're right!"

"A mockup," Rikard said.

"No, look, this is real!"

"Real skin and scales made to look like an Ahmear," Grayshard said. He got down off Ming's shoulders and slithered up to the figure. He shaped himself into a column and reached out a rope of fibers to touch the Ahmear. "It is an Ahmear," he said, nearly losing control of his vocalizer.

"How in heaven's name the Tschagan got an Ahmear I don't know," Raebuck said, "but they sure as hell did, and they mummified it to prove their victory. I've seen this thing on tapes lots of time, and I always thought it was just a statue. The Tschagan wanted people to believe that they were superior, even to the Ahmear, but nobody believed it, because the Ahmear had left this part of the galaxy long before the Tschagan even came into existence."

"Come on," Sukiro said, "let's get the crown and go."

Raebuck glanced at the major, then the two of them started carefully to climb up the coils of the mummy. When they stood on its top coil its head was still out of reach so, one on either side, they went up its crossed arms and sat down on its shoulders. Its head was nearly as big as Raebuck's body. They took hold of the crown on either side and tried to lift it off.

"It won't move," Raebuck said.

They tried again, but were afraid to damage the mummy, or the crown, which simply refused to come off.

"We'll have to just leave it," Rikard said.

"Maybe we can move the whole thing after all," Sukiro suggested. "Push on the platform."

Petorska gave the side of the throne an experimental shove, and the platform did move a couple of centimeters.

"We'll never get it up those narrow ramps," Falyn objected. Nelross was trying to get the goons to resume a defensive formation.

"Maybe I can help," Grayshard said. He slumped forward onto the lower coils of the Ahmear and crawled up its body as easily as he had crawled along the floor. He came up between Sukiro and Raebuck and reached up with his tendrils to probe under the edge of the crown.

"There are anchor wires of some kind under here," he said. He probed further, brought more of his tendrils into the interface between head and crown. "There is electrical power of some kind," he went on. "There, I have disconnected it."

He withdrew his tendrils as Sukiro and Raebuck, between them, at last lifted the large, heavy crown from the figure's head.

Grayshard slithered back down to the deck. Then, taking turns and handing the crown back and forth so they could clamber down, Sukiro and Raebuck followed until at last all three were once again standing on the deck.

"Now let's go," Sukiro said as she brandished the crown triumphantly. Then she looked up at the Ahmear's face just in time to see its eyes look down at her.

2

"Oh, my God!" Sukiro said, and stared up at the domelike eyes, which now were glowing with an internal light.

"I must have triggered something when I unfastened the crown," Grayshard said.

"Those aren't artificial eyes," Rikard said as he backed off from the enthroned figure. Everybody else was backing off too.

The eyes glittered, as if the thing were looking from one

person to another. Colder and Charney started to aim their weapons. "Hold your fire!" Sukiro shouted.

The Ahmear slowly flexed, at first just a general twitching of its whole serpentine body, then it began to move its crossed arms and a ripple ran down its coiled length.

Sukiro suddenly realized that she was still holding the crown. "Here," she said, offering it to the Ahmear, "here, take it back."

It paid no attention to her. Now it slowly stretched out its arms, as if they were cramped from being folded for so long, and turned its head from side to side. A convulsive ripple ran down its bronze, green, and dark blue length, and then it reached up with its upper set of arms and felt its head, where the crown had been. Jasime, Yansen, and Glaine raised their blasters.

"Hold your fire, dammit!" Sukiro shouted, and those who had not already done so backed out of the alcove onto the stage.

The Ahmear lifted itself up on its coils until its head was more than four meters above the platform. It leaned forward, looked around, and at last directed its glowing gaze at the people in front of its alcove. It spoke, "Ahh glagtha savish'kath-arn." Its mouth, besides the fangs, had a double row of carnivorous teeth. Its voice was a smooth bass, and strangely resonant, but with a catching quality to it. It unmistakably cleared its throat, shook its head, seemed to glance down at Sukiro's side where the crown now hung from her twitching hand. She lifted it up again, offered it to the Ahmear. It barked as if in laughter and slithered down off the throne.

The goons, in spite of their training, couldn't help themselves. They backed farther away, some turned as if to run, others raised their weapons. Only Rikard held fast, shouting, "Don't shoot! Don't shoot!"

By now Sukiro had fallen flat on her face. Raebuck had sat down hard, and was just staring. The goons who had not run to the edge of the stage were crouched or prone or seated similarly.

There was something, Rikard sensed, other than just the sight of this being which was affecting them. Colder and Glaine were still trying to take aim, though their hands shook, but before they could fire, a paralyzing thought came into all their minds, and those still standing, even Rikard, sat or crouched or fell down. The Ahmear was not only alive, it was telepathic.

Rikard, half-paralyzed, watched as the Ahmear, paying them

no further attention, came out onto the stage. It looked around the auditorium as if expecting to see other people down on the floor.

Rikard heard irises snapping. He managed to roll to one side so that he could see the back of the auditorium, and saw the blurs of Tschagan streaking toward them from the far arches. He felt the Ahmear send its telepathic command again, but it was not aimed at him, and it was as though he had been touched with just the edge of the thought. But the Tschagan, one by one but in rapid succession, suddenly stopped motionless, in postures of running, and crashed forward, thrown down by their own momentum.

The Ahmear moved toward the edge of the stage. Some of the Tschagan became able to move again, and scurried away. The Ahmear, it seemed, had decided to let them go. Rikard began to recover and sat up. Other Tschagan became mobile and ran away.

The Ahmear turned and looked at Rikard. The goons were recovering too, though they continued to cower. Even Sukiro was terrified of this being. The Ahmear looked from one to the other—as near as Rikard could tell with its bulging dome eyes —and its gaze seemed to rest on him, Denny, and Sukiro, as if recognizing them as leaders. It ignored the others.

Then Grayshard rose from where he had lain slumped by the base of the throne, and *projected* his own brand of chemo-tele-pathic paralysis. The Ahmear almost seemed to smile, and a sound that could have been a chuckle came from its throat, but though Rikard felt the full force of Grayshard's attack the Ahmear was unaffected. Grayshard gave up his *projection* almost at once and slumped back down to the deck.

The Vaashka paralysis quickly cleared from Rikard's mind and he felt, peripherally, a sending from the Ahmear. Judging from Denny's reaction, the sending had been directed at her. She just shook her head, her face a rigid mask, but there was something about that attempt at communication that Rikard found familiar.

The Ahmear then turned its attention to Sukiro, and once again Rikard "overheard" its sending. But the major just rolled over on her face, utterly rejecting the Ahmear's attempt at communication.

And now Rikard remembered where he had felt that kind of telepathy before—it was the same as that used by the Taarshome, those creatures he had found beneath the ruins of Kholtri, and which he had reintroduced to civilization on the Federation capital of Seltique. It was not as strong as the dragons' sending, or as refined, or as all-enveloping, but it was the same kind of thing, a pure electromagnetic effect, without the chemical component that was a part of Tathas and Vaashka sendings.

The Ahmear turned its attention to Rikard. He felt the communication, more focused but still open to all hearers, and yes, it was indeed the same as that form of telepathy the Taarshome used—until now the only truly telepathic species known in the Federation or elsewhere. But unlike the Taarshome "speech," there was no instantaneous translation into terms Rikard could understand.

Even so Rikard got a sense of amusement mingled with condescension, curiosity, determination, relief. Denny and Sukiro had not been able to deal with this form of communication because they had not experienced it before, but Rikard had acted as spokesman for the Taarshome, and as the Ahmear turned its attention elsewhere Rikard sat up and called out to it—just a half-formed greeting—in the way he had been taught by the dragons of Kohltri.

He must have done the right thing because the Ahmear coiled back from him as if amazed. It looked from Rikard, to Denny, to Sukiro, to one or two others who happened to be looking directly at it, as if it couldn't tell who had "spoken." It sent a short message in return, not in words but in images, which Rikard interpreted as meaning, "How did you learn to do that?" The images were a rapid succession of each face the Ahmear could see, and a strong sense of question. Rikard struggled to his feet, and sent back an image, of himself, "Me," and tried to form a sensory image of speech with the Ahmear as his audience. In effect, "I can talk to you—I think."

The Ahmear coiled up, like a snake poised to strike, but somehow without the sense of threat. It looked at Rikard, its head more than a meter above his, and stared at him as if it were confused. Its thoughts seemed turned in but Rikard could still overhear traces, and now he could detect an overtone of anger and fear, though not at him or the goons, or of them.

Rikard took a step forward, the Ahmear leaned back. Rikard formed an image in his mind of himself—as best he could—and in his mind enunciated the words, "Rikard Braeth," then added the image-concept. It was a clumsy attempt. He couldn't, after all, speak only in true imagery.

The Ahmear's thoughts became still, as if it were trying to conceal them, then the response came, and with it a vocalization, "Endark Droagn"—or at least, that was how Rikard heard it.

This time Rikard spoke his own name as he made another attempt to send a mental image of "self." As he did so the others around him began to relax, some of them turning to watch these first attempts at communication. The Ahmear—Endark Droagn—pulled its—his?—lips back in a terrifying simulation of a smile—and as it did so seemed to become aware of Rikard's anxious reaction. It—he—stopped, and sent a sensation that Rikard could only interpret as "greeting."

Out on the auditorium floor more and more of the Tschagan were begining to rouse too. Endark Droagn offhandedly projected a violent thought toward them. Unlike Grayshard, his telepathic ability was controllably directional. Those Tschagan who were able simply ran for the arches.

Endark Droagn focused on Rikard again. Rikard got a sort of image of a pyramid of people, with Rikard at the top, flanked by Denny and Sukiro. He paused a moment, then created a similar image in his mind, with Sukiro at the peak, then himself and Denny immediately below, and the corporals and goons under Denny. It was hard to convey the mixed leadership. He said, "Sukiro is our leader, Denny commands the troops, but I am leading the exploration—theoretically."

By this time most of the others had regained some semblance of composure, and though all of them were still cautious and afraid they got to their feet and stood, albeit at a safe distance, watching Rikard and Endark Droagn. Whether any of them could sense the telepathic part of the conversation, Rikard couldn't tell, but it hardly mattered. At the same time more of the Tschagan on the auditorium floor were regaining their senses and staggering, so slowly as to be visible, toward the arches and away.

Endark Droagn mulled over Rikard's last communication and at last replied to the effect, ˜But you are the one who can talk to me.˜

Rikard answered, to the best of his ability, speaking words as he did so for the sake of the others, ˜I've had some practice, with a race we know as the ~~Taarshome.~~ Your speech is much like theirs.~

~We knew the Taarshome, long ago,~ Endark Droagn said. ~How did you come to meet them?~

~Some of them came back to a world that is now ours. They wanted to join with us again.~

~I sense a long story,~ Droagn said. He gestured with one of his four arms back at the still recovering and retreating Tschagan. ~How did you get past those villains?~

~Very few of them are awake, and until just now there were no soldiers among them.~

Droagn watched as the last of the Tschagan made their clumsy way out through the arches. ~Much has changed since last I was aware,~ he said as he turned back to Rikard. ~Who are you, and why are you here?~

"We have come,~ Rikard said, ~to find the people who have been raiding our worlds—not the Tschagan, but others, who steal the brains from our people and have been using this derelict as their base.~

~Derelict? It was not so when I came.~

~That must have been a long time ago. We thought you were a mummy, set up for their propaganda. How come they didn't kill you?~

"They could not, and besides, I was useful to them.~

~You worked for them?~

~Of course not, they put me into that device so that my— *psychic power*—could be used by them.~

~You seem to be able to paralyze the Tschagan, and drive them away at will, how could they have gained control over you?~

~I was careless, and they used machines I could not defend against when I was overwhelmed by their numbers.~

~And why did you come?~ Rikard glanced at Sukiro who, he thought, was beginning to be able to hear Droagn's responses, though the Ahmear did not vocalize them. The expressions on other people's faces indicated that they, too, were beginning to understand. ~Your people left our space very long ago,~ Rikard went on, ~why did you come back?~

~To recover the Prime, a simulacrum of which your leader is still clutching.~

Sukiro could indeed understand Droagn's sending. She self-consciously dropped the crown. Raebuck stared at it with surprised disappointment.

~I've been in stasis since I was captured,~ Droagn went on. ~How long ago was that?~

"As near as we know," Raebuck said, "the Tschagan stole the crown about a thousand years after they came to power in their own space."

Droagn apparently could understand her spoken speech, for he said, ~I heard of that shortly after it happened, maybe a *century* or two later, and decided that was a good time to retrieve it. A few hundred *years* is awfully brief for the changes I see around me.~

~More like twenty-five thousand years,~ Rikard said. He tried to form an image in his mind of what a standard year was, and the commonly used concept of numbering in base ten.

Droagn paused as he translated these ideas into his own terms. After a moment he began to lower himself slowly onto the deck. He sent back to Rikard a parallel concept, an idea of a second, minute, day, year. The terms were not identical to those Rikard knew, but near enough, and Rikard confirmed the estimate of the time elapsed.

~That's not possible,~ Droagn said.

"It is," Raebuck said as she came up to stand beside Rikard. "The Tschagan were in power for fifteen thousand years before the Vengatti led the rebellion against them, and that was ten thousand years ago. If you came here shortly after the Tschagan stole the crown, then you've been in stasis for nearly twenty-five millennia."

~Well, hell!~ was the telepathic equivalent of Endark Droagn's thought. ~I guess that blows everything.~

3

The Ahmear's last comment was so unexpected that for a moment the whole group was nonplussed—except for Denny.

"We've got to get moving," the sergeant said, "and it doesn't much matter in which direction."

Sukiro looked disappointedly at the false crown at her feet.

"How do we get out of here?" Rikard asked Raebuck. But before she could answer, Droagn "spoke" again.

~Just go out those doors,~ he said, pointing at the arches.

"The Tschagan are out there waiting for us," Rikard told him.

~Tough luck,~ Droagn replied, ~that's the way I'm going to go.~

"Do you know a way to get to the surface?" Rikard asked, speaking and sending at the same time.

~I know several,~ Droagn said, ~but I'm not leaving just yet.~

"Look," Sukiro said, "we got you out of stasis, who knows how long you'd be there otherwise. Help us in return to find a hatch so we can call our ship."

~After twenty-five thousand years,~ the Ahmear said, ~you might as well have left me. I thank you, and you can come with me if you want to, but I'm going after the Prime. That's why I came here in the first place.~

"Let him go out the front door," Falyn said, "he'll distract the Tschagan"—she looked pointedly at Raebuck—"and we can find another way out."

"There should be a stage entrance around to the side," Raebuck said. "At least the tapes showed Tschagan officials entering from offstage somewhere."

"What I'm worried about," Falyn said, "is if the pirates can use the comcons, and come looking for us as we go up. We haven't really gone that far away from their base."

Droagn had gone to the edge of the stage, but now he turned back. ~These pirates,~ he said, ~these are the brain stealers you spoke of?~

"Yes," Rikard said. "They have destroyed half a million people so far."

~And how many of these brain stealers are there then?~

"We're not sure," Sukiro said, "but I guess about a thousand or twelve hundred altogether."

~You tackled a force that large all by yourselves?~

"We've taken casualties," Sukiro said, "we're not up to full strength."

Droagn looked out at the auditorium floor, and it was as if he was seeing all the Tschagan bodies for the first time. ~You seem to have acquitted yourself fairly well so far.~

"We've been lucky," Rikard said. "When Grayshard *projects*, they slow down enough so that we can see them well enough to shoot at them. Without him we'd have been wiped out by now, even though, until the last attack, none of the Tschagan had weapons."

Droagn surveyed the group again. ~Which one is Grayshard?~

Grayshard stretched up like a loose basketwork column. "I am."

Droagn seemed confused. ~There's nobody there.~

"There is indeed," Grayshard said, and set a short, sharp *projection* at Droagn.

~I can't feel you,~ Droagn said. ~There's no *neurostructure*.~ He looked enquiringly at Rikard. ~That's an automaton, isn't it?~

"Didn't you feel his attack?" Rikard asked.

~What attack? Look.~ He sent a tight beam telepathic signal at Grayshard. The Vaashka didn't waver. ~See, he doesn't respond at all, that's just a construct.~

"On the contrary," Sukiro said, "members of his race are the masterminds behind the brain pirates. They make their victims mindless with their psychic attack."

Droagn's eyes glowed as he stared at Grayshard and he snaked closer to the Vaashka. Grayshard crept backward a bit, apprehensive of this being who was invulnerable to his psychic weapons.

~I see,~ Droagn said, ~I've heard about a race like this, not animal as we know it but a fantastically advanced form of

fungus. But how can a mind such as his have any affect on
you?~

"We don't know," Rikard said, "but he can. And the pirates
have soldiers of his race, who ride on zombies they've created,
and if you meet them, you won't be able to stop them with your
own psychic abilities, and"—he looked at Grayshard—"can
those zombies use blasters?"

"Of course they can," Grayshard said. "They may be simple,
but they are capable of perfect control of the bodies they ride.
Those carrying the *warriors* and *administrators* take direct
orders from their masters, and work as if they were parts of one
body."

~Then I'll just have to avoid them,~ Droagn said, and went
back to the edge of the stage and slid off to the floor.

Raebuck stared after the retreating Ahmear, then exchanged
disappointed glances with Sukiro.

"There's nothing you can do about it," Rikard said to her
gently. "Now we've got to get out of here, while Droagn buys
us some time."

Raebuck nodded.

"It would have been the greatest find of all time," Sukiro said
to her.

Raebuck took a deep breath, then went toward the left end of
the stage. The others followed. "I hope I can find the way," she
said.

Then Droagn called to them from the floor. ~What the hell
did you use to kill these people with?~

Rikard paused to look back. "Blasters, most of them." he
said.

Droagn was fingering one of the corpses. Then he looked at
one of the rails that had been blown apart. ~I've never seen
such destruction, how could the Tschagan be any threat to
you?~

"They move too fast for us to see."

"Ha!" Droagn said, an actual vocalization. ~That makes
sense. Ah, tell me, are these brain pirates you came here after
armed the same as you?~

"Rather heavier," Sukiro said. "We brought in only our lightest weapons, because we didn't want to damage anything. The
pirates don't seem to care."

Droagn went from body to body, then looked back toward the

stage just as Grayshard was remounting Ming's shoulders. ~Are you being directed now?~ he asked the goon.

"No," Ming said, "I'm just giving him a lift."

~Let me see one of those ~blasters,~~ Droagn said.

"You've got to be kidding," Sukiro told him, "you're dangerous enough as you are."

~Show me how one works, then.~

Sukiro gestured, and Raebuck went to the edge of the stage, aimed her light blaster at one of the more intact corpses near the stage, and fired. The blaster bolt blew a thirty centimeter hole in the body.

Droagn stared at the remains of the corpse, wiped spatters of its ichor from its face. ~That's a terrible weapon,~ he said.

"Not at all," Sukiro told him. She gestured to Denny who drew her heavier, sergeant's blaster and shot away two rail seats. Chips and splinters flew, and the shots left shallow holes in the surface of the deck. Droagn backed off.

Sukiro said to Droagn, "The raiding parties, if they come back, and they're due back right now, are armed more like this." She held out her own blaster, larger even than Denny's. She went to the edge of the stage and shot down at the floor. The bolt blew a hole all the way through into the chamber below. "But don't let that worry you," she went on, "you can avoid them, I'm sure. Let's go, Raebuck."

~Wait a minute,~ Droagn said anxiously, ~are these pirates following you?~

"I have no idea," Rikard said, "probably not."

"What are the chances, Grayshard," Sukiro said in an audible aside, "that the pirates would like Droagn's brain and body?"

"If they could take him undamaged," Grayshard said, "he'd bring a tremendous price, the only known slave Ahmear brain. And whoever had his body to ride would have immeasurable prestige, though of course they couldn't ride it in public."

"Come on," Rikard said, "let's get out of here. There's no chance the pirates will even know he's here." He was embarrassed by the ruse, and by playing along with it.

~I believe you, Rikard Braeth,~ Droagn said, ~but I prefer not to take that chance. Let us strike a bargain. I came here for the Prime, and I will not leave without it. I know where it is. Come with me, and I will protect you from the Tschagan as best I can—~

"Grayshard can do that," Sukiro said.

~But he can't find you a way out,~ Droagn went on, ~and I don't believe you can either, Jania Raebuck. Your uncertainty is all too clear, and we are not where you think you are. Help me find the Prime, and I will take you back to the surface, if you will protect me in turn from those pirates, should they appear. And I may need a way to get off this station, if my ship has been damaged which, considering the nature of the Tschagan, and the amount of time that I've been here, is almost a certainty.~

"My friends have been playing with you," Rikard said, "hoping to bring you to something like this."

~I know that, but those blasters are real. And too much time has passed, if I get out of here I'll be rather at odd ends, and I need to learn the present situation among whatever star nations now exist before I go back to find my people. You can help me with that. Do we have a deal?~

"We do," Sukiro said.

~Then come with me.~ Then Droagn started snaking up the sloping auditorium floor toward the arches.

"Let's do it," Sukiro said, and they all came off the stage after her.

But instead of going out one of the arches, the Ahmear led them to a corner at the back of the auditorium, where he fingered an area of the set of triple dark blue stripes. A service hatch slid up, beyond which was a very broad ramp that spiraled both up and down. The walls were cream colored instead of light blue, and there was only a single triple black stripe, not dark blue, along the wall, at shoulder height. The ceiling was more yellow than amber, and the floor was pebbled, a bluish gray.

~This is the way most of the trophies were brought in,~ Droagn said, ~and it leads straight to a ship's hatch at the surface. But first I want to go down. Do we still have a deal?~

"We do," Rikard said, and they followed the Ahmear deeper into the now not so derelict station.

4

The ramp descended a long way, with here and there a landing, at each of which was one of those service hatches which nobody but Droagn seemed to know how to work.

"How do you know about this stuff?" Sukiro asked the Ahmear.

~I studied their architecture.~

"The Tschagan just let you do that?" Rikard asked incredulously.

~Of course not. A few of their stations fell into our hands, back when they were just coming out of their system.~

"I didn't know there were any Ahmear around then," Raebuck said.

~A few of us stayed in this part of the galaxy, just to keep an eye on things as it were. We kept out of people's way mostly, but the Tschagan found out about us and didn't like us even being around. I guess we were too much of a counterexample. Anyway, they decided to try to take one of our bases—there were only ten of us in the crew—I wasn't one of them of course, that was before my time—and they lost.~

"What happened to them?" Rikard asked.

~I don't know, shipped back home I suppose.~

"So that gave you access to their ships," Sukiro said. "How did you get to their station?"

~They towed it in themselves, and set it up sunward of where our base was located. It was just a small red star, no habitable planets, but that was the way we liked it—keep out of people's way. We are not at all a warlike race, though we used to be way back in our history, but when somebody comes shooting we can defend ourselves. This happened in a couple of places, and we wound up with three of their stations under our control. No sense trying to give them back, so we took them apart to see how they worked and all.~

"This was before your time," Rikard said sardonically.

~Several hundred of your years before I was born. But then when I learned that the Tschagan had sacked Tromarn, the last place where the Prime was known to have been, and that there was no trace of the Prime after that—it wouldn't have been destroyed by anything short of a fission blast—I guessed that the Tschagan had taken it, and so I did some research, and decided that the Tschagan had it on their capital, where they kept everything else they'd stolen.~

"You knew that their capital was a giant space station?" Raebuck asked.

~It made sense. Their worlds were too vulnerable, you can move a station somewhere and hide it—as they did, after all. And since the Prime had been missing for something like half a million years, and was the only one of our devices we'd ever let fall into alien hands, I figured I'd go get it and bring it back.~

"All by yourself," Sukiro said.

~Why not?~

"You have your own personal starship, I suppose."

~Of course, or had. If the Tschagan haven't taken it apart.~

"But how could you know anything about this station," Rikard insisted, "from the other one's you studied? Surely it's a different design, and much larger."

~Larger, yes, but the basic scheme is the same. All the equipment works the same way. All the stations, and their larger ships, too, have these service ways. I think it's a racial holdover.~

"So how come," Sukiro said, "none of the rest of your people tried to get this Prime if it's so important?"

~I guess none of them thought to try. And besides, your space was an awfully long way off. The few Ahmear left out here on the frontier had been called back after the Tschagan affair. It took me a good half of a year, in your terms, to get here.~

"Distances are relative," Sukiro said, "how fast was your ship?"

~It takes a couple of days to get between our closest stars.~

"You came halfway around the galaxy on a chance?" Rikard said.

~I'm afraid I was not considered a very good citizen. A year or so away from home seemed like a good idea. I guess it turned out to be a bit more than that. There never were very many of us, by your standards, and we tended to roam around a bit. By now, there may be none of us at all back where I left them.~

At last Droagn stopped at one of the landings and opened a service hatch. They entered a broad corridor with a low ceiling and no doors. But this was just another of the service ways, which apparently interpenetrated much of the interior portions of the station.

"How much further do we go?" Sukiro asked.

~At the rate we're moving, at least another half hour.~

"You were in trouble with the law?" Raebuck asked.

~I guess you could say that. I'd rather not be, but life is otherwise pretty dull.~

"Sounds like you and Rikard ought to get along," Sukiro said.

~Indeed.~ If Rikard could judge, the Ahmear was smiling.

"Are there a lot more at home like you?" Denny asked in parody of the stock question.

~Something useful was usually found for people like me to do,~ Droagn said. ~I just didn't care to go along with it. I'm no criminal, I've never hurt anybody intentionally. I like to think that I've even done some good in my time. Bringing home the Prime would have been a real coup.~

"How come your government," Sukiro said, "if they knew where the Prime was, didn't just come and take it?"

~They'd tried negotiating with the people who had it any number of times. But nobody wanted to give it up. You have to understand that we're basically a peaceful people, and we didn't want to just *slither* in and take it.~

"But *you* were going to steal it," Rikard said.

~Hardly stealing, taking it from people like the Tschagan. Besides, I thought it would be fun.~

Indeed, Rikard thought, Endark Droagn was a kindred spirit.

~After all,~ Droagn went on, ~it was our policy to keep to ourselves as much as possible. But there are an awful lot of worlds out there, and lots of peoples. I couldn't just sit at home, I wanted to go places, do things. It's gotten me into plenty of trouble before.~

"So you came looking for the Prime," Rikard prompted.

~Well, yes, like I said, I thought it was a good idea to get away for a while. You folks don't seem too impressed by my telepathy, but the peoples where I live—or lived—were either frightened of it, or wanted to acquire it for themselves. No need to be frightened, I can't read your mind, though I can feel your neurological presence. And as far as I know, unless you have the talent˜—he looked at Rikard oddly—˜a racial characteristic, I'd thought until now—˜

"I was taught by the Taarshome."

˜Of course. They can do wonders. Anyway, unless you have the genes and the neurological structure for it—or are taught by the Taarshome—there's no way you can acquire telepathy. It's not what people think. And how you Humans can hear and understand me I don't know.

˜Anyway, I was just looking around on Li'kha'n and let myself get found out. One of their governments raised a ruckus with our Resident there—the people of Li'kha'n didn't know we were telepathic I guess—and things got kind of hot for me. But that was where I heard about the Prime—never mind how —and when my local mentor got all excited about what I'd done, I decided I could squash two bugs with one rock—disappear until things cooled down, and bring back the Prime into the bargain.˜

"And started off by going to your local library to study Tschagan architecture," Rikard said.

˜Well, not exactly. I went to Fremorsh, where my people are well known and accepted, and, ah, sort of told them a story. By the time word got back home, I'd learned what I needed to know and was gone. If I could have brought the Prime back, I would have been a hero. Maybe I still can be, if I can find my people again.˜

"On your own personal starship," Sukiro said.

˜It was only second hand, and not very big. Ah, my people have, over the millennia, developed a rather higher standard of living than most of the starfaring species we've met. Private starships are not that uncommon.˜

"And what did you do for a crew?" Sukiro asked.

˜Robotics. What else?˜

"And when you got here," Rikard said, "what did you do, just knock on the door and walk in?"

˜Of course not. Service hatch.˜

"But how did you avoid the Tschagan?" Denny wanted to know.

˜Well, that was a bit of a trick, they *can* move awfully fast. But I can see them, even so, and I can 'feel' their neurostructures, so I know when there're nearby. But I wasn't careful enough. When I was doing my research, I spent most of my time studying these service ways. I should have paid more attention to the sensing devices they have built into the walls. So somewhere along the way I must have tripped something, or maybe left other traces—I spent nearly ten of your days learning my way around.

˜In any event, after a while, they were on to me, and started trying to hunt me down. It was damn frustrating, because I'd just found out where the Prime was being kept, and it was a good ways off from where I was. They set a trap for me, and I fell for it.

˜I was cornered—there were maybe sixty or so of their soldiers—and they used some kind of electronic device I'd give my lower right arm to find out more about. It knocked me out and I was taken prisoner.

˜They tried to kill me—I guess they wanted to make a mummy out of me like they did with the other important prisoners they'd captured—but when they couldn't they put me into stasis. And except for a lot of strange dreams, that's all I remember until I woke up just now.˜

By this time they had come to the end of the corridor, and Droagn led them out through a service hatch onto a broad walkway above a dark space, the floor of which they could not see, as the ceiling was lit only over the walk and their headlamps were not bright enough to reach bottom when they looked over the chest-high railing. If there were walls, they were too far away to be visible.

"What kind of place is this?" Denny asked.

˜I have no idea, but the Tschagan seldom come here, so I suspect it's off limits except to technicians.˜

The railed walkway was five meters wide and, like most of the corridors, the ceiling above it lit up as they approached a darkened section, and dimmed after they left. Each section of illumination was only ten meters long, so they walked along in what was in effect a moving spotlight.

Several times they came to places where another, similar walkway crossed the one on which they were traveling, and once came to a section that was twenty meters wide and long, with one-meter catwalks angling off from the corners. Droagn did not make any turnings, but led them straight on until they came to where the walkway ended in a large iris, that was not set into the wall but suspended in the dark space, on a column ten meters wide which went both up and down into the darkness.

As was to be expected, on the other side of the iris was a spiral ramp. But this was a regular ramp, with the familiar pale blue walls, two triple stripes of dark blue, and milk-glass floor. They descended three levels, then went out an iris into an intersection of four corridors. And here Droagn hesitated for the first time.

~I was attacked here. I think we go that way.~ He pointed to the right.

After a while the corridor came to an end and they entered a large room. There were no furniturelike artifacts here, but there were a dozen or so of the round, black-topped tables, and counters along all four walls, each of which also had two doors. There were closed cabinets above and below the counters.

"This looks familiar," Raebuck said. "The museum I was looking for shouldn't be far from here."

~If you mean,~ Droagn said, ~a place where the Tschagan kept their trophies, then you're right. But how did you know?~

"I saw tapes made of the Tschagan propaganda broadcasts. I suppose there must be other museums."

~I'm sure there are, but I'm interested in only this one.~

"Because here is where the crown, ah, the Prime is kept."

~Exactly, but again, how did you know?~

"Because I saw it in that museum, or thought I did. It was just in the background, they were showing off something else instead, but I'd seen pictures of the Prime before, and I thought I recognized it. I didn't tell anybody about it, I was sure other students had made the connection, but I guess they never did. And then when we found you, and you had the false crown on your head, I thought that was it."

~How much do people know about this Prime of mine?~ Droagn asked, with something akin to wariness in his telepathic question.

"Not as much as they'd like. It's the only functional Ahmear artifact known to exist, the oldest artifact in the known universe. Generally it's referred to as the Crown of the Serpent. Everybody thought it was lost forever after the Tschagan razed Tromarn."

~And yet you recognized it in the background of a film made for other purposes. I will not let you have it, you know.~

"I know. But let's hurry up and find it so we can get out of here."

~The way is through there,~ Droagn said as he pointed to the near door in the left hand wall.

Beyond the iris was a short corridor, at the end of which was an antechamber, separated by open arches from a large room, three levels high, but without balconies at the upper levels. The floor of the room was perhaps two hundred meters on a side, and filled with stands, freestanding shelves, high pedestals, and low platforms, on each of which stood some kind of object, with other, larger things standing on the floor itself, or sometimes suspended from the ceiling, and other things attached to the walls, or on brackets.

It was a veritable wealth of stolen art, electronic devices, furniture, small vehicles. There were paintings, sculptures, tapestries, ornamental objects of every kind. There were ancient cars, small aircraft, space runners, even several oddly proportioned bicycles. Some of the electronic devices—communicators, stand-alone computers, perhaps home appliances—were broken, others were intact and possibly functional. There were beds, thrones, fragile chairs made of ancient wood, steel shapes designed for physiologies now unknown in the Federation or in any of the nearby star nations. Some items were smaller than a fist, and stood on their own special pedestals. Others were collections of similar objects sharing a shelf.

There were too many things to make sense of any of it. Rikard found that he was holding his breath, excited by the scope of the collection, wishing he could spend hours just looking around. And what would even a fraction of it be worth, if he could "liberate" it.

Droagn led them quickly past the displays to the far side of the room, where more arches opened into another part of the museum. The collection here was much the same—overwhelming—and arches in the distant side walls revealed hints of even more treasures stored away.

But Droagn had no time for any of this. They went on to yet a third room. Rikard sensed the Ahmear's excitement, and became apprehensive as they neared a display of what looked like tubular street signs. Immediately behind these multicolored rods was a chest-high pedestal, on which sat the duplicate of the crown Endark Droagn had worn while in stasis.

Except that it seemed somehow alive. Droagn slithered up to

the pedestal, his head towering above it. Rikard, Raebuck, and Sukiro were right behind, and watched as the Ahmear reached out with his upper two hands, took the crown—the Prime—off its pedestal and turned it over and over. There was power in the thing, even though there were no lights, no hums, no outward indications. It just *felt* alive.

Something special was happening here, and everybody seemed to sense it, but nobody knew what to do about it except watch as Droagn put the crown on his head and turned to face them with a strange expression which Rikard, sensing the Ahmear's telepathic overflow, could only interpret as triumph. Droagn's eyes glowed fiercely, his arms trembled as he lowered them to his sides. He coiled his lower body under him and rose himself up even higher.

Then the light went out of his eyes, and he relaxed so that his head was no higher than Rikard's. All four hands reached up to touch the crown tentatively. He took it off, looked at it again, touched it here and there.

˜Oh, well,˜ he said. ˜I guess it doesn't work on Humans.˜

"What were you going to do?" Rikard asked.

˜Just try it out. I would have kept my end of the bargain. But it is disappointing.˜

"I guess. What is it?"

˜An amplifier. It enhances part of our natural telepathic abilities, so that the wearer can communicate over longer distances than normal, and even control other beings to a certain extent.˜ He put it back on his head and stared at Grayshard. ˜It still works,˜ he said, ˜I can feel the Vaashka now. But it was made a long time ago, the technology has long been lost, and I guess it had to have been tuned somehow.˜ He removed the crown again, turned it over and over, then put it back on. ˜As convenient a way to carry it as any,˜ he said.

"Can we get out of here now?" Sukiro asked. She was staring at the crown with a poorly concealed covetousness.

˜I think that would be a very good idea,˜ Droagn said. ˜I—I think our hosts are beginning to wake up.˜

"The Prime can tell you that?" Denny asked.

˜No, it just enhances my own awareness of other neurosystems—I can feel yours quite strongly—and I'm getting a distant background sensation of increasing Tschagan mental activity. Of course, it could just mean that there's a group of them coming this way.˜

"Then let's get moving," Sukiro said. "And let us know when they get near so we won't be taken by surprise."

~I'll do that,~ Droagn said.

But instead of going back the way they had come, Droagn led them to an alcove to one side. ~No sense taking a round-about way,~ he said. ~We can go straight up from here.~

The back of the alcove was a large iris, which opened onto a ramp broad enough to allow three goons to walk side by side. They went up.

"How many of those Primes are there?" Sukiro asked Droagn as they ascended.

~Only this one, now. There never were very many, and those were kept for administrative use. Originally the system was to have been used as a weapon, but it didn't work that way.~

"I thought the Ahmear were pacifists," Raebuck said.

~Oh, we are, now, and have been for millennia. In fact, the system of amplifiers, of which this crown was the Prime, or the central controlling amplifier, contributed in its own way to our giving up our primitive, violent ways.

~Our normal range of communication is—ah—about two kilometers in your terms. With the amplifiers we could talk to each other anywhere on a planet, and from the ground to low-orbiting stations. After a while we developed other means of doing this, without the control functions, and every Ahmear child is so equipped at birth.

~The control system was still used for a while, to coordinate complex activities—ah, such as military maneuvers, and later certain exploratory expeditions. But eventually most of the system was just allowed to deteriorate, or was destroyed rather than thrown away where other peoples might find it.

~This device, however, was—ah—misplaced, and then it fell into ShaVaGa hands, and then was lost.

~We went through several changes of culture in the meantime, and lost a lot of history in the process. And lost the knowledge of how this thing was made and properly used at the same time. I don't know what someone could do with it, with the proper training. Or what our scientists and technicians could develop from it if they had it.

~That was my intention. We have—or had—a need for better communication over interstellar distances, and the Prime could have helped solve that problem. Maybe we've already solved the problem by now without it.~

They did not go all the way to the top of the ramp, but turned off at a landing where they entered a small room. But instead of going out the iris, Droagn opened another of the service hatches. ~There was probably an entrance like this down in the museum,~ Droagn said, ~but I didn't want to take the time to find it.~

"Are our 'hosts' getting any nearer?" Sukiro asked.

~No, but there are more of them awake now.~

The hatch did not lead to a ramp or a corridor, but to another room, big enough for all of them, and without any other exit. There was a bank of controls beside the iris. Droagn touched a silver button with a cryptic black symbol on it, and a panel slid shut over the iris. ~Service elevator,~ he explained. He touched another button, and they could all feel the increase of gravity as the elevator went up.

When the vator came to a stop they were still a long way from the surface of the station, and had to take another vator. The well down which they had dropped—how long ago?—had taken them very deep indeed. Again they stopped short of their destination, but there was no third vator here, and they had to go by more normal ways.

The corridors here were all two levels high, and there were few side doors. Ascending and descending ramps opened off small alcoves. They went up whenever they could.

As they came up one ramp Droagn slowed, made a soft hissing sound, and held out his hands to stop them. ~I smell villains afoot,~ he said, ~between us and the next ramp.~

Denny and Nelross led their goons out the door at the top of the ramp. Even though the iris snapped shut, the rest could hear the immediate sound of rapid and repeated blaster fire from beyond it. Then Denny poked her head back in through the door.

"We got a few," she said, "but the rest got away."

~It should be safe now,~ Droagn said, and the rest of the party went through the door into a corridor.

Several times during the next hour, as they went from ramp to ramp and level to level, they came across small parties of Tschagan. Sometimes one of the noncoms led an attack, but most of the time Grayshard and Droagn were able to use their peculiar psychic powers to drive the caterpillars away.

They passed through an area different from any they had visited before. Narrow ramp tubes led them up for short distances, then they ascended a long set of tiered ramps clinging to the wall of a huge chamber more than ten levels high, its ceiling supported by large columns, and with narrow balconies around the upper levels and around the columns connected by narrow catwalks with knee-high rails. They met few Tschagan, and those Droagn quickly drove away.

In one place they entered a chamber with no visible walls or floor, a dark place of freefloating catwalks that formed a maze in the air. Here there were occasional platforms like open rooms or offices, larger floors on which were typical "furniture," or floor-standing objects like those they had seen so many times before. Many of these now hummed, or blinked, or sometimes changed shape in slow, subtle ways.

They went over another huge open space, on broader catwalks this time, where occasional spotlights in a distant ceiling shone down into the spaces between the walkways, illuminating metallic and crystalline objects—machines of some kind—on the floor equally far below. They went through a succession of three-level cubical rooms, each with a huge floating object in the center, all lit now, blinking, clicking, sometimes rotating on an oblique axis.

There were small areas similar to those they had traversed before as well. And still, the few Tschagan they met were easily avoided or driven off. ˜But there are more of them coming awake, now,˜ Droagn said. ˜I can feel them, a background hum. They are not pleasant to listen to.˜

"Is it us?" Rikard asked, "Are they waking up because we got so far into their capitol station?"

˜I think it's because *I'm* awake,˜ Droagn said. ˜They were using me, they admitted as much when they put me in stasis. I think that somehow they were able to tap my telepathic abilities and use them to prolong the stasis effect. Even in stasis, after a thousand years you grow old, and then you die. And prolonged stasis can have a damaging effect on the nervous system and the psyche. I know they used stasis whenever they traveled, their starships are no faster than ours, or yours, and for them, a three day trip would seem to take far longer, subjectively—not that they're that swift intellectually, of course.

˜I had dreams while I was in stasis. You're not supposed to do that, but Ahmear are different, after all. One image that recurred was of somehow expanding to fill all space—that would be when they linked me to their central controller, and I became aware of the vast number of Tschagan connected through it to me. I remember feeling motion, not of my body so much as my mind. Time didn't seem to pass so much as cycle. I'm sure a psychologist would be able to interpret each of my dreams in terms of what was being done to me, since they weren't really dreams after all, but subliminal perceptions of reality.

˜And now that I think about it, the last of those dreams was at the end of a long period of utter peace—the time the station was completely shut down I'll bet. Little sparks . . . a kind of swirling off to one side—that would be when the first of these villains began to wake up. For a long while there hadn't been any awareness at all, so I'd guess the entire personnel had been put under—makes sense if they had an emergency they wanted to wait out.

˜And now they're all waking up, not all at once, just a few thousand at a time, if I can trust my senses. That false Prime, it wasn't just a mockup, it was the device by which I was connected to their stasis controller. When you took it off me, that was when they started to wake up.˜

"And now," Falyn said, "the stasis devices are shutting off automatically, in an orderly fashion."

"That's what I would guess," Sukiro said. "It will take a while before they're all awake, but then, my God, how many are there?"

˜Five or six million.˜

The remains of the three goon squads, a force that could intimidate cities, felt very small indeed.

At last they came to an area which, though different from the vestibule to which they had entered, was obviously the foyer to an external hatchway, with its floor of steel instead of milk-glass, and walls of ribbed steel instead of pale blue enamel. Along the side walls were platforms on which rested the vehicles that could only be space-cars, and at the far end was the air-lock iris. They opened this cautiously, in case there was no pressure on the other side, but there was. Ahead of them now was the broad, spiral ramp leading upward.

As they ascended Sukiro tried to reach the shuttle, or Captain Brenner on the gunship, by means of her comcon, but got no response by the time they had come to the top of the ramp. "They may be over the horizon," she said. "We don't know how far around the perimeter we've come."

"We've got to go out onto the surface, then," Denny said.

But many of the surviving goons had been wounded, and their armor had taken damage so that they were not proof against hard vacuum. They would have to wait below, in the vestibule. Rikard took off his impromptu Vaashka shield so he could put his vacuum suit on again, to accompany Sukiro and the goons with intact suits out onto the station's skin. Meanwhile Falyn, with Grayshard and Droagn, led the wounded below.

When Falyn reported that they were safely out of the lock area, Sukiro had Jasime go around the ledge that surrounded the ramp to the controls at the back of the hatch. Jasime didn't know how to recycle the air, so when the hatch opened, the atmosphere inside the ramp rushed out past them. They waited a moment, to clear the traces of frost off their face plates, then went out onto the surface. They were on a circular pad like the one at the other hatch, with the semi-dome rising behind them.

Once again Sukiro tried to signal the gunship, but could get no response. She tried on several emergency and service frequencies, hoping one of them would carry the distance, and at last she got an answer. Rikard had a radio in his suit helmet, and Sukiro had cut him into her personal circuit so that he could hear what was going on.

"We read you, Major," the voice from the gunship said. "Where the hell have you been?"

"It's a long story, Brenner. We need help."

"So do we," Captain Brenner replied. "I don't know how they avoided our scanners, but they did."

"Who did?"

"The raiders. All of a sudden, there they were. We never saw them at all until they were within optical range. They blew out our engines, and all the shuttle bays. Then they landed, near where you went in, and destroyed the shuttle there. We can't move."

PART
<u>SIX</u>

PART

SIX

1

For a moment Rikard couldn't believe what he had just heard, and apparently neither could Sukiro, who was just breathing deeply.

"What the hell happened?" she said at last.

"I don't know," Brenner answered. "We didn't even get a chance to return fire."

"Completely sensor-transparent," Sukiro muttered. "We've got to take that ship intact. How many casualties?"

"The entire engineering section. We're drifting out of orbit, but we're not going to crash."

"All right," Sukiro said. "How many personal propulsion units do you have?"

"Enough for everybody on board."

"Good. I want every goon into one and down here on the double, and have them bring down an emergency com-link field-node. Use every available optical scanner and keep all weapons fully manned. We'll take out the raiders from inside, and if we can capture a ship we'll come up and get you."

"Be sure and signal when you do, I intend to blast anything that moves."

"You do that. We'll have a beacon set up down here by the time the goons are ready to come out."

She broke contact and started giving instructions to the goons who, in fact, were already starting to rig the beacon. Quickly three telescoping rods were planted on the surface of the station, their top ends linked together. The beacon was attached at the top, and several emergency power packs were connected together and to the beacon by a long cable and set on the ground between the tripod's feet. Then the tripod was extended to its full height, something over ten meters.

"Maybe we should call in some help," Rikard said to Sukiro.

"We'll have thirty goons here inside of twenty minutes."

"I mean another ship."

"If we can take the raiders' ship, we'll be just fine."

"As long as it isn't booby-trapped, or we don't damage it when we take it—if we can locate it at all."

Sukiro turned to look at him. It was not easy to make out her expression through the faceplate of her helmet.

"I'm not used to calling for help," she said. Her voice was tight. She was silent for a long moment, then turned away. "But I think you're right. A lot of good it will do us. It'll take a gunship four days to get here from Shentary."

"Then we'll present them with a victory. And besides, we'll need more than one ship to carry all those prisoners and the brains."

"I guess you've got a point," Sukiro said, then, "Wait a minute, we've got some trouble downstairs."

"What's happening?"

"Good God, the raiders have come. Is that damn beacon rigged yet? We've got to get below!"

One of the goons turned from where he or she was adjusting a jury-rigged control panel. Rikard couldn't hear that end of the conversation, but almost at once Sukiro said, "Good, let's go."

As they hurried into the lock Rikard said, "I can't hear anything."

"Switch to Channel C," Sukiro told him, then, "I've lost them too. Somebody said something about raiders, then they moved out of range."

The last goon into the lock ran around the catwalk to the back, even as the others started descending the ramp, and triggered the lock closing mechanism, then jumped off the ledge to join the others.

"How will they get in?" Rikard asked as they spiraled downward.

"The best way they can," Sukiro answered.

They came into the vestibule. It was empty, but dust was stirred up everywhere and still hung in the air. Everybody cracked their helmets, the only way they could communicate with each other until the com-link field-node came down. Rikard removed his outer gloves too, so that he could complete the connection between his hand and his gun. And now he could hear, somewhere off in the distance, the sounds of blaster-fire.

The room beyond showed blaster damage. One of the other two irises was blown completely away. "They've got heavier weapons," Sukiro said.

They quickly went from room to room, following the trail of damage—smoked walls, pocks and holes in walls and cabinets, blasted tables, still burning electronics once concealed behind wall panels. The sounds of shooting got louder, and they hurried in the direction from which the noise was coming.

In the next room they found bodies, three pirates—or maybe four, it was hard to tell the way the blaster shots had blown them apart. The room beyond was empty except for damaged and destroyed Tschagan "furniture," and beyond that, three more pirates lay dead, strung out along the corridor. An iris at the far end was standing open, blocked by part of another body.

"On the double," Sukiro commanded, and the goons ran toward the open iris. The first there stopped short and started shooting through the door. By the time Rikard got there, right behind Sukiro, the battle on the other side had turned to a rout. They had come on the pirates from behind, and the floor of the large room was littered with a dozen still smoking corpses. The survivors had already fled.

There were four other irises to choose from. "Sukiro here," she shouted, "where are you?"

Three blaster shots in rapid succession gave the signal and the direction, the far door on the left. Sukiro's group hurried through it into a room where the pirates were just leaving. There was an exchange of fire, two pirates fell dead. But in the next room Hornower was hit and disabled, as the now fleeing pirates raced away through side exits. In the room beyond they found Choi with his helmet and head blown off.

"We're coming through," Sukiro shouted.

"Watch your fire," someone yelled back.

They passed through an iris into a long corridor. The remaining goons were two hundred meters or so down it. There were three dead pirates on the floor in front of them.

For just an instant it seemed to Rikard that the two groups of police would fire on each other, but recognition was swift. The goons rejoined in the middle of the corridor.

"At least," Sukiro said, "there were no Vaashka warriors with them."

"I don't think that was their main party," Falyn said. "There were only about fifty of them, and they must have sent people out in other directions."

"Let's get back outside," Rikard suggested. "We've got reinforcements coming, and we can pick any pirates off as they come out the hatch."

"That's a damn good idea," Sukiro agreed.

But then irises all up and down the corridor snapped open, just long enough for the raiders on the other side to fire once quickly. Most of the unaimed shots just pocked the wall, but a few passed through the group. There was no chance for return fire.

"Get down," Denny said, and blasted away the nearest iris. Sukiro took out another, beyond which Rikard could see pirates, taken by surprise. The goons facing the two blasted portals opened fire as Denny and Sukiro opened a couple more. Sukiro's weapon was powerful enough that the pirates on the other side of the iris were knocked backward by the blaster's blow-through.

They started back toward the airlock but as they passed more irises they snapped open, admitting more enemy fire. Denny and Sukiro did what they could to remove this advantage, but there were more pirates behind them now, and the iris ahead, though Sukiro had blown it away, let pirates in concealment in the room beyond fire with impunity.

"In here," Sukiro said, and led them into a side room. She blew out the far iris as they entered, Denny blew away those on either side, and the goons gathered in the center of the room, facing outward, with Rikard, Ming and Grayshard, and Endark Droagn crouching down in the middle of the group.

"We'll take it one room at a time," Sukiro said.

And then Rikard felt the first whisper of a Vaashka attack. "Seal up!" he shouted. His helmet wasn't adequate protection, even with the face-plate closed, so he groped in the space suit pack on his back, where he'd stowed the fragment of Grayshard's clothing he'd been using as a shield.

"Seal up!" the noncoms shouted even as he did, doing as they commanded. The goons responded quickly, but Gerandine, Brisabane, and Valencis, all of whose suits were fractured, slumped to the deck.

Rikard struggled against the oppression of the Vaashka attack as he dragged the shielding material from the pack and wrapped it around his head. The relief was immediate. But now every goon who's armor had been breached in combat was lying on the deck, facedown or with their arms over their heads. They could not defend themselves from the Vaashka warriors.

~Don't give up so quickly,~ Droagn said. He coiled himself up and picked up four goons, one under each arm. ~Take the easy way out,~ he went on, and slithered toward the far side of the room—away from the hatch.

Sukiro could not hear the Ahmear, but she understood what he was doing. "Pull back," she ordered, and the goons who were able assisted their stricken comrades away from the raiders.

That left only Rikard and Sukiro to cover their retreat. Together they backed out the way the others had gone. Sukiro's powerful blaster fired methodically at any movement in the room beyond. Rikard gripped his weapon, and as time slowed, picked his targets carefully. He felt Sukiro's hand on his shoulder, guiding him backward.

The goons that could still fire did so, the blaster bolts passing frighteningly close to Rikard and Sukiro. It helped.

As they retreated, they were able to make each shot count. Sukiro's blaster did more damage, but Rikard never missed. He backed as quickly as he could, feeling as though he were moving in slow motion under the influence of his time contraction. Then his .75 clicked empty. It seemed to take forever to take a fresh clip out of his belt and slip it into the weapon's butt.

They retreated as fast as they could. Rikard paid no attention to anything but the occasional glimpse of a raider coming into view. He only fired when he was able to take aim, many times he had to let a target go because it would take even him too long to bring his weapon to bear. Once he nearly fell when, backing through an iris, he stepped on Petersin's body.

His head and neck were protected from the Vaashka attack by Grayshard's clothing, but not his face. A Vaashka warrior, several rooms away, appeared momentarily right in front of him and he felt himself cringing. Sukiro's blaster fire made the Vaashka, riding its two zombies, duck back.

Rikard tried to keep pace with the major, even so, but the Vaashka effect was increasing. He wanted to stop, to sit down, to hide under a table, or inside a cabinet. Even with his accelerated senses, the effect was almost overwhelming.

But then the thought came to him, vague, half nightmare, why not turn that effect to his advantage, go ahead, slow down, if he looked at things in a certain way, the Vaashka attack augmented his time sense instead of countering it.

He let the feeling take hold of him, and now he seemed to be floating, backwards, watching the achingly slow movement of his enemies. There were so many of them. He fired, watched a pirate jerk backward as the heavy slug slammed through his chest, even as he was picking another target. He fired again as the spot of his sight entered the central circle of his target, and moved the gun away before the bullet had traveled half the distance.

He lost track of everything except aiming, shooting, and reloading. He continued to back away from the still advancing raiders, and subliminally became aware that there were fewer and fewer blaster shots coming from behind him. And then the inevitable happened. He reached for a fresh clip, even as he was squeezing off the last shot in his gun, and his hand found nothing at his belt. He was out of ammunition.

For an instant of time that seemed to go on forever, but that probably lasted less than a second, he froze in place. Deprived of his only meaningful activity, his mind went blank. He watched, though he did not care, as a raider carefully aimed at him and fired, and only at the last instant twitched aside. The bolt hummed past his head, the charge of hydrogen plasma crisping his hair.

He twisted in place, turned one hundred eighty degrees, started to run after his companions. His head was now fully shielded from the Vaashka attack. For a moment he thought he was alone, then he saw Sukiro, standing half in an iris, firing past him at the enemies now behind him. He rocked his weapon back in his hand so that the connection between his special glove and the gun butt was broken. His time sense returned to normal, so quickly that he seemed to be flying. He ran for the door and jumped through it even as Sukiro stepped out of the way. The iris closed, then fused as blaster shots struck it from the other side.

Sukiro grabbed his arm as he passed, and steered him toward a side entrance. As they ducked through she let go his arm and took a blaster from her holster and handed it to him. He looked at the weapon as they ran through the room. It was a regulation goon blaster. Then he holstered his .75 and took the police weapon in his right hand. He had never fired a blaster before.

They hit another iris at a full run. Or rather, they would have hit it had not the mechanism been designed for even faster approaches than that. Rikard had the longer reach, his hand was stretched out in front of him, aiming at the latch-plate. He didn't even feel it. The iris snapped open, they were through, and it snapped shut behind them again.

The room they were now in was larger, and as they hurried toward the far wall an iris snapped on their right and a goon stepped through.

"This way," Fresno shouted, and they changed direction in midstride. Fresno thought to keep the iris open for them, but stepped back when he saw they had no intention of slowing down. The iris snapped closed, but again, when Rikard reached out his hand for the latch-plate, it opened without causing them a half second's loss of motion. As it was, they nearly bowled Fresno over as they came through into a corridor.

"Which way?" Sukiro asked as they paused to let Fresno recover himself—a mere second's wait. The goon pointed to a ramp, at one side of the corridor, leading down. They ran again, for a moment leaving Fresno behind. The goon's power armor caught him up again quickly, and had Rikard had power assist they could have gone faster. "Don't stop at the doors," Sukiro said as they raced down the ramp. "Just hit the latch-plate on the run."

They came to the bottom of the ramp and raced along a corridor to where it elled. Taking Sukiro's instructions literally, Fresno charged through an iris at the corner. Snap, snap. Sukiro and Rikard came to it side by side. Snap, snap. Fresno was still ahead, going toward another door. They followed, through two more rooms, then into another corridor at the far end of which they could see several of their companions, in pairs, the whole helping the wounded.

They ran through two more rooms and another corridor, and finally caught up with the rest of the platoon in a short, two-level arcade, with a large, cube-shaped object in the center. Their relief at being together again was short-lived. No sooner had they stopped to take stock than irises on all levels and both sides snapped open to admit raider blaster-fire. Aside from the cube, only two meters on a side, in the center of the arcade, there was no cover, and at that the cube protected only one side.

Endark Droagn was the first to recover from the surprise of this attack. He dropped the goons he was still carrying and took their blaster, one in each hand. Maybe there was something in the way his eyes were constructed that allowed him to aim them all in different directions, but whatever it was, each of his shots was good, either hitting a raider in a doorway or blasting an iris. ˜Move that thing aside,˜ he shouted.

For a moment no one understood, then Falyn, Charney, and Jasime put their shoulders to the cube and pushed. Other floor objects had been too massive to move, in spite of their sometimes small size, but this one was different. It moved so easily that the three nearly fell on their faces.

Underneath the cube was a service hatch. Droagn lurched toward it, dropped one of the blasters, reached down and opened the hatch, even as he fired with his other three hands. Then he dropped the guns, grabbed a couple of the nearest still disabled goons, and dove down the hatch head first. The rest of the party, firing for cover and at least partially protected by the cube, quickly followed.

Again Rikard and Sukiro were the last to enter the descending ramp. Rikard scooped up one of the dropped blasters as he entered the service hatch. He and Sukiro backed down, as rapidly as they could, firing with both hands, and when the first of the raiders appeared in the opening above them, blew them away. The ramp spiraled until the curve of the ramp concealed them from the raiders now in full chase. They continued to back and fired up at the near curve of the ramp to keep the raiders from following too closely. In turn, the raiders fired blindly down at them and the blow-through from their blaster shots rained superheated gas and molten metal around them.

"All at once," Sukiro said. They each fired their weapons three times in rapid succession, then turned and raced down the ramp after their fellows.

The ramp ended in an octagonal chamber ten meters across. There was nobody there, and the dust on the floor was so churned up that they couldn't tell by which of the other seven doors their party had exited.

"We're sitting ducks," Rikard said.

"Not yet," Sukiro told him. She dashed back to the side by which they had entered and flattened up against the wall between the corner and the door. Rikard saw her plan and went to the opposite side. But now they would hit each other if they fired at people coming out the door. Rikard dropped flat on his face so he could aim upward, and Sukiro did the same.

As she did so, three pirates burst through from the ramp.

Rikard and Sukiro fired and took out all three. A moment later, two more came at full speed, saw their comrades too late, and were blown apart as quickly. The next raider came out simply due to momentum, and fared no better. No more came after that, though they could hear their enemy, on the ramp, muttering and cursing to each other.

And then—Rikard couldn't tell how many—a group of raiders leapt through the door and hit the floor rolling, firing back at Rikard and Sukiro as they did so. Their aim was spoiled by their motion, and was directed toward standing targets, and by the time they saw that Rikard and Sukiro were prone, it was too late, they were gunned down. But another group followed in the same way, spread out, and aimed lower this time while others reached their weapons around the corners of the doorway to fire blindly. Only the fact that Falyn and Glaine suddenly appeared at irises to either side, doubly armed and blasting at every exposed pirate, saved Rikard and Sukiro from destruction. This sudden defense surprised the raiders sufficiently that Rikard and Sukiro were able to kill those Falyn and Glaine missed.

Sukiro was nearest Falyn, Rikard Glaine, and while their rescuers filled the ramp entrance with a volley, they dashed toward their respective exits and out.

Glaine did not hesitate but led Rikard through another door into another octagon room, just as Falyn and Sukiro entered it. They all ran out yet another iris, up a short corridor into a third octagon room, then Sukiro and Glaine suddenly stopped. Behind them, Rikard could heard the sounds of heavy blaster-fire.

"Yah haa!" Sukiro shouted. "That's our people! They've hit the pirates from behind!"

2

The turnabout was almost instantaneous. The retreating goons, even the disabled and the Vaashka-struck, took new heart and, under Denny's command, turned against the raiders once more. They were the Goon Squad, after all, and the only thing to do was to go on the offensive, as few as they were. Only the worst of the wounded, Rikard, and Grayshard now riding on Endark Droagn, stayed to the rear.

The reinforcements, led by Sergeant Iturba and communicating by means of the com-link field-node, pressed the pirates from the other side, what had been their rear. They were armed with the heaviest of blasters, with which they blew out doors, smashed holes in the walls, and even occasionally shot holes in floor or ceiling. The pirates didn't have a chance. There was no place for them to go, and soon nowhere to hide.

The pirates from the returning ship, as they later learned, numbered over five hundred, and the base crew had originally been more than two hundred, but counting for casualties, fewer than six hundred of the raiders survived. Against these were fifteen of the original platoon, four of which were wounded, and thirty reinforcements. The pirates didn't have a chance.

The Vaashka had little or no effect on the reinforcements, whose armor was kept tightly sealed. The original platoon, now that their com-links were working again, sealed up too. And because of what Sukiro told them about the Vaashka, the reinforcements instituted a simple policy of blasting every one they saw.

At last, as their numbers were quickly decimated, the pirates started throwing down their arms in surrender, and eventually, in a complex of connecting rooms, the battle ended.

It took a while to get things straight. Wounded or Vaashka-affected goons disarmed and restrained the pirates. A few Vaashka, mostly administrators, were found still alive and taken prisoner. Grayshard instructed the goons on how to contain them, and how to disable the three Vaashka warriors that had escaped destruction. The blue-collar Vaashka driving the zombies were no problem, they were not intelligent enough to act on their own.

Rikard and Sukiro went from room to room, moving through the cowed and defeated pirates, more than five hundred of them filling several chambers. Most of these were Human, but many were Srenim, who seemed to have been in charge of the others, taking their orders directly from the Vaashka.

As Rikard and Sukiro finished the circuit of the prisoners, Rikard thought he saw a familiar face among the pirates on the far side of the room.

"What is it?" Sukiro asked. Rikard pointed. The man with whom he and Darcy had made the deal back on Nowarth was now looking at them.

Rikard and Sukiro went to meet him. As they neared, Djentsin said sardonically, "Well, if it isn't Jack Begin."

"Indeed it is," Rikard said. "Is this the other business you had to attend to?"

"As you see," Djentsin said bitterly.

"And when were you going to find the time to get the Leaves of Ba'Gashi?"

Djentsin half laughed. "They're in my suite, here on this station. I found them in one of the museums here."

"What's the matter," Sukiro asked, "your masters not paying you enough?"

Djentsin stared at her contemptuously. "They are paying me very well indeed," he said, "but what does that matter compared with recovering the Reliquiture? I fully intended to live up to my part of the bargain," he went on to Rikard, "but how about you? You can just take the Leaves now."

"How much of a hero would you be," Rikard asked him, "if the Archipopulos knew how you had gotten the Reliquiture?"

"That was just a trade with you," Djentsin said angrily, "and has nothing to do with this business."

"Just what is your part in this?" Sukiro asked.

But Djentsin stiffened his face and turned away.

"He was the one who recruited us," another pirate, angry and despairing, said.

"You must have needed money awfully badly," Sukiro said to Djentsin, "to have sold your own people into slavery like this."

"I never did," Djentsin shouted, "I never sold my people! What are you to me, or these other non-Human beings, to me? I'd do it again, and would continue to do it for as long as necessary. You're not important, only the Reliquiture is important. I don't care what you do to me, I would have quit this business as soon as I had the Reliquiture anyway. 'Jack Begin,' or whoever you are, you can have the Leaves, just take the Reliquiture back to Derolos."

"We have no deal anymore," Rikard said.

"But what is the Reliquiture to you?" Djentsin pleaded. "You can become my people's hero now, you will be honored forever, please!"

Rikard turned away, embarassed by the man's broken composure. "I'll do what I can," he said, "but I can make no promises."

"Indeed you cannot," Sukiro said. And as she spoke two special members of the goon squad came forward, in answer to her silent com-link command.

"Msr. Djentsin," Sukiro told the pirate, "I hereby place you formally under arrest on the charges of kidnapping, murder, conspiracy, resisting arrest, and almost anything else I can think of. I must inform you that our present circumstances constitute a state of emergency, and that on my authority, this station is now under martial law. Your normal rights of defense must be put aside as long as my police are still in danger from your other expeditionary team. If you assist us now by answering my questions, what you say will not be used as additional evidence against you. Will you cooperate, or must I use forceful measures? I can only guarantee that should that be necessary, you will not be physically or psychically damaged."

"What the hell," Djentsin said, and his voice broke. "I don't care. What do you want to know?"

Sukiro's interrogation was not harsh. With Rikard and the two special goons as witnesses, she asked the broken pirate questions, and Djentsin answered. Yes, there were two fleets of raiders, working more or less independently. Yes, the second team was out, and could come back at almost any time, an hour or ten days from now, he didn't know. Yes, the pirates had sensor-proof equipment, supplied by the Srenim, but he knew nothing about how it worked, the Srenim despised Humans and confided nothing in them.

The bodies stolen were indeed to be sold on the black market on Vaashka worlds. Djentsin didn't know how widespread the illicit practice was.

"It is more common," Grayshard said at this point, "than I would like to believe, or than most of our governments would care to admit. Using animals as carriers is not that much different from Humans or other species eating the meat of specially bred stock. Adapting wild animals to the service might be compared to your eating similar wild animals, when all such are supposed to be protected by law. Using the bodies of sentient beings, as these 'zombie' riders have been forced to do, is comparable to cannibalism."

"And what about the brains," Rikard asked.

"It is a complex thing," Grayshard said. "A Vaashka can *link* itself to neurological tissue, and resonate to its functions. I have not done it, I cannot describe the effect, except that it is exhilarating, and addictive. The more developed the neurological tissue, the more advanced the brain, the more powerful it is, then the greater is its effect on the Vaashka who indulges. The brains of intelligent creatures are the most effective of all, as you would guess. The interaction is both more intense, more interesting, and in a perverse way more prestigious. Many Vaashka indulge in vat-grown neurology, as your people consume alcohol. There is no harm and no stigma in that. It is tissue that was once independent that is addictive, and the more intelligent the source, the more addictive it is."

Sukiro found this all very interesting, but she had more questions she wanted to ask Djentsin, and Rikard decided to leave her to her job.

By this time the pirates were completely under control, and those who were fit were pressed into service to tend to the wounded of both sides, eventually to carry them back to the pirate headquarters, where they would be boarded on the raiders' ship. The Human raiders, leaders and followers, presented no problem, but the Srenim refused to cooperate at all. These were all carefully restrained with security flex. At last they were ready, and with two of the Human raiders guiding, they started back toward the pirate base by the shortest route.

But the base was some distance away, and as they went, they found lights already on in some rooms, and the ceiling lit in distant sections of corridor, and in one or two rooms a comcon screen was glowing, though blank. The pirates were as surprised by this as Rikard and the first platoon of goons.

"Well," Colder said, "we knew the Tschagan were waking up."

"Who are the Tschagan?" a pirate named Smith asked.

"The people who built this place," Rikard told him.

"But it's been a derelict for thousands of years."

"Not really, just under stasis."

It turned out that none of the pirates had had any experience with the Tschagan, and indeed didn't know who they were. But one or two of the Srenim, overhearing the conversation, began to pay attention.

Grayshard was still riding with Endark Droagn, who was accompanying Rikard and Raebuck, who were close behind Sergeant Iturba, Sukiro, and Djentsin. "It would seem," Grayshard said, "that there were always a few Vaashka warriors present among the custodial staff. They would be sufficient, I think, to keep away any of the few Tschagan who were awake during the pirates' occupancy of their base here."

"Why didn't the Tschagan wake up their whole complement," Sukiro asked, "when they knew there were intruders here?"

"I don't know," Grayshard said.

˜I don't think they could,˜ Droagn said. ˜With me plugged into their circuit, they were in a form of stasis that they wouldn't want maintenance technicians to be able to override.˜

"That would mean," Rikard said, "that all the attacks we experienced, at least until we got to the auditorium, were from the equivalent of janitors."

"Somebody woke up some soldiers," Sukiro said.

"There had to be some provision for arousing higher echelon administrators," Denny said. "Maybe when we diddled with that comcon, it set something off."

"But surely the raiders experimented with the comcons when they first found this place," Iturba said.

"No, we didn't," Djentsin said. "We never touched any of the electronics. It was totally alien, and we just assumed there was no power."

"But you had to use power for life support," Sukiro said, "and to keep those brains and bodies."

"We brought our own generators in for that."

"Then it had to have been the comcon," Rikard said. "I find that hard to believe, but it's just possible that when Falyn punched those buttons, that was the first time any of the elec-/

tronics had been used, and we somehow inadvertantly sent a signal."

"Ahh, I don't think so," Raebuck said. "More likely it was when I was fiddling with that big machine and turned it on."

"What does it matter what woke them up," Charney said. "What matters is that they are awake, and there's millions of them, and even a platoon and a half of goons won't be able to handle that many. We've got to get off this station right now."

"That's exactly what we intend to do," Sukiro said.

"What are you talking about?" one of the goon reinforcements, named Quinn, asked.

"This station isn't a derelict," Rikard said. "The people who built it are still on board. They were in stasis until just a few hours ago."

The remnants of the first platoon quickly informed their fellows as to what had happened, what the Tschagan were like, and how they had fought. Only the Srenim seemed unconcerned, though they listened intently.

"Do they know something we don't know?" Rikard asked Droagn.

~They could, and that makes me nervous. It's one thing to sneak into a place like this secretly. It's something entirely different when they know you're here and come looking for you.~

"You can't be sure that they're all going to wake up now," Raebuck said.

But even as she spoke a comcon screen blinked on. There was only a brief flicker-image of a Tschagan face looking at them before the screen went blank again. But the screen stayed on.

~I think they are all waking up now,~ Droagn said, ~and they are obviously very aware of us, and know where we are.~

"Do you feel air moving?" Denny asked suddenly.

"I do," Rikard answered, and so did everybody else.

"They've turned on the main ventilation," Falyn said.

"And look." Raebuck pointed at one of the strange, round-edged objects standing on the floor, set diagonally into the corner of the room they were passing through at the moment. It was blue, a meter tall, half a meter wide, and three meters long. It was striped and smeared with grayish dark brown, with things like red fingers sticking out of the middle of each face. The fingers were moving in and out.

"All the equipment is being turned on," Charney said.

"How long," Rikard asked Droagn, "would it take them all to come out of stasis?"

~It's hard to say. It feels like they're waking up about a thousand at a time, but I can't feel the whole station. It's been a while since I was disconnected from the circuit. I'd guess they could arouse the whole population in a matter of days, maybe a lot less.~

"I still don't understand why they put you in the center of the stasis circuit," Rikard said. "They had to have some other way of accomplishing the same thing, they couldn't depend on you coming and being captured."

~They just took advantage of the situation,~ Droagn said.

"It's really quite simple," Raebuck told them. "The Tschagan liked to dominate people, and use them. I think it gave them a kick knowing that a member of one of the most powerful and mysterious species in the galaxy was enslaved to their machine and them."

~That would certainly have great appeal,~ Droagn said. ~And I think we'd better hurry. It's hard to judge distances, but I can feel a number of Tschagan coming in our direction, and I don't think they're very far off.~

They hurried on toward the raiders' base, even as more and more of the objects in the rooms, the lights, the occasional electronic devices came on or began to move or change shape. They could all hear a slight humming now, further evidence that the derelict was a derelict no more.

"They're coming up to full power," Sukiro said. "What do you want to bet that they intend to try to reassert their position in the galaxy?"

"No bet," Rikard said. He nodded at a comçon screen as they passed. There, full in view, and slowed so that the Humans and others could clearly see it, was the face of a Tschagan.

3

The goons found it difficult to keep all their prisoners under control, but as more comcon screens came to life, and as other equipment behind panels in walls came on, the pirates became as eager as anybody to get back to their ship and away.

At last they came to the perimeter of the pirate base, where rooms had been cleared out but not yet converted to their new uses. The pirate leaders began to feel more relaxed, but as they went through an iris into an area that had been modified as a kind of common room dining hall, they found the Tschagan there ahead of them, waiting motionless until the first of the group had entered. They became almost invisible as they moved to attack.

Before the police could react the Tschagan opened fire, and a fusillade of shots came through other doors around the large room. The goons were still fully armored and not hurt by the small caliber projectiles, but the pirate prisoners were unprotected. The police returned fire and retreated from the room, but not before thirty or so of the prisoners nearest the front fell wounded or dead.

"Everybody back out," Sukiro commanded. "Keep the prisoners to the rear." With so few police, and so many prisoners, it took several seconds for the group to respond. The first platoon, though their weapons were lighter, kept to the fore and, when the irises in front of them started to snap, were the first to get off their shots. The more heavily armed reinforcements added to the barrage belatedly, and destroyed the irises in the process.

The Tschagan, in ambush, had not been ready for so quick a response, and it was several seconds before they attacked again. That was enough time for the police to get their prisoners moving away from the base. But the second attack, when it came, was from the two forward flanks. Again, the police armor was proof, but nearly twenty pirates fell dead.

Grayshard and Droagn were in the middle of the group, a room or two back from the attacks, and at first didn't know what was going on. But as soon as they got word of the ambush Grayshard had Droagn carry him back to where the other Vaashka were being kept. Sukiro and the sergeants were busy organizing the retreat so Rikard went along to keep track of things.

Corporal LeClarke, in charge of the Vaashka, wasn't pleased with either Droagn or Grayshard, but Rikard explained the effect the Vaashka warriors had on the Tschagan and LeClarke reluctantly let Grayshard talk with the prisoners. Rikard could not even hear their communication, half chemical and half telepathic, but the conversation obviously disturbed the prisoners, who waved tendrils and fibers around, changed form from spheres to columns to low disks and back again, and otherwise seemed to be resisting Grayshard's suggestions.

But apparently he was persuasive. "They will help us," he told Rikard. "They have no choice, defend against the Tschagan or die here."

It took a little further persuading on Rikard's part to get LeClarke to go along with the idea, but at last she gave in and, with four other heavy goons, accompanied Grayshard and the three Vaashka warriors as the rest of the group moved around them to the rear. When the first of the enemy bullets came through open or blasted irises, the four Vaashka, Grayshard and the three prisoners, projected their strongest attack. The gunfire stopped immediately, but the pirates nearby, without armor, also succumbed, and fell. None of the Srenim seemed affected.

Nelross and Falyn were present and knew what had happened. On their command unaffected pirates from farther back came forward to pick up their fallen fellows and carry them away. Grayshard held off until the first of these had managed to escape, but then had to project again when the Tschagan rallied. Rikard, LeClarke, and the heavy goons opened fire at the same time, and then retreated along with the others. Some of the pirates, nearly comatose from the two Vaashka assaults, had to be left behind.

The next Tschagan attack was longer in coming. When Grayshard and the Vaashka warriors projected, all Tschagan within range slowed drastically, and Rikard and the half-squad of heavy goons exacted a terrible toll. The Tschagan wore no armor at all, and even near misses burned them or, if hitting a wall or piece of "furniture," exploded with sufficient force that the side-flash and flying fragments also did considerable damage.

They fell back across a corridor and through two more rooms, where Sukiro, Iturba, and Denny were doing their best to regroup. This was complicated by a number of the pirates who, fearing the Tschagan more than arrest, were begging for their weapons back so that they could help defend.

"I think we've got to let them do it," Rikard said.

"I agree," Sukiro said, "but only the light weapons."

"Not the Srenim," Djentsin told her. Sukiro had been keeping him close to hand. "You can't trust them, not with anything."

"The Vaashka don't have any effect on them," Rikard pointed out. "And they've been listening to our conversation too much."

"All right then," Sukiro said. She gave an order that all Srenim were to be double-bound and taken directly to the rear, while the noncoms passed captured weapons around to those pirates who seemed to them to be most trustworthy.

This task was not yet finished when all the irises on the side toward the pirate base began snapping, and a fusillade of bullets poured into the group. The defenders simply laid down a cover fire, blasting out walls and doors, firing through every opening. The air filled with smoke as electrical equipment caught fire, and several of the soft Tschagan artifacts burst into greasy flames. Sukiro directed them to keep up the fire until every wall surrounding the rooms in which they stood had been breached at least once, and blaster shots had gone into rooms beyond.

Then she called a cease fire. The area around them was ruined. Tschagan body parts lay everywhere, and thirty-four more pirates had fallen. There was less damage on the side away from the base, and here all the unarmed pirates, the Vaashka administrators, and the Srenim were gathered. The remaining troops, pirate and police, formed a protective arch between them and the direction of the Tschagan assault.

"Time for drastic measures," Sukiro said. She cleared an area in the middle room, then blasted a hole through the floor. The decking was half a meter thick, and it took a second shot to make a hole big enough for a goon in armor to pass through. Sukiro stepped into the hole, firing between her feet at the floor in the room below as he fell in the low gravity, and a second time even before she hit. Three heavy goons followed immediately, then the unarmed prisoners were herded through into the chamber below.

As the rest of the group waited their turns, irises several rooms away began snapping as the Tschagan at last launched another attack. Grayshard and his Vaashka warriors projected, the police and armed pirates fired through every opening, and the attack stopped. The rest of the group descended.

They dropped, one at a time, down one level, then another. Rikard, Droagn, and Grayshard with the goons carrying the three Vaashka warriors were the last to go. At the third descent they met Jasime and Raebuck, who were directing people toward a down-ramp. The others were far ahead. At the bottom of the ramp they passed through several rooms. In each of them, the comcons were glowing.

"I'll bet they're recording everything," Jasime said.

"Not very good propaganda," Rikard said, "they're losing far more than we are."

"They'll just edit the damn tapes," Raebuck said as they at last rejoined the rest of the group, who had paused in a large and otherwise empty room.

There were far fewer of the pirates now, and Lakey, Valencis, and Woadham, with their damaged armor, had fallen. "The best thing we can do is run," Sukiro said.

"How far?" Iturba asked.

"Until we find a way out. We've got to get word to the rest of the Federation. If we don't, and the Tschagan bring this station up to full function, who knows what kind of threat they'll pose, especially if they take us by surprise. That's got to be our highest priority, regardless of cost."

"We won't get out by going deeper," Denny said.

~It is still the best way,~ Droagn countered, ~though it's not the shortest. I can take us to my ship, I think.~

"How can you do that?" Falyn asked.

Droagn tapped the crown that he still wore on his head, now half-concealed by Grayshard's tendrils. ~One of the side benefits,~ he said. The heavy goons didn't understand this, but Falyn was satisfied.

"Can your ship hold all of us?" Sukiro asked Droagn.

~No, only three or four, but there should be other ships in the same place.~

"Are you in contact with your ship now?"

~Not contact, but I can 'feel' where it is.~

"Then let's get moving," Rikard said.

But Endark Droagn was not as confident of his way as he was pretending to be. He hesitated at irises, and changed direction frequently. "Are you sure you know what you're doing?" Rikard asked him quietly.

~I'm looking for the path of least resistance,~ Droagn said. ~There are Tschagan not that far away.~

"Are we being pursued?" Grayshard asked.

~Not at the moment.~

They passed through strange territory, huge chambers where elevated walkways led between sunken offices, with no other partition or ceiling support. Some of these 'offices' were only half a meter or so below the level of the walkways, others were as much as three meters lower, and had side ramps leading down to them. Each had a black-topped pedestal table, but no other 'furniture.'

After ten or twelve of these huge chambers the nature of the architecture changed. The rooms were now not so large and were all on one level, but there were only open arches connecting them, no irises. There was plenty of furniture here, and those which could blink, or hum, or move, or change shape, all did so.

This eventually gave way to rooms of a more moderate size, but here each room was bisected or quadrisected by sunken walkways. Each room was half a meter or a meter lower than the last, and the walkways sloped down as they passed through.

They left this area at last to enter a short, broad corridor, with no other doors except a large iris at the far end, fifty meters away. Here Droagn stopped.

~We've got to go this way,~ he said, ~but there are Tschagan beyond that iris.~

"Then let's do it right," Sukiro said. She brought the goons who were carrying the Vaashka warriors up to the portal, but to the side so they would be out of the direct line of fire. Droagn and Grayshard took up a position with them. Then she organized a triple rank of heavy goons, right in front of the iris. The rest of the company she kept back. Then, taking the greatest risk herself, she reached out with a prybar and touched the latch-plate in the middle of the iris. As she did so, the Vaashka projected as strongly as they could, and the ranked heavy goons opened fire. Several of the shots hit the edge of the iris, fusing it open.

When they went through they saw one or two blurs departing through irises on the sides. The far wall was half blown away. The floor of the room was covered with the charred residue of a number of Tschagan. There were no weapons.

"Through here," Droagn said as he came in, and led them to one side, where he opened a service panel in the wall between two irises. Beyond it was a long, yellow corridor with what looked like a gray conveyor belt set into the blue gray floor. It wasn't moving, but as soon as Droagn slithered onto it, he started sliding away at great speed.

As quickly as they could the others followed. It was a conveyor running along the hall, an archaic form of molecular belt. It did not itself move, but anything or anyone on it did. Rikard wondered how one could come back the other way.

The company was spread out as they whisked along. They passed several nodes, places where the corridor widened and one could step off the belt if one wanted to. Once they came to a place where the corridor and its belt split in two, in gradually increasing arcs to right and left. Droagn led them to the left. As Rikard passed the fork, he wondered how it was that none of them had gone the other way by mistake.

They went on for a long way, Rikard could not guess how many kilometers. He wondered just what kind of range Droagn's Prime had, that he could "feel" his ship so far away. They took another fork, to the right this time, and later passed one angling backward. It seemed to Rikard that they were descending as they went along.

Then Droagn slithered off the belt at a node, and as he did so the goons and pirates closest behind him slowed. Those in the rear kept up their full pace until it seemed they would crash into the ones ahead, but the belt was "intelligent" and didn't let that happen.

The service hatch at the back of the node led them into a three-level arcade. As the first of them entered they saw the blurs of Tschagan, all of whom quickly left.

"They know where we are now," Sukiro said, then to Droagn, "Were you aware of them?"

~There were few,~ the Ahmear answered, ~and felt like those we destroyed before, mere technicians. Blaster-fire would have brought the attention of others. But we must hurry now.~

He crossed the arcade to the far side where a spiral ramp, one of two in that wall, led upward. On the third level balcony he turned right and out a broad open arch into a long corridor.

They raced along until they came to a mid-corridor ramp leading down, and went down again, even as swarms of Tschagan came at them from behind. These were armed, and in the narrow confines of the corridor, their fire was devastating. One of the Vaashka warriors and two of the administrators were torn apart by bullets, many of the remaining pirates were killed, and even two of the heavy goon reinforcements were wounded and had to be helped along by their fellows. It was small comfort that the goons' return fire was equally as devastating, that by the time the last of them had gotten to the ramp, none of the Tschagan soldiers were left.

The ramp led them down through another parallel corridor, then farther into a transverse corridor where Droagn led them to the left.

"Where are we?" Rikard asked.

~I have no idea, only that my ship is ahead. At least there don't seem to be many Tschagan here.~

The corridor was not very long, and they had to pass through a succession of rooms. Each of these held one, two, or three devices of the types they had seen before, but unlike the area they had just left, all of them seemed to be still shut down. After a while, even the ceiling lights were off, and they had to turn them on as they passed through.

"Even granting," Rikard said to Sukiro, "that most of the Tschagan could still be in stasis, it seems that this place is awfully understaffed."

"What I'm wondering," Sukiro said, "is where they've been sleeping all this time. We haven't seen anything like a dormitory."

At last Droagn stopped. ~The ship dock is above us,~ he said. ~We've got to go up now, find a ramp.~

They checked out every iris and, one room over, Yansen found what they were looking for. They ascended quickly, but the ramp went up only one level.

~Here,~ Droagn said, pointing at a blank wall. But it was not truly blank, there was a service hatch, and beyond it was a gravity shaft. Droagn, carrying Grayshard, and six heavy goons went first, then the others followed, ten at a time, all the way to the top, where it ended in a kind of vestibule.

As the last of the police reached the vestibule Droagn suddenly shouted, "Tschagan!" ~They're coming from all sides.~

The police barely had time to face the walls before the irises, two on each side, opened with a crushing hail of bullets. The goons' return fire was instantaneous, smashing walls and irises, blasting Tschagan bodies to vapor and slime. Nearly half the remaining pirates, including all but two of the Srenim, were killed, as were two of the Vaashka warriors and all but one of the administrators. Droagn and Grayshard escaped injury, but Sukiro was hit. Petorska and Charney were killed, and three of the heavy goon reinforcements were wounded. Grayshard and the surviving Vaashka belatedly projected, and the attack turned. Goon blaster-fire tore away more of the walls of the vestibule and of the rooms surrounding.

"We will not survive," Grayshard said when the firing stopped. "There are too many of them."

"But they're not very creative," Rikard said. "There's a definite pattern to the way they've been attacking us. We can counter that pattern, and—"

But before he could finish a burst of gunfire came from a snapping iris several rooms away, rooms the walls of which had been blown away, leaving a clear shot between Rikard and the iris. Though Rikard wore no armor his leathers and meshmail served the same purpose, and should have been proof against the small caliber weapons the Tschagan were using. Would have been, perhaps, if he hadn't taken a full burst in the chest.

For an instant it was as if his weapon-induced time dilation had come on of its own accord. The world around him seemed to stop. He felt no pain, just a tremendous force pushing him backward. He was half surprised to see his feet flying up in front of him. He was going to fall. He tried desperately to get his hands behind him, but they seemed to be waving around in the air at his sides.

And then he hit the deck, sitting, and time returned to normal. His chest felt like he had swallowed something huge and it had gotten stuck halfway down. He saw, without caring too much about it, that the iris from which the shots had come had been blown away by blaster-fire. He felt very much like lying down, so he did.

He felt Droagn's voice in his mind, though the Ahmear's words were not directed at him. ~Here!~ Droagn said. His face came into Rikard's view as he bent over him. Sukiro was yelling something about getting out of there—just when they'd gotten it all opened up. It was hard to focus on Droagn's eyes, there were no pupils. He felt somebody take his arms on either side, it was Raebuck and Sukiro. They helped him to his feet. He tried his best to run along between them, but his legs weren't working properly.

They went through an iris into a room, the details of which escaped Rikard completely. He was just beginning to figure out that he'd been shot, and was wounded, probably badly. His chest no longer felt huge, but did begin to hurt. That frightened him, he wasn't used to pain. He was able to get his legs to work a little better as they went through the room and into another. The shock of being shot was beginning to wear off, but now he felt weak and uncoordinated. He wasn't sure, but he thought there was no fighting going on at the moment.

He didn't try to keep track of the people around him. It took all his attention just to hold on to consciousness. They went through this room and into a large space that, for the moment, completely eluded his comprehension. Then even as the pain in his chest became sharper, and he began to be aware of his legs actually working, if clumsily, the scale of the place became clear. They were in a starship hangar, a place that could never have been built on a planet, only on the largest of space stations. Standing on their ends, supported by gravity fields, were dozen of starships of all sizes and shapes.

The iris by which they had entered the ship museum was large, broader than high, but there were no other irises within sight along the long wall. When everybody was inside, two goons fused the iris shut, to slow down the Tschagan at least a little bit.

Endark Droagn rose as high as he could on his coils and looked around. ˜I can't see it,˜ he said, ˜but it's here, over that way.˜

Now that they were not running Rikard was able to carry some of his weight. He felt something dripping down from his chest to his belt and seeping through into his pants. But the pain in his chest got no stronger, and though he felt weak, his thoughts were clearing.

Each ship, most of them variations on the familiar Federal spindle shape, stood on end, the tip of its flicker spike floating a meter or so above a circular platform as big around as the widest part of the ship above and a meter or so above the general level of the deck. Only about half the platforms were occupied, and there was enough room between them to see far into the distance. The ceiling of the whole hangar was lit, but not brightly, and Rikard could not see the far walls.

Droagn led them between the ships for perhaps a kilometer, and then stopped. ~There it is,~ he said, and pointed at a strange craft a few hundred meters farther on.

There were what looked like three habitation disks, stacked on top of each other, with only the smallest of domes atop that, and below them a long spindle that tapered smoothly from half the diameter of the lowest disk to one quarter that, where there were three more smaller disks of different sizes. Rikard could see nothing that looked like a power sphere, or a fuel sphere, and in place of the telescoping cylinders of an inertial drive there was a dodecahedral shape, and instead of a flicker spike there was a long rod ending in a small ball no more than three meters in diameter.

But portions of its hull had been removed. In one place a mass of wiring hung from a gaping hole. ~I guess I have to go with you after all,~ Droagn said.

"I've never seen anything like it," Sukiro said, staring at Droagn's ship in utter fascination. It was not that big, but larger than a typical Federation scout.

"He said he could carry only three or four of us," Denny said.

"Look at that wiring," Falyn said. "How can you run a starship with wiring?"

"We've got to find another ship," Sukiro said. She stared around the hangar in a futile effort to find one that looked familiar.

Behind them they could hear the sounds of the Tschagan trying to break through the sealed iris. It wouldn't hold for long, the Tschagan would have heavy equipment for repair work, and it was just a matter of time before it was brought and set to the task.

"The further we go," Rikard said, shocked at the sound of his voice, "the longer they'll have to look for us once they break in."

"Save your breath," Sukiro told him, but she and Raebuck started walking him away from the sound of the Tschagan.

"You can't judge the capacity by the size," Denny said as they passed ship after ship.

~I think I can,~ Droagn said, ~to an extent. That one is mostly hollow, but I'd bet it was a cargo ship.~

"It looks like one," Sukiro said. "I think. But more important, we've got to find one that's functional." She turned to Droagn. "Can you tell that too?"

~Not very well,~ Droagn answered. ~But I can tell if a ship has residual power.~

They did not go in a straight line, but rather tacked off to the right and wove between ships, in order to put as many of them as possible between them and the iris. They passed by several ships that were obviously nonfunctional, or obviously too small, or that Droagn said had insufficient internal space in spite of their size. But at last they came to one that Droagn said seemed to have lots of room inside as well as residual power.

They had thought Droagn's ship was unusual, but this one was even stranger. There was a clearly defined flicker spike, but it had seven small rings around it. Above that was a bundle of vertical cylinders, probably six around a central seventh, in lieu of the inertial drive. Then there was a wasp-waist, with a thin disk at the narrowest part, and above that a half-sphere surmounted by a larger sphere, with another sphere the size of the first atop that.

"Is there anything better nearby?" Sukiro asked Droagn.

~I can't tell.~ The Ahmear reached up to adjust the crown on his head. ~I really don't know how this thing works.~

"If we can get inside," Iturba said, "the Tschagan will have a hard time finding us, and it sounds like they've almost broken through the iris."

"That's a good point," Sukiro said. "The trick is, where is the hatch, and how do we get to it?"

"I think I can help," Grayshard said. "Take me to the ship."

Droagn slithered over to the platform above which the ship was floating, and up onto it. ~What's holding the ship up?~ he asked, ~I thought the gravity would cut off here.~

"More likely a specific repulsion field," Falyn said as Grayshard climbed down off Droagn's shoulders and over to the tip of the flicker spike.

The Vaashka reached up with a bundle of fibers and took hold of the spike, then crawled up it toward the first of its disks. They presented him no obstacle, he just flowed around them. And where he flowed the surface of the ship was stained a dark, thin, iridescent red.

Grayshard continued to climb, almost as quickly as he could move along the ground, spread out in a web of fibers so as to present as much of himself to the ship's surface as possible. He slowed a bit as he navigated the overhanging cylinders of what they assumed was the inertial drive, then went more quickly again up the first part of the wasp-waist. He had to spread himself very thin as he crawled along the underside of the disk above that, but there was never any question about the firmness of his hold. Where the way was more difficult, the trail of red corrosion he left behind just got darker and more iridescent. Even if he had fallen, the air resistance over his now greatly distributed surface area would have let him land unharmed, especially in the station's reduced gravity.

As he climbed, Sukiro issued commands to the goons, who spread out, facing in the direction they had come, prepared to meet an attack.

"I've got a hatch," Grayshard called down from the equator of the largest, central sphere.

"Can you open it?" Sukiro called back. Back at the hangar entrance there was a rapid series of small explosions, then silence.

"I think so," Grayshard called down. Though the iris was not visible from here, the goons were ready, and the surviving pirates, now fewer than two hundred, took cover behind them.

From the iris came a strange ripping sound.

~They're inside,~ Droagn said.

"So am I," Grayshard called down. "Just a minute."

The people below waited. There were no further sounds from the iris. ~They're taking their time,~ Droagn said. ~Relatively speaking.~

Then there was a whining from overhead, and Rikard looked up to see a hexagonal opening in the side of the largest sphere, from which a beaded cable was descending toward the deck.

"Let's not waste any time," Sukiro said. "Wounded first."

The end of the cable touched the edge of the platform. The wounded goons who were able to immediately started climbing. Those who could not were carried up by other goons using their armor's power assist. Raebuck picked up Rikard and lifted him up toward the hatch. Droagn followed immediately after, coiling tightly around the cable and using all four hands to good advantage. The cable creaked under his weight.

The chamber inside the hatch was of a peculiar shape, neither cubical nor spherical nor wedge shaped, but oddly angled with no clearly defined deck. Several of the inner surfaces had other hatches, now open as those who had come in first made way for those to follow. Beyond were other spaces, equally as irregular if larger.

Grayshard was pressed against the side of the external hatch, a bundle of his fibers disappeared into the crevices of a control panel. Rikard couldn't help but think how useful a talent like that would be in opening safes and other locked doors. Droagn's head appeared in the outer hatch, then the goons with Rikard carried him farther into the strange ship.

There were no features to this next chamber, but panels on most of the surfaces hinted that whatever equipment and furniture the original owner had used was kept out of sight. It was still crowded in here, as the pirates began to come in through the hatch, so they moved farther in.

The next chamber was much as the first, somewhat larger, and longer. Here there were what looked like handles set into the walls, between the corners and panels, where there weren't other hatches. It didn't look like there were corridors here at all.

At last Rikard heard a thin whining sound coming from the area of the outer hatch, and a moment later a dull thud as it closed. A moment after that Sukiro came through the hexagonal inner hatch between chambers. "Which way's the damn bridge?"

"We're looking for it," Falyn said.

"This place has been stripped," Sukiro said. "Look at those brackets."

"I thought they were handles," Rikard said.

"Maybe this is a dead ship after all," Falyn said.

˜There's power here,˜ Droagn said, ˜I can feel it.˜

Then somebody called from another part of the ship, and word was relayed, they'd found the bridge—maybe.

"Find room for everybody," Sukiro told Iturba. Then she started toward the supposed bridge.

"I'm coming too," Rikard said.

"The hell you are," Sukiro told him, "you're bleeding all over the place."

Rikard looked down at the slanting surface on which he was sitting. There was more blood there than he liked to acknowl-

edge was his. His shirt was soaked with it, and the front of his
pants—and now his seat as well.

~I'll carry him,~ Droagn said as Grayshard came into the
chamber. The Ahmear reached down and picked Rikard up with
all four arms, making him as comfortable as possible. Droagn
felt as if he were made of iron.

They followed directions from other goons in other
chambers, all polyhedral, of different sizes and shapes, until at
last they came to one that was very much larger, perhaps ten
meters across. Its outer walls were composed of so many facets
that it might almost have been spherical.

And it did sort of look like a bridge. At least there were
what could have been viewscreens, set into many of the faces
of the chamber, though they were placed almost at random.
And there were several clusters of instruments and possibly
controls, projecting from some of the larger facets, but they
too were positioned in nonsensical places. Except for one set,
which composed a half-meter sphere held in the middle of the
chamber by four finger-thin rods, tetrahedrally arranged, connecting it to the walls. The only thing wrong was that it was
out of reach from any of the slanting surfaces that now served
as the deck.

All the able goons present set the gravity-enhancers in their
armor to reverse, so that they could float around the chamber
and look over the equipment. There were signs that there might
have been other furniture here, but it had long since been removed.

"At least the electronics seem undamaged," Jasime said.
"None of the panels have been tampered with."

"Keep your hands off everything," Sukiro ordered.

And then Rikard felt a wave of dizziness. He was glad
Droagn was holding him so securely. He lost interest in what
was going on around him and just let himself relax.

~He's passing out,~ he heard Droagn say, wondered for a
moment who the Ahmear was talking about, then felt himself
being put gently on the slanting deck.

"We need a medic here," Raebuck called. Her voice sounded
very far away, but when Rikard looked for her, he saw she was
kneeling over him. Almost at once another face came into view.
It was Sameth, one of the goons who had been left on the
gunship. How had he gotten here? His helmet was off, and he
was trying to undo Rikard's jacket. Rikard fluttered his hands

up to keep the goon away, but Raebuck undid the fastenings, and she and Sameth opened his jacket and his meshmail.

"He's been hit three times," Sameth said. He shook his head. "I don't have the equipment to deal with this." His face receded as he sat back.

"Oh, well," Rikard sighed, or thought he did. He wasn't feeling too much pain now, just a distant ache in his chest. The blood, the lack of pain, the feeling of lethargy and dizziness. His wounds were fatal. Dammit, it wasn't fair, there was so much to be done. . . . They shouldn't be wasting time with him, they had to warn people about the Tschagan.

"Don't talk crazy," Raebuck said. "We're going to get out of here."

"I don't think so," Rikard said. His voice was a mere whisper.

"Be still. Save your strength."

"Do as she says," Sukiro said. Rikard could barely turn his head to see the Major kneeling beside him. Where had that other goon gone?

"Where's Darcy?" Rikard started to say, "I need to talk to Darcy."

"After we get you to a hospital," Sukiro told him.

Nearest one's only four days away, Rikard said, or thought he did, but the words sounded like coughing instead, and he saw drops of blood splattering on Raebuck's armor.

A creamy white tangle of coarse fibers, tipped in red, swam into his view. He heard a monotonous voice saying something, but it was a moment before the words made any sense. "Can you trust me?" Grayshard had asked.

Rikard tried to breathe, but he was strangling on something. He coughed again, deliberately, to clear his throat. "What have I got to lose," he said.

Then the tangle of fibers that was Grayshard descended on him, over his face, and he could feel the Vaashka's tendrils weaving a web around his head, along his upper spine. For an instant he felt utter panic, the Tathas were going to eat him, and then he felt a wonderful dark lethargy spread over him, not a nightmare, and he remembered that Grayshard wasn't a Tathas after all, and let himself sink down into a kind of trance.

He watched, unfeeling, uncaring, as goons crawled along the surfaces of the bridge, as Grayshard worked thick strands of tendrils into each of the wounds on his chest, as Denny, on the edges of his vision, moved here and there, as Raebuck at last stood up from his side and went to stand beside Sukiro. Where was Droagn?

The movements of the goons seemed to take on a symbolic significance. He felt strange movements inside his chest, a counterpoint to that movement, that also held mystic meaning somehow. He saw Droagn at last, looming up behind Sukiro and Raebuck, felt reassured by that somehow, saw a thin matting of white tendrils cover his face, woven into complex patterns he couldn't understand.

Though there was no pain, none at all anymore, it seemed as though there were thousands of tiny fires in his chest. He could almost see the light shining out of him, illuminating the basketwork writhing in front of him, underlighting the faces of his friends. His chest seemed to swell, then to shrink. There was a feeling of—departure?—then a pearly gray sense of distance and rest.

And then, as if he were just waking up, he came to his senses.

He looked up, through the network of Grayshard's tendrils, which dropped down out of sight as Sukiro knelt beside him. Endark Droagn was behind her.

"You're going to be all right," Sukiro said.

"I think he is," Grayshard said. The mechanical nature of his voice could not conceal his fatigue.

Filled with a sense of wonder and surprise mingled with relief, Rikard sat up. He had been convinced that he was going to die. He looked around the strange chamber and had to restrain himself from laughing. Thinking about the trouble they still had to deal with helped. Everybody was looking at him, with ill-concealed expressions of fascination. Beside him, Grayshard was a flaccid pile of fibers.

"This one needs help too," a strange voice said. Rikard turned and saw the one surviving Vaashka administrator "standing" in the doorway. Private Colder accompanied him, her face both frightened and angry.

"This thing," Colder said, "I couldn't stop it."

"What do you want here?" Sukiro demanded. She started to draw her blaster though she didn't dare fire it in here.

"This one," the Vaashka said—it had a voicebox like Grayshard's—"puts shame on me. S'he has expended much. I can fix."

"You just stay where you are," Denny said. She had drawn her jolter. It couldn't damage the ship but it would shock the Vaashka.

"Let s'hem come," Grayshard said. "I need help."

The Vaashka came forward a bit. Denny backed away but kept her jolter aimed. Then the Vaashka flowed toward Grayshard, and when it got to him, entwined its tendrils in his. "This one is a hero," the Vaashka said. "S'he deserves to live."

There was a moment of silence, then Grayshard used his vocalizer so the others could hear, "You still must pay for your crimes."

"If I must then I shall," the Vaashka said.

After another moment Grayshard began to bunch himself up. "I will need rest," he vocalized, "but I thank you." The other Vaashka squashed down flat on the deck. "And you need rest too," Grayshard said to Rikard. "The healing has begun, but it is not finished. I have done all I can."

Rikard stared at the figure of Grayshard, which reminded him so much of the terror of the Tathas. Then he reached out and put his ungloved right hand in among Grayshard's tendrils. It was a token handshake. "I owe you my life," he said, "and I won't waste it. But if we don't get out of here, more than one life will be wasted."

He started to stand, and Raebuck and Sukiro helped him. "Does anybody know how this ship works?" he asked as he got to his feet.

"We haven't figured it out yet," Falyn said. "I don't know if we ever will." She looked up at the central sphere of controls and screens, where five goons were using hand-held sensing devices.

"That's not the right place," Rikard said. He looked around until he saw a small panel on one surface within reach of what now served as the deck. "That's it," he said.

"How do you know?" Sukiro asked.

"Call it instinct," Rikard said. "Now help me get over to it."

4

Sukiro and Raebuck helped Rikard to his feet, then, with Droagn following and with Grayshard again on the Ahmear's shoulders, helped him to the small console he had pointed out.

The whole of the console was maybe a meter across. The main feature was a set of seven hexagonal viewscreens clustered in the center, and from each screen but the central one was a radiating line of toggles and blank circular readouts, and at the end of each line an arc of five push buttons.

The surface on which the console was located was slanted at a rather large angle, and it was easier for Rikard to lie on his stomach on the sloping deck than to try to stand in front of the console and lean forward. He made himself as comfortable as he could and looked over the array. Even as he did so, the central screen came to life, though it remained blank.

"Who did that?" he asked. He rolled onto his side so he could look around the chamber. There were goons at every other console except the one suspended in the middle of the room.

"Did what?" Dyson asked.

"I touched the middle screen here," Yansen said, halfway around the nearly spherical wall.

"That makes sense," Rikard said. "Now everybody, hands off, and keep your eyes on the screens."

He touched the middle one in front of him. There were murmurs from around the place. "It's gone off again," Yansen said.

"This one was on too," Lisobria said, "and now it's off."

Rikard touched the central screen again. At each workstation, the central screen of a group, or the only screen if there was just one, came on. He touched each of the other screens in turn. They lit up, as did the corresponding screens, where they existed, at each of the other workstations.

There were other features besides the screens, toggles, readouts, and push buttons. One was a slightly raised shape, remi-

230

niscent of that of the ship, between the bottom line of controls and the next one left. Rikard touched it, and one of his outside screens cleared to show a portion of the hangar deck.

"Anybody else get a picture?" he called out.

The response was about half affirmative, and each scene was different, though all were of the outside of the ship.

"Wait a minute," Fresno said. "There's something moving out there."

"What is it?" Sukiro asked.

"I don't know, all I can see is blurs."

"The Tschagan are still looking for us," Denny said.

"Let them," Rikard said as he felt a weight settling down on his shoulders.

It was Grayshard. "Just getting a better look," the Vaashka told him. Several of his tendrils, singularly or in clumps, waved in the air over the console. Others waved in other directions. The tendrils near the console clumped, then separated to form new tendrils as old ones came apart. Rikard watched in fascination. "My 'eyes' are at the ends," Grayshard explained.

Then Grayshard slid off Rikard's shoulders and down onto the slanting deck beside him on the left side. "It's not quite the same," he said, "as it would be in one of our ships, but I'll wager that the people who made this ship had no symmetry, or at most radial symmetry."

"That makes sense," Rikard said. "From the layout of the console, I'd guess radial."

˜Of course,˜ Droagn said, ˜and I'd guess they were also buoyant in their atmosphere. That would explain the decks.˜

"I've never heard of anybody like that," Rikard said, "but I think you're right. The Belshpaer were radial, this console would have seemed normal to them, but their decks would have been level."

"Does that help you make any sense out of all this?" Sukiro asked.

"It can. No right or left, no front or back, and in this case no reason to stay on the floor. So the controls would be arranged by a different logic."

"And one not that difficult for me to figure out," Grayshard added.

"But why do you think this is the master panel," Sukiro asked, "instead of that one in the middle of the room?"

˜That one,˜ Droagn said, ˜is for general display. It's almost all display panels, there are very few controls. And all the other panels on the walls are in clusters, the one where Rikard Braeth lies is isolated.˜

"My thought exactly," Rikard said.

Droagn, on Rikard's right, reached out a finger, touched the central screen, then touched the one on the upper right. Another image formed, adjacent to the one on the central screen. It showed an area of the hangar above floor level. ˜They still have to account for thrust and direction in a spacecraft,˜ Droagn said.

Grayshard, clumped together on Rikard's left, bunched a mass of tendrils and with it touched the center screen, then one on the lower left. Most of what the screen then showed was the platform under the ship. And the central screen now showed distant Tschagan, moving from platform to platform, pausing at each almost long enough to be seen before going on.

"Our friends are being cautious," Sukiro said.

"So we've got a navigator's console," Falyn observed, "will it control the whole ship?"

"Only one way to find out," Rikard told her. He shifted his position so that he was crouching over his knees, which left him both hands free. But for the moment he just leaned on them, between the radial arms of the mysterious controls.

"Toggles are obvious," he said, "though who knows what they do." He touched a blank readout disk. It came on.

"I just realized," Sukiro said. "This ship has power even though it has been here at least ten thousand years."

"Are we connected to the Tschagan station in any way?" Falyn asked.

Rikard looked at the meaningless readout. It displayed a collection of dots and squiggles, which were not arranged in any array or pattern he could discover. "I didn't notice any connections when we were outside," he said.

˜The bottom of the ship,˜ Droagn said, ˜was—ah—one meter above the support pad, if that means anything.˜

"Tight-beam broadcast?" Sukiro suggested.

"The Tschagan are getting closer," Fresno warned.

Rikard touched the raised outline of the ship and then a screen. A diagram appeared, showing what was obviously the ship, in schematic form. "Love it," he said, then touched an area on the schematic that corresponded to the hatch by which they had entered and then another screen. An enlarged view on this other screen showed the hatch itself. "Love it! Now how do I lock that thing?"

He touched the image of the hatch, it opened. He touched it again, it closed.

"We'll have to take it for granted," he said, "that it's locked if it's closed."

"What did you do?" Dyson called to him. "The Tschagan on the hatch side are all staring at us, if I can judge."

"They saw or heard the hatch opening," Raebuck said.

"Damn," Rikard muttered.

"They still have to get up to it," Sukiro said. "But now they know where we are."

"I think we've got trouble," Corporal LeClarke said. "A bunch of Tschagan have gone off to some equipment over to one side."

"Nothing we can do about it," Rikard told her. He turned his attention back to the schematic and touched the representation of the ship's lower sphere—which might have been analogous to the power sphere on a Federation ship—then another unused screen. The display showed a simulated panel, its hexagons all showing single dots.

~Let's guess those are zeroes,~ Droagn said.

Rikard touched one of the simulated hexes, then another screen, but nothing useful happened. "Some things require more direct control," he said. "Probably an anti-idiot circuit."

"Are we going to blast off before we open the hatches?" Sukiro asked.

Rikard pointed to another area on the schematic. "That's the drives," he said, "I just want power." He looked at the readout from the power sphere—if indeed that was what it was—and noticed that some of the lines between hexes were thicker than others.

"First digit is here"—he pointed at the central hex—"and it goes this way." He traced a spiral out counterclockwise.

~Gotcha,~ Droagn said, ~and look here.~ He pointed to another display which, until now, had been non-functional. ~Base eight.~

"You're right," Grayshard said.

"So how does that help us turn on the power?" Falyn asked.

Rikard tapped the central hex of the power display eight times. The symbols flickered, changing from one shape to another, then turned back into a dot. But the second hex in the spiral now showed the first symbol to appear after a dot.

"They've got a platform outside the hatch," Fresno said, "and they're using some kind of cutting tools."

"All right," Sukiro said, "have a squad ready to blast them when they cut through." She turned back to Rikard. "Can you close off inner hatches?"

Rikard looked at the schematic. "I think so."

Rikard, Droagn, and Grayshard continued to examine the controls. They tried them out cautiously, and learned more with each experiment. Sometimes they tried things that had to do with life support, or internal communications, and sometimes things they didn't understand at all. These last they quickly abandoned.

"We have to learn the logic first," Rikard said.

They continued to experiment, until at last, between the three of them, they thought they had an idea of how to control the drives. But they could not test this knowledge since, as Sukiro had suggested, they couldn't go anywhere with the station's hatches closed.

Fortunately the Tschagan outside seemed to be having trouble cutting their way into the ship. It was, apparently, well armored. But more Tschagan were arriving, and some of them were bringing in equipment that looked to some of the goons like heavy duty mounted blasters, though they could not have been.

At last Rikard thought they could turn on the power, and with Grayshard's and Droagn's concurrence, did so. They could all feel the ship respond, a subtle vibration, a movement of the air. But not all the telltales on the schematic came on, many remained dark. Rikard, Droagn, and Grayshard reevaluated the mathematics and tried again, and this time the whole ship came alive.

And outside, the Tschagan were zipping around like the angry insects they were. There was no dust at all within a hundred meters of the ship, and the blurs of the moving Tschagan were seen all over the place.

"How about weapons?" Sukiro asked. "We could blast our way out."

Falyn leaned over Rikard's shoulder, and pointed to several places on the schematic. "Those?" she suggested.

"They won't be blasters," Rikard said, but he put them on

another display, which now showed what they knew were power readouts, and something more besides, which seemed to be a special coordinate system.

~Might be worth a try,~ Droagn said.

"Read it this way," Grayshard said, and started to try to explain how he thought the system worked, but Rikard interrupted him.

"It's just like my built in ranging system," he said, "only the symbols are different." And it worked by touch. When he touched a portion of the screen, a series of radiating lines centered on the spot, and after a moment a small circle followed. Rikard wasn't aiming at anything, just over the tops of the nearest ships. He touched the schematic, where now several small lights were glowing in the waist between the bottom and middle spheres, and there was a brief, intense flicker of blue light.

"UV laser," Sukiro said. The bolt left a dark scar along the far roof of the hangar, where the weapon happened to have been pointed.

The Tschagan outside were startled by the shot, and had all dashed away, but when they saw where the shot had gone they came back. They brought up heavy weapons and opened fire. They were projectile weapons which, judging by the flashes they produced when they hit the skin of the ship, fired armor piercing shells.

The ship's armor was good, however, and nothing penetrated, but yellow signals lit up on the schematic. Rikard brought enlargements of those areas to other screens, and from the diagrams shown guessed that the shells had done some small damage to the hull. If the Tschagan concentrated their fire they could probably breach the hull in time, and then the ship wouldn't be spaceworthy.

It took several tries but Rikard and his two companions eventually figured out how to turn on the antigravity lifters. But once they were independent of whatever it was the Tschagan had used to keep it afloat, the ship began to rock and tilt. They couldn't maintain balance from just this one console. They set the ship back down again, and while the Tschagan outside scurried around almost invisibly, set several goons at other control stations and quickly instructed them as to what to do. The Tschagan's confusion gave them the time they needed to learn how to maneuver the ship on its own lifters.

~We still have to get out of here,~ Droagn said. ~I think we could blast our way through the hull right overhead.~

"I wouldn't count on it," Rikard told him. "I suspect that the hull armor is far too strong for even UV lasers. It's designed to withstand meteorites, after all. And besides, I don't want to cause any more damage than we have to. But we can try to blow out the hatch."

The three of them worked together. They lifted the ship again, and slid and sidled over toward the hatch, a dome in the roof of the hangar a dozen ship-spaces away. But as the ship left its docking pad it fell off the pad's supporting field. It was a drop of less than three meters, but they could all feel the crunch as the ship's flicker spike touched the deck.

Outside, the Tschagan were thrown into a frenzy. At least they weren't shooting at the moment.

Rikard and his impromptu crew got the ship back up off the deck and, learning as they went, kept it upright as they moved it between other ships toward the hatch. Telltales on the schematic showed that the short fall had caused considerable damage to the jump spike, but as far as Rikard could tell it was still functional.

The Tschagan started firing again, aiming at the damaged bottom of the ship. Under Rikard's direction the ship moved over an empty gravity pedestal. It lurched up toward the ceiling, spoiling the Tschagan's aim.

He brought the ship down off the other side of the pedestal, more gracefully this time—it didn't hit the deck. But as they passed another ship the two brushed sides and they started spinning.

It took a moment to stop the spin, and when they did they found that they'd drifted to one side. But at least they were nearing the area below the hangar's hatch.

Grayshard and Droagn, leaving Rikard in charge of the ship's movement, went to other, nearby control stations, and started learning how to aim the ship's weapons. They blasted a group of Tschagan manning a cannon, which sent other Tschagan nearby running for cover. They hit another ship without causing any noticeable damage, blew a hole in a far wall, and smashed yet another ship to pieces. The Tschagan retreated in disorder. But the weapon couldn't be brought to bear on the hatch which, by now, was directly overhead.

"Everybody grab hold of something," Rikard called out. "Get

word to the others, we're going to tip over." He did not wait for a reply, but delicately fingered the controls on his display console. As the ship started to tip, it slid away from its position, in the direction its base was pointing, and started to topple. Quickly he righted it.

"Shoot when you can," he shouted to Grayshard and Droagn. He performed the clumsy maneuver again, and in the instant when the ship was tipped but still in control, they fired upward at the hatch.

The ship slipped, Rikard righted it. The shot had hit the edge of the hatch without causing damage.

"Once again," Rikard called. This was the third time, and his crew and gunners were ready for it. They were able to keep the ship more or less under control, though it continued to slip and tilt, and Droagn and Grayshard got off three shots before they had to right again. The last shot hit square on the center of the hatch.

It blew open. The atmosphere in the hangar rushed out, a storm of dust that obscured all the vision screens. Rikard held the ship steady, and after a moment the dust was gone and the rush of air stopped as the station's inner seals closed.

"Hang on!" Rikard shouted. "We're going through!" He slowly lifted the ship toward the blasted hatch, fragments of which still hung in the opening. The ship brushed against the broken and twisted metal valves as it pushed its way out, and telltales on the schematic showed minor damage but no breaks in the hull. The ship got stuck for a moment as its central sphere came up against a solid piece of the hatch. Rikard pushed the ship up harder. They could feel and hear the tearing as the ship pushed its way through. Then suddenly they were out into space.

Rikard slumped back exhausted. "Get us away from here," he told his crew, "away from the surface until we can figure out the inertial drive."

Droagn and Grayshard came back to his side. "I think this is the communications system," Grayshard said, indicating various areas on the console.

"Try to call the gunship," Rikard told him.

Grayshard did so, but though the console screens and telltales indicated that he was doing the right things, he could get no response.

"This ship," Falyn said, "probably uses a different range of frequencies."

"You and Grayshard get on it then," Rikard said, "over there. I've got to get the inertials working."

Grayshard went with Falyn to a nearby console, and Sukiro took the Vaashka's place.

Droagn pointed at an area of the schematic. ˜Could that be the inertial drive?˜ he asked.

"One way to find out," Rikard said.

With Sukiro and Droagn offering advice, Rikard manipulated the alien controls. Droagn's suggestion seemed to be right, and the drive seemed to be working. But if Rikard could read the telltales correctly, there was little fuel left in the craft—that was something modern ships hardly ever had to worry about.

The inertial drives were controlled by a track-ball device, set to one side of the central display of screens. But the ball not only rotated and spun in its socket, it responded to pressure. Thus direction and speed of rotation and pressure all contributed to the working of the drive, and it took Rikard a while, testing the drive at its lowest functional setting, to even begin to get the hang of it. But at last the urgency to move overbalanced his need for caution, and he pulled the ship up and away from the derelict—clumsily it was true—and moved the alien vessel out to what he judged to be five of the station's diameters from it.

"Hold on," Sukiro said, "I think I've got direct contact with the ship. We must have come over the horizon relative to it."

And as the other goons in the bridge acknowledged similar contact, Grayshard and Falyn gave up trying to figure out this ship's communicators.

"Hold on," Sukiro said again, and then fell silent as, via her com-link, she told the crew of the gunship that they were coming, and described the alien vessel so Brenner wouldn't fire on it.

At the same time Iturba was in communication with the com-chief on board the gunship, and told her about the alien ship's communicators, and after a moment the speakers came on so that Rikard, Droagn, and Grayshard could also hear what was being said.

Captain Brenner reported that nothing had happened on the gunship since the rest of the goons had gone down to the station, but some repairs had been done, though the drive itself was totally nonfunctional. The gunship's inertials were damaged but working, their weapons were fine, their communications were functional, and they were ready for action should the pirates on the station come out.

"They won't," Sukiro told him. She quickly described the battle, ending that the survivors had all been taken prisoner and were on board. "But there's a second pirate craft," she concluded, "that could come at any time."

"We've got you located," someone on the gunship reported, then gave a string of numbers that were relative coordinates.

Rikard did not understand this, but Sukiro instructed him on where to go. After a few moments Rikard saw a blip on one of the external screens. That was the gunship. Clumsily, the two craft maneuvered toward each other.

"We've got other craft on our detectors," the crewman on the gunship said. "They're small, but they're coming up fast, from over the horizon."

They could only be Tschagan ships, and there were several dozen of them. They were probably fighters, and were closing quickly.

Rikard and the others working the consoles of the alien ship had not had a chance to try out its long range scanners, and couldn't get a reading on the Tschagan craft. They had to depend on the reports from the gunship, which now, at least, was well within visual range, and saw the flash of its blasters firing.

The Tschagan fighters, when at last they came into view, were strange open structures without any streamlining. Fortunately, the laws of physics kept these ships from moving as fast, relatively speaking, as the Tschagan did themselves. But all of them were well armed, if one could judge from the muzzle flashes, which were clearly visible on even the most distant of them.

"Let me take the weapons," Grayshard said, and moved to a console near the one that Rikard was commanding. The screens which showed the side of the alien vessel from which he shot blinked brilliant blue as he fired, but without computer assistance he hit nothing.

Rikard let his hand play over the trackball control of the inertial drive and set the ship rocking and spinning in an attempt to avoid the enemy fire. This seemed to be effective, since the telltales on the schematic showed that they weren't being hit very often, and the shots that did hit damaged only the skin.

The gunship was getting closer to them, firing its blasters at the enemy as it did so. There was nothing wrong with its ranging systems, one shot out of every eight or ten hit a fighter, with devastating results. But there were more and more Tschagan craft all the time.

Sukiro crouched beside Rikard, and together they tried to maneuver the ship so that it could dock with the gunship.

Meanwhile, Grayshard was beginning to develop a strategy. The Tschagan ships frequently passed within a certain distance of the gunship before arcing away. He watched the next fighters to approach and just aimed at the place where he figured they would begin their turn. He did in fact hit two of the fighters out of thirty shots and, given that he had no computer assistance, that was impressive.

Rikard's ship and the gunship were now near enough that they had to turn off the inertials and use grappler fields in order to dock. Rikard had no idea how to do that on his ship, so he just shut it down and left the task up to the pilot of the gunship, with its finer control.

All this time Grayshard was laying down a barrage of UV laser fire around the edge of the gunship, which in turn continued to fire protectively around Rikard's ship, as the two moved together. The Tschagan fighters were only lightly armed, and though the two larger craft took a lot of hits a single shot did little damage. But now the Tschagan started concentrating their fire on the gunship's habitation saucer and the alien ship's top sphere.

At last, with a shock that knocked everybody out of place, the two ships connected and locked onto each other.

"Can this ship jump?" Sukiro yelled to Rikard.

"I think so," Rikard answered.

"Good enough." Sukiro ordered the gunship crew to board the alien vessel.

The voice from the gunship responded, "As soon as I can find your hatch."

Rikard rotated the alien ship so that the hatch was facing the gunship. The voice from the gunship said, "Got it," and grapples came out from it, and a connecting tube snaked out between them.

Both ships continued to fire during the maneuver. The tube connected, the hatches on both ships were opened, and everybody on the gunship except the weapons crews started coming on board the alien ship.

5

"Set all weapons on automatic," Sukiro told the ten remaining gunners on the gunship. "Set an automatic release on the hatch connection, and get ready to abandon ship."

But even as she got an affirmative reply, the Tschagan craft all suddenly broke away and headed for the station's horizon.

Both gunship and alien ship stopped firing. Then a frantic voice from the gunship said, "There's one hell of a big flicker drive warming up."

"My God," Rikard said, "it's the station."

"Get over here," Sukiro yelled to the gunship crew. She didn't have to yell, they could have heard her subvocal just as well.

The crewman on the other end said, "six seconds . . . five seconds . . ."

Rikard's senses hung poised, as if he were clutching his gun. If the Tschagan station did indeed have a jump-drive big enough to move it—and what a god-awful big drive it must have been—and if it jumped while the gunship and his alien craft were still this close, the warp of the drive would smear the two ships into dust and gas. There were still the ten gunners on the gunship, and maybe a few others. The hatch connector was still in place between the two ships.

". . . four seconds . . ."

Rikard watched in horrified fascination as his hand, seemingly of its own volition, reached out to the inertial drive controls and jammed them on hard. The wrench of the separating hatch tube was lost in the wrench of acceleration. He angled the alien ship away from the now not so derelict Tschagan station, that was not really just a space station after all but a giant starship. Alarms went off as atmosphere went out the breached hatch. Then inner locks shut down automatically.

". . . three seconds . . ."

He could see the gunship on the central screen of his console, receding. Its inertial drive came on—had one of the gun crew gotten to the bridge in time? And what was that other ship that had suddenly appeared—the second pirate ship? It opened fire on the gunship. With his right hand Rikard continued to work the inertial controls for all they were worth. His left hand hovered over what he hoped was the jump controls.

". . . two seconds . . ." The voice was resigned. The gunship's inertials pulsed again. Rikard jabbed at the jump drive.

The alien ship flickered once. Alarms went off everywhere. They came to rest, still moving with the velocity imparted by their inertial drive. The Tschagan station was no longer visible.

". . . one se—" A sudden flare, off to one side, showed them where they had been.

"They blew up my ship," Sukiro said.

But almost immediately there was a larger flare, that grew and spread for long seconds. The Tschagan supership had jumped too, and the gunship and the pirate ship had become one with the dust of space.

PART
SEVEN

1

It was a long moment before anybody could react.

"I pity any pirates left alive on the Tschagan ship," Dyson said.

"I pity us," Sukiro said, "if we don't get word of the Tschagan back to the Federation." Her voice was flat, emotionless. "Anybody who could build a flicker drive big enough to move a station like that is not to be taken lightly."

"The hell with the Tschagan," Lisobria said, "I don't want to die here."

Denny glared at her, then turned to Rikard. "Can this ship jump again?"

Rikard looked at the schematic. The drive section was dark. "I don't think so," he said.

Private Goren, stationed at the hatch, came into the bridge. "We lost three crew who were in the hatch when we broke loose," he said. "Everybody else is all right."

Rikard turned around when he heard no response. Sukiro was staring into a blank angle of the wall, in a state of emotional shock. Out of a total complement of eighty, only fifty-five of her crew and goons were still alive, and fifteen of them were wounded. No police force had suffered more than ten percent casualties since the Goon Squads had been founded seven hundred years ago.

"Heavy losses, Major," Denny said brutally. Her tone was intended to break Sukiro out of her mood. "And we'll have one hundred percent losses if we can't jump out of here or call for help."

Sukiro stared at her, then her face lost its blank expression. She turned back to Goren. "Did Captain Brenner make it?" she asked.

"He did, and would like to see you."

"Bring him forward."

Goren departed, and a moment later Brenner came into the bridge. It was obvious that he was taking the loss of his ship very hard. It was all he could do to control himself.

Sukiro stepped up to him and grabbed him by both shoulders. "Did you send out a distress call after you were hit by the pirates?" she asked.

"Of course," Brenner said, in a very small voice. "Standard operating procedure when a police craft is disabled."

"And what was the response?"

"I had gotten none by the time—by the time—"

Sukiro shook him as hard as she could. "It's my fault," she said, "not yours."

"I should have stayed with the gunners," was all Brenner could say.

Corporal LeClarke had come quietly up to the pair. She put her arm around Brenner and led him back through the hatch.

"The first thing," Falyn said, "is to make sure that the life support on this ship is functioning, and then maybe we can figure out how to make the communicators work."

Rikard turned back to the console. "At least we can breathe the air," he said, "but I wouldn't place any bets on the food." His hands fluttered over the readouts.

Droagn leaned over his shoulder and said, ˜It begins to make sense if you look at it like this.˜ He pointed to the power section of the schematic. ˜It looks different, but it's where the power should be. Same with the various drives. Everything is analogous to the ships I know—˜

"And to Federation ships," Rikard said.

As Droagn went on, Grayshard slithered up to join them and contribute to the analysis. "Communicators, see"—he touched the part of the diagram in question and brought up a control version on another screen—"the symbols are different, but they really work the same way."

˜Their number system is base eight,˜ Droagn said, ˜and we know the possible frequency range for deep space communications, maximum and minimum. We should be able to translate their scale into terms we understand.˜

"I believe you're right," Rikard said. He turned to Sukiro. "What's your helmet frequency?" Sukiro told him.

Rikard diddled with what he now thought was a tuning scale. Then Sukiro suddenly said, "I got static."

Droagn reached out, touched a part of the scale on the screen and "dragged" it to another screen where it was enlarged.

"Aha," Rikard said, and diddled some more.

"Good clean signal," Sukiro said. "Nothing on it, of course."

"But now we know what that frequency is in their terms," Grayshard said, "and now we can figure out what frequency we need to call for help."

Sukiro grinned. "By damn I think you can."

"You just have to look at it the right way," Rikard said.

"Well," Denny said, "maybe *you* do."

"We were just too pressed for time before," Rikard said, "had too much to think about. See, it's only the variant symmetry that's confusing, a matter of shape and terminology rather than of real function. It really all makes sense."

"I'm glad you think so," Falyn said.

˜But of course it does,˜ Droagn said. Then Rikard tried Sukiro's personal com-link frequency to calibrate the scale.

"Assuming we have the power," Sukiro said.

"We should have enough to last us until we starve to death," Rikard told her.

"Or die of thirst," Denny said, "if these people didn't drink water."

"It might get kind of sticky in here during the next few days," Falyn observed.

But their progress made everybody feel better, and Rikard continued to work on the communicator, to try to identify the right frequency, assisted by Private Leeds, who knew Federation technology.

"What if the Tschagan come back?" Yansen asked.

"Why would they want to," Dyson returned, "just to shut us up?"

"Are they really a threat?" Private Satorian asked.

"We had better assume," Raebuck said, "that they're the worst threat possible. There may not be many of them left but we don't know how well equipped they are to try to reassert their former place in the galaxy, and if their flicker drive is any example then they're formidable. And I'd wager they can increase their numbers quickly. Maybe not this year, or this decade, but from what I know of them they'll eventually come back, looking for trouble and dominance. They might decide to try to establish themselves somewhere outside the Federation, and some of the smaller star nations would be especially vulnerable to their depredations."

Rikard looked up from the controls. "This ship has a tachyon communicator very similar to ours, any idea which way to aim it?"

"Can you do a spherical broadcast?" Sukiro asked.

"That's the easy way, but it would take a lot of power."

"How much power do we need, besides life support?"

"None I guess. But we'll have to monitor what we use. This ship doesn't have a permanent fuel cell like ours do, and there isn't much fuel left. If we start to run too low, we'll have to cut the broadcast."

"There should be an automatic monitor," Sukiro said.

"I'm sure there is, if you think we can figure out their computer system."

"So we'll keep an eye on it ourselves, and broadcast full power until we either get a response or figure out how to do a tight beam—or until the lights start to go dim."

"If it comes to that," Rikard said as he turned back to the panel, "we'll probably all be dead anyway." He touched a few points on various screens. "That should do it."

He felt very tired. He drew a deep, shuddering breath and sat back on his heels.

"You've exerted yourself too much," Grayshard told him. "You must rest now."

"I intend to," Rikard said. He twisted around so that he was sitting, facing into the room, and lay back on the slanting deck beside the console.

LeClarke came back into the bridge. "Brenner's resting," she said. "Someone had a sedative."

"I think Rikard could use one too," Sukiro suggested.

"No," Rikard protested, "I'm just going to sit here for a while." He looked up at the major and sighed. "I guess the Leaves are lost again," he said to her.

"What about the Reliquiture," she asked, "do you want to give that back?"

"I think I'll let Darcy decide that," he said.

Sukiro looked at him a moment. "She gave up on you," she said at last.

"It doesn't matter," Rikard lied. He'd figured once that he and Darcy would be together for a long time. But whatever they had had between them, it was over now.

He looked up at Sukiro again. She nodded once and left him to his thoughts.

Rikard sat there for a long moment, then pulled himself to his feet and went over to where Endark Droagn and Grayshard were waiting, at the far side of the chamber.

As Rikard neared, Droagn turned to him and said, ~I'm afraid that my interests will not be best served by staying in your Federation, but everything I used to know is twenty five thousand years in the past. Have you any suggestions as to what I might do with myself?~

"You don't relish being the center of attention of every ethnologist and xenobiologist in the Federation?" Rikard asked ironically.

"That hardly seems to offer much freedom of movement or privacy," Grayshard said. "Now, in my case, my *predator* fellows can fill in for me quite nicely, and I suspect they'll have to put up with it. But I have no intention of staying where I would be only a curiosity."

"I've got a signal," Fresno, who was monitoring the communicators, said. Everybody turned to watch and listen as he turned up the volume. There was a moment of static, and then a voice came in.

"—calling on 2750. This is System Watch on Shentary. We got your signal, but it is very weak. Please repeat. Attention ship in distress calling on 2750. This is System Watch on Shentary. We got your signal, but it is very weak. Please repeat."

"This is Task Force Pirate," Fresno replied. "Let me switch to tight beam." He diddled with the console the way he'd seen Rikard do it.

"I'll take care of it," Sukiro said. She went to the communicator. "Turn the volume down," she said to Fresno. He did so.

"Looks like we're going to be saved," Rikard said to Grayshard and Droagn. "And I'm not going to stick around either. I'm thinking of taking a little private tour, you know, just to pull myself together, get over a few things."

~You think you can get me away from your people?~ Droagn asked. ~You can sell the Prime if you need money.~

Rikard almost laughed. "No need for that," he said, thinking of the hoard of dragongems that even Darcy didn't know about.

"I'd like to see some of your Federation," Grayshard said. "Discreetly, of course. I have no reason to go home, mind if I tag along?"

"We were a pretty good team there, weren't we?" Rikard said.

"Help will be here in five days," Sukiro announced. Then she noticed how chummy Rikard was being with Grayshard and Endark Droagn, both of whom were self-professed rogues. Though she continued to smile her expression became that of the professional cop. "I guess you three have got some other plans," she said.

"The only plan I have," Rikard said, "is to book passage as soon as we reach a Federation world."

Sukiro stared at him a moment longer, then sighed. "I guess you've done your share. How about your friends?"

"I thought we might team up for a while." He looked directly at Sukiro. "We're taking the crown with us."

Sukiro looked back at him. Her expression was unreadable. "To hell with the crown," she said, then turned away. "I just hope I'm never assigned to your case," she muttered over her shoulder.

Rikard grinned, then laughed, and scratched the palm of his right hand.